KW-484-262

GOLDEN GATE PEOPLE

Recent Titles by Virginia Coffman from Severn House

The Jewels Series

EMERALD FLAME
THE WINE-DARK OPAL
TIGER'S EYE
A SPLASH OF RUBIES

The Moura Series

MOURA
VAMPYRE OF MOURA
RETURN TO MOURA

The Royles Saga

THE ROYLES
DANGEROUS LOYALTIES
THE PRINCESS ROYAL
HEIR TO A THRONE

GOLDEN GATE PEOPLE

GOLDEN GATE PEOPLE

Virginia Coffman

This first world edition published in Great Britain 2000 by
SEVERN HOUSE PUBLISHERS LTD of
9–15 High Street, Sutton, Surrey SM1 1DF.
This first world edition published in the USA 2001 by
SEVERN HOUSE PUBLISHERS INC of
595 Madison Avenue, New York, N.Y. 10022.

Copyright © 2000 by Virginia Coffman.

All rights reserved.
The moral right of the author has been asserted.

British Library Cataloguing in Publication Data

Coffman, Virginia, 1914-
    Golden gate people
    1.   San Francisco (Calif.) - Social Conditions - 20th century - Fiction
    I.   Title
    813.5'4 [F]

    ISBN 0-7278-5624-3

All situations in this publication are fictitious and
any resemblance to living persons is purely coincidental.

Typeset by Hewer Text Ltd.,
Edinburgh, Scotland.
Printed and bound in Great Britain by
MPG Books Ltd., Bodmin, Cornwall.

BISHOPSTOWN
LIBRARY

CORK CITY
LIBRARY

CORK CITY LIBRARY	
04894977	
LBC	08/02/2006
	£17.99

One

H e didn't like the sound of the job, especially when the woman was a byword in San Francisco for her bossy ways.

"Sorry, Ben. Normally, I get along pretty well with women, but . . ."

He knew his own managing editor, bossy but male, was trying to let him down easy.

At his refusal Ben merely said, "Ha!" and buried his face in his beer mug, one of the last before the idiotic new Prohibition law came into effect. After a long, pleasurable draft, Ben Riggs raised his head. He stared out the tavern window at the latest cargo liner cutting through the Golden Gate waters.

"Well, we did hold your job open during the war. But it's tough now, with all you doughboys pouring in, wanting jobs. And then, you were one of the last back in, so naturally . . ."

Denis Mallory finished off his Martini in one gulp, almost choking on the olive. But he managed to play it lightly. "Damn! I might as well have the Spanish flu with the rest of the poor devils."

"The pay at our place is lousy," his ex-boss reminded him. "Whereas, the Kyles could buy and sell us, if they had a mind to. Trouble is," he added ruefully, "nobody has a mind to these days."

As a hint that veterans returning from France were not as bad off as they might be he added, "This flu thing is no joke. My brother-in-law and one of the kids were quarantined over the armistice celebrations. Bad business. I had a cousin who died a few months ago."

"Thanks, buddy. You are a joy to have around."

Denis Mallory was making circles with the bottom of his glass on the big white napkin, but he grinned as his ex-boss looked at him.

"What do you figure to do?" the boss asked guiltily, though he didn't know why. It wasn't his fault the Kaiser had kicked up his heels and caused a war. He saw Denis Mallory's smile and was pleased that the younger man didn't act as though he might be to blame. He returned to his first suggestion. "You ought to at least think about the Kyles, Mallory. With your looks and your way with women. My God! You could have any woman in our office." He added, trying for flippancy, "Including my wife. Why not give it a try?"

"Your wife?"

"Skip that. But a job as assistant manager of the Kyle organization could be a nice way to work yourself to the top. All you have to do is put your charm to work on Old Man Kyle and the Iron Maiden. Ought to be a cinch for you. And I can fill you in here and there. They know me. I've been out there a few times when there's a story blowing their way."

Mallory nodded, amused in spite of himself. It was a challenge, but how easy it sounded when Riggs talked about it! Maybe he could overlook a few reminders of his inferiority to a female boss. He might play the charmer. That shouldn't be too hard. Boring, but not that difficult. Of course, they always thought they knew best when they ran things.

Ben Riggs took a deep breath and got out his wallet.

"Let me get this. I owe you one."

When Denis Mallory shrugged and let him pay for the round, Riggs' conscience eased. He could afford to be generous.

They said goodbye outside the saloon and Ben Riggs thumbed his felt hat to the back of his balding head while he tried to think of some more encouragement for Mallory's job-hunting.

"There's more to the Kyle Baths than a bathhouse."

Denis gave his doubtful opinion of that.

Riggs shrugged. "Well, it's a job. Assistant Manager. There's a few dollars in it." He tried one last time. "They really are advertising for the job. I saw the add in the *Journal* before we put the paper to bed this morning. Shows you."

"It shows me," Denis agreed, "they never could hold their people. Too much management upstairs."

"Well, I'll send you a reference. It may help you out wherever you want to try next. And that architect friend of yours, Larry Hoaglund, was talking to me a few days ago about the good times you guys had before the war. He might have a few ideas. You're sure there's nothing doing on the other rags?"

"Nothing. Anyway, you've been swell. Maybe when I'm running the works for old Kyle, I'll be able to repay you for the drinks."

He started up the hill past the big Ghirardelli Chocolate Factory toward the street car.

Ben laughed at Mallory's unruly dark hair blowing in the San Francisco wind and yelled, "For God's sake, get a hat! Or at least a beret."

Denis waved a response but didn't look back.

It occurred to him as he looked around for car tracks – there was no hum of car cables nearby – that he might as well look into the Kyle Baths proposition. The place was somewhere this side of the Presidio. The thought annoyed him. It was as if fate was pushing him to another useless turndown.

Well, why not? When it came to that, why not check off everything in town? At least he was being thorough.

Next step would be Oakland, and that meant commuting by ferry boat across the Bay. He didn't mind the boat, but he hated the wasted hour or more each day. There had been enough of that in France. After the last eighteen months he felt ambition gnawing at him. He had to get somewhere. Accomplish something.

He started off with a long stride, glad of the invigorating wind. He had missed it during those long months. Somehow, when he enlisted, he had seen himself fighting fear, losing a leg, even dying, but he hadn't believed the thing he would feel most was the pointlessness of it all. Never getting anywhere. Maybe two yards of mud gained after days and nights. Make that weeks.

He hadn't missed women. There were French girls, charming, vibrant. Lonely. But they wouldn't replace the loss of two ambitious years out of his life. Before he went overseas he had never dreamed he wouldn't come home to proud employers, fighting for his services at various newspapers. Or elsewhere.

The world had been his oyster. He had been sent off amid cheers and solemn promises from two editors that they would remain faithful. They hadn't. But then, neither had he. So he had nothing to complain about. He laughed to himself now at the naivety of Cal-Berkeley's twenty-year-old sophomore-class Wonder Boy who thought the world was his oyster.

A woman came up the hill, passing him with a bottle of milk and a long loaf of fresh bread in her string bag. She made him think of Paris. Paris with the lights out and faces wan, anxious. Faces that had seen four years of what he complained about for eighteen months.

He was ashamed, but that didn't make his depression go away.

Well, off to the Kyle Baths.

A few minutes later he was almost blinded by the sunlight glittering off the glass roof of a peculiar building that ran in steps down the face of a low cliff. It was an imitation of the celebrated Sutro Baths built between Land's End and the Cliff House. Did the Kyles really believe they could compete with the product of Adolph Sutro, who had been the leading light and the Mayor of the city at the beginning of its greatness?

The world's most celebrated swimming champions had won their wings – and their medals – at Sutro Baths. The Kyle Baths dealt in other athletic accomplishments as well, but in none of them had they ever been able to compete with Sutro Baths. The best that could be said for the Kyle Baths was that it might prove to be the fourth or fifth in its field.

Kyle seemed to feel that all it needed was a daughter who was little better than a child to compete with the great Dr Merritt,

4

who had so brilliantly carried on the work of her father, Adolph Sutro, for thirty or forty years. Denis had admired the doyenne of Sutro Baths, as all the city did, ever since he had lived in San Francisco. And he was sure the only reason Kyle was trying to compete with Sutro's talented daughter was out of personal jealousy of Dr Merritt. He couldn't win at that game.

But Jason Kyle's ambition was better than nothing, he supposed. With this in mind he saw to it that he didn't slump or look anxious. He was careful to adopt the old, easy self-confidence that had always been so much a part of his nature before the war.

He had been walking faster and soon found himself crossing the cliffside road in front of the Kyle Baths, noting that it had been paved but not very well kept up. Someone ought to get on to the city about that. It reflected on the property in the area. The importance of city taxes should be brought up before the City Hall.

Cars, mostly Fords, and one long touring car with isinglass windows, passed along the street in front of the Baths, but they seemed to be turning off and heading for the Presidio Drive. The traffic, in what appeared to be a new parking lot beside the Baths, was confined to a pretty riff-raff clientele, almost entirely male. He suspected they paid their fifteen cents admission to spend the day there. Not necessarily on athletics, but just loafing around.

He crossed the street and headed down the first flight of stairs under the worn wooden shingle:

KYLE BATHS
JASON KYLE, PROPRIETOR

The place had never interested him before the war and didn't strike him as anything to rave about now, but clearly the Kyles were mighty proud to show off their name.

On the first level below the street the stairs spread out to make room for the cashier's cage on the left. The cashier was a good-looking female of forty or possibly more. She impressed him with her pleasant smile as she looked up from a ledger and dipped her pen in an ink bottle set into the end of the counter. She remained busy but greeted him, "Good afternoon, sir," and then went on dipping her pen.

He took a few steps over to her, gave her his best smile. She reminded him of his aunts in England, but, unless her look was strictly for the public, she seemed warm and welcoming. He pulled out a heavy silver dollar – the usual currency of San Francisco – and accepted his change.

He had no intention of entering the pool or the tennis courts, or studying the terrifying exhibits of prehistoric man that were, bizarrely, littered around the bathhouse, not to mention a gigantic man-eating lizard he had met in his paleontology class long ago. The cashier pointed out to him the place to receive his swimsuit and the dressing room. He thanked her, enjoyed another of her warm smiles, glancing at her name above the cashier's window:

MRS SANTINI, HEAD CASHIER

He had meant to ask where he could reach the manager of the Baths, but decided instead to give the place a once-over. He could already hear the unique, hollow sounds which echoed against the glass roof from the main pool.

It was after school had been let out and the sounds came pleasantly from the youngsters playing in the big sand pile. A few others, in their early teens, were timing each other as they slid down the slide to the pool. A race was coming in two weeks and they were obviously taking it seriously.

As far as the rest of the baths were concerned, a few benches on three sides of the pool were occupied by what seemed to Mallory a number of disreputable males, huddled there, legs, feet, shoes or boots, and all.

The Kyle Baths certainly needed management.

Denis walked on down the stairs, then saw a curious creation

6

on a billiard table in a side room. The exhibit seemed to be a church. He turned and went into the room and recognized the west face of Notre Dame Cathedral in Paris. Even the gargoyles were there.

He had thought he was alone and was startled when a figure in white rose up from under the table with a dust cloth in one hand and a feather duster in the other.

A cleaning woman. Her pale golden hair was partly confined by a bandeau of some kind and her tall, slender form was sheathed in a beltless white dress that looked clean enough but in style was at least ten years old.

He had been taken aback by this apparition and found himself staring at her, speechless, until her pale eyebrows went up and her shapely mouth looked almost as if she might smile any minute, though she didn't.

"You were looking for somebody, mister?"

Her voice might be musical but the words had the broad, very clear enunciation of the West Coast. It disappointed him.

"Sorry. I didn't mean to disturb your work. But I've heard about the Baths. I was just curious. That's a miniature of Notre Dame in Paris, isn't it? Beautiful work. The original, I mean. Not that this isn't a fine piece of work."

Her eyes lighted.

"Have you seen the original? You are lucky. This was built by an old Frenchman. He was homesick."

"My people live in England. I've been on sketching holidays in Europe."

She had been rhythmically rubbing her cloth over the cathedral's great westerly façade. He could see that she had become interested when he mentioned sketching.

"Do you sketch French buildings? Historical ones?"

He was amused. Very few cleaning women looked this interested when someone mentioned sketching, and especially French cathedrals. He pursued his advantage.

"I have done, but not often."

She was looking thoughtful as she dropped the cloth and

7

waved her duster around the miniature cathedral, along with a tornado of dust. It wasn't a very good piece of art but obviously the cleaning woman cared for it.

Some of the building before him was made of clay, some of painted wood, and the flying buttresses were pretty shaky. Some sort of metal had seen its way in as well.

She looked a bit anxious as she saw him frown.

"I'd like to see your British work too. But this is authentic, isn't it? I was told so by the artist."

"In its way," he assured her. "Perhaps his first attempt at anything so comprehensive." He was beginning to hope she would be impressed by his knowledge. It would be a better introduction to her than if he merely told her he was looking for a job.

"For the work of an amateur – I mean – a non-professional, quite admirable."

He felt that she was still under the spell of his cultured tone.

"Your French work might be popular here," she suggested. "You might . . ." She hesitated. "I mean to say, would you consider selling some of your sketches of France if you were asked?"

"I hadn't thought of it." Which was true enough.

"They could be hung around this room. You have some, I suppose."

Some of his articles in the *Evening Journal* had been adorned by his sketches. Most of them were political and got some nasty reactions from the readers of the "other" party. He had certainly sold sketches to his buddies in France, but they would hardly qualify for this room. They had been done at the behest of fellow doughboys and were all females in the place Pigalle.

No need to go into that with this girl, whether she was a "Kyle" or not. For one thing, take away those cleaning woman's rags and she would be a beauty. Maybe it was Old Man Kyle who gave the family such a nasty name.

He debated mentally whether he should tell her the truth about himself and just possibly land the job. She might even have a

8

sense of humor. On the other hand he himself did have a sense of humor of sorts and he decided to play it through.

He shrugged, grinned, and said, "I could show you a bit of my work. Samples, you might say. And see what you think." Mischievously, he added, "There isn't anyone else who must vote on it, is there? Besides your employer, of course?"

She looked away a few seconds, then raised her head. He was amused by the reaction. She would make a beautiful model herself for – he didn't know what, but he would like to try.

She smiled softly. "I'm sure it would be all right. I could ask Mrs Santini."

"When should I bring them? The sketches," he added eagerly, like a good amateur. "I'm sure we could come to terms, Miss – Miss . . ."

"The cleaning woman," she said with an enchanting smile.

"Wonderful," and as he left her, he meant it.

Marina Kyle went on dusting Notre Dame's flying buttresses, but paying furtive attention to the departure of the self-assured young man whose name she still didn't know. Not American-born, she thought, though his language was certainly American. There was a slight accent in that voice. Perhaps the west of England, judging by a Devonshire woman she had once known.

The cashier, Mrs Santini, caught her smiling to herself, although half an hour ago she had complained of a headache. Now, as she watched her, Mrs Santini looked back up the long, wide flight of stairs to see what had so much interested her boss.

"Good-looking enough to be in films; dangerous but attractive, don't you think?"

Marina shrugged. "Like a lot of them just out of uniform. What he is doing here in the Baths I've no idea. He said nothing about the job. He's an artist, I think."

Mrs Santini devoted a couple of minutes to watching the stranger's exit, after which she returned her attention to Marina in a worried way.

"You don't look your best, Miss Kyle."

9

Marina laughed, but it seemed to the motherly Mrs Santini that she really was looking extremely pale and tired.

"Excuse me, Miss Kyle, but you've been working awfully hard, what with two of those handymen out and now a cleaning woman. You'd ought to go home and lay yourself down this afternoon."

Marina looked around, pushed back her straggling lengths of hair, and agreed.

"I think I will. Thanks for the advice, Rosa." She wrinkled her nose and looked around. "We're practically deserted. I think we're going to have to close down before the authorities do it for us if this damned flu epidemic gets any worse. I thought it would be almost over by now."

She began to peel off her pinafore and ancient overdress. "We're not doing any good here. Close up and go home, dear."

"Got my receipts to tote up but then I might dismiss the crew, except the watchmen, and walk over to the cable car. Hard to get a transfer this time of day."

Marina Kyle turned tiredly.

"Don't be silly. Take a taxi. Charge it to our account. Heavens! North Beach isn't that far away . . . Good-night, dear."

Mrs Santini looked after her with the devotion that had lasted during the younger woman's lifetime.

No doubt about it. Marina Kyle surely looked overworked. It was the shortage of help, thanks to the accursed Spanish influenza that had finally reached the West Coast.

Two

D enis Mallory spent most of the next few days at the French exhibits in various museums, being unexpectedly inspired, and sketched until his finger pads were numb.

Since the great earthquake and fire thirteen years before, some of the rebuilding had been hasty and temporary, but there were additions to various collections, plus the pieces Denis remembered.

When he started out to sketch he told himself that Marina Kyle, if the cleaning woman was indeed the Kyle girl, would be unlikely to know the difference between good and bad art. And were sketches really art, anyway? But something surprising took over his sketching materials and he was surprised when he stepped out on the area of the new Civic Center to discover that his working fingers cared, whether he did or not.

Normally, it would have been depressing to run into so many flu masks on the street and especially in the cable cars. Those sunken, worried eyes stared at him above the mouth coverings, obviously wondering if he was contagious and whether he could expose them. Since he had gone through a siege of flu himself two years ago as a "Welcome to France", he was reasonably sure that after his exposure to hundreds of flu victims since, he must have become immune.

The constant reminder of the masks blowing around him in the afternoon wind was not pleasant, but the wind itself was invigorating and restored his sense of life and ambition.

He had to admit finally that it just might be his recent encounter with the corn-silk lovely at the Baths.

He put away his sketch pad, looked around to get his bearings, and started off to complete his little errand to the Kyle Baths.

He transferred twice by street car, always in the general direction of the Golden Gate, and walked the rest of the way toward the Baths.

It was here at the wide entrance of the Baths that he received his first jarring barrier – a large, hastily painted sign across the stairs leading down:

QUARANTINE!
By the Health Department of the
CITY AND COUNTY OF SAN FRANCISCO!

He looked around. A few people, mostly wearing flu masks, were wandering along the cliffside road. He couldn't imagine where they were going or what they were doing out here, but they didn't seem to be going anywhere in particular. It made him think of the endless "forever" he had often felt in the trenches.

He devoted some attention to what was going on behind and below the chain that stretched across the staircase, but neither saw nor heard any sounds in the bathhouse below.

Deserted, obviously.

What had happened to the corn-silk beauty? Surely she hadn't gotten the influenza so quickly! He didn't know her from the man in the moon but he didn't like to think of her suffering with a dangerous disease. Not only did he barely know her, truth to tell, he didn't know for sure who she was!

Wondering about this and vaguely aware of distant fog horns out in the Golden Gate, Mallory was interrupted by a male voice behind him.

"Baths are closed. The flu, you know."

Hoping the flu victim of the Baths was not the girl he had met a few days ago, he swung around and saw a smooth, carefully groomed man studying him.

Denis said, "Has it spread that quick? I was here not long ago. Everything was all right then."

The stranger shrugged casually. "Came down all of a sudden. Funny, too. Marina looked delicate, but this took us all by surprise."

The fellow must know Marina Kyle very well. He seemed intimate enough. For no legitimate reason, Denis resented him. If, of course, the girl Denis Mallory was looking for really happened to be Marina Kyle.

Denis's manner became cooler. "Miss Kyle wanted me to show her a few sketches. Is she quite ill?"

"I'm afraid Marina can't see strangers yet. Even I see her only once a day, and I know her as well as anyone. What are the sketches about?"

Denis found himself even more angry with this pompous fool. "How bad is she? I mean, I found her charming. And kind."

"Oh, she's all of that. She can be a real charmer when she wants to be. But as she always says, she's my girl. I've known her since the Year One. I suppose you have your sketches with you. As something of an avocation, I am the sponsor of the Cavenaugh Gallery."

Denis tried to back down from his dislike of the man. It also astonished him to realize how much Marina Kyle had been in his thoughts since the day before yesterday. Working on the sketches might have encouraged his thoughts, but he couldn't deny them.

He could kick himself for asking a favor, but he tried: "When Miss Kyle is better, I wonder if you'd mention the Paris and English sketches and the artist, who wishes her well. I'll try again to see her when she is feeling better."

Cavanaugh was very casual over his girlfriend's illness. "Certainly. Want to give me your phone number?"

This was humiliating. "I've just gotten back in town. I don't have a phone in yet. But as soon as I do, I'll leave the number with the cashier here, along with a sketch or two. That's all right?"

"Of course – you can leave the sketches with me if you like. They might cheer her up."

He accepted the two sketches Mallory took from the folio. The

13

man's smile was easy, but he looked more ruthless than he sounded. His chill account of Marina Kyle's illness reminded Denis of his father's people – the old ladies who were left had banished his youthful father from the family in England after his marriage to an Irish-American servant girl with neither money nor ancestors. This time was long gone by but the small amounts of Denis Mallory's salary that he had been able to scrape together for them following their loud hints during the early stages of the war had gone unacknowledged. They died without any more communication with him.

"Not bad," Marina's supposed boyfriend admitted about the sketches with a certain amount of indifference. "I'm Blake Cavenaugh, by the way." He said it as though it was a matter to remember.

"I'm Mallory," Denis returned without enthusiasm.

Blake Cavenaugh stuck the sketches under his arm and said, "Hmm. Europe isn't my big interest. But you never know how Marina will feel. Anyway, the best of luck. This is your address?"

Denis despised himself for even hinting at his own anxiety, but he nodded and Cavenaugh studied the words on the envelope, a little puzzled.

"Montezuma Street? Where is that exactly?"

It was actually a rented room in a lean-faced house of the Excelsior Tract. In what locals called "the Mission District". Not slums but pretty far from the wealthy Kyles' world.

Cavenaugh started up the street and called over his shoulder, "I'm afraid Marina won't have much time for you. She's not very sociable."

Denis turned away, not wanting to be seen watching the fellow, but it occurred to him that he not only hadn't seen the Kyle girl, he still didn't even know where she lived.

By this time, half a dozen passersby had sauntered over to the quarantine sign and peered down the stairs to the big, locked chain sealing off the lower level. Having satisfied their curiosity about the dark bowels of the Kyle Baths, they strayed off to several "flivers", cranking and then rushing to get into their seats. An older man in uniform headed for the Presidio Grounds, interested in the distant bungalows and houses of the military. There seemed to be nothing of interest to Denis, who was about to turn away and wander over to Fisherman's Wharf for a lunch of sorts, when he heard footsteps on the stairs below the quarantine sign.

He took a few steps, looked down the stairs, and saw Mrs Santini. She called to him.

"Sorry, sir. Miss Kyle isn't able to see you." She came on up the stairs and, to his surprise, held the quarantine sign up over her head to talk to him. "I wonder. Would you like to get another look at the interior? It's a terrific location. No business now. They've locked us up. But I often think some day it could be quite nice all fixed up again, and no flu, of course."

He gave her his name, ducked under the chain, hung it up again and started down with her.

"And I'm Rosa Santini," she told him.

They shook hands, well pleased with each other. The hollow sounds crowded around them even more closely. His first reaction to the huge place hadn't left him. He still saw possibilities for the future of the Baths without liking anything at all about the eerie place as it appeared today.

"What a place for a café overlooking . . ."

"The swimming baths?" she joked.

"No. Gardens, maybe. Something of that sort, where the large pool is."

She nodded. "Go on. My sainted husband had ideas like that."

"Well," he went on, inspired. "Maybe a fancy restaurant, French-style. Using one of those balconies overlooking the gardens. With a little sidewalk café lower, near the gardens. With . . ." His imagination surprised him and Mrs Santini, who seemed to be enlivened by the idea.

"What else? Go on."

He tried to laugh off his own sudden spurt of ideas, but it was clear that she had been sincere about her interest.

15

"Oh, maybe umbrellas over the tables, with sounds of rain overhead, like the cafés in Paris during rain showers."

Mrs Santini looked at him oddly. "Miss Kyle mentioned my husband's ideas to me long ago. She was just a child, but his description must have gotten to her." She shook her head. "But you have – or I should say Miss Kyle would have a fight with Mr Jason. He's kind of old-fashioned. Nothing inventive for him."

"Well, it's not my property. I suppose the owner does have some rights, even if their taste is out of date."

He got to the subject that interested him more at the moment. "How serious is Miss Kyle's condition? She seems like a lovely person."

To his surprise she suddenly changed her tone, spoke in a louder voice, unlike the warm, intimate way in which she had seemed to discuss changes with him. She said emphatically, "All business, sir. Nothing but business."

She had spoken with such decisiveness that Denis was puzzled and started to look behind him until her foot came down on his toe with a playful pinch. He took the hint, unpleasantly aware that someone was listening to them.

He backtracked. "Incredible that one man, her father, I mean, should have created a world like this, almost singlehandedly, as you might say."

"Thank you," a smooth, jovial voice said behind him. "My little girl has become quite a fair assistant to me. A pity the poor child may have inherited her mother's weakness but . . ." He went on, though Denis paid little attention. He was aware of Mrs Santini's sharp, sudden breath. Evidently, Jason Kyle's remark about his daughter's weakness had irritated Mrs Santini. Denis shared Mrs Santini's annoyance.

Mrs Santini introduced them. "Sir, this gentleman is here with sketches Miss Marina wishes to see."

"Oh?" Kyle looked him up and down. Denis remained cool. He was prepared for the arrogance of at least one of the Kyles and went on, "I don't imagine sketches would be very successful in the atmosphere of the Baths here."

Mrs Santini said innocently, "Anyway, Mr Cavenaugh didn't seem to like them." She sighed.

Jason Kyle was passing the sketches back to Denis but, as Denis reached for them, privately cursing Mrs Santini for interfering, Kyle took the sketches again and reconsidered the work Denis had so carelessly given him at Mrs Santini's nod.

"Well, Blake's tastes run to stocks, bonds, shipyards, and steamer runs to Hawaii. I give him a little advice now and then about his art exhibits."

Denis saw Rosa Santini's eyebrows go up and guessed with amusement that Jason Kyle's influence on his friend Cavenaugh was a trifle exaggerated. Kyle went on with self-satisfaction, "These sketches are not bad, you know. Not bad at all."

He nodded to Denis, hesitated, looked Denis over, and then suggested, "I might let my little girl see them when I visit her. The child is in the hospital right now. She seems to have been the last to catch the infernal flu. What do you think, Rosa? He has come about the job, I presume? He's a better prospect than any of the others we've interviewed. He might help us. At least, until Marina recovers. But once I take the girl in hand again, I'm sure things will work out satisfactorily. Meanwhile . . ." He gave Denis a pleasing smile, almost a grin. But there was no mistaking his arrogant superiority. Denis was prepared for that.

For Denis, this job, which he certainly needed, had one great advantage. It would keep Marina Kyle in sight. He hoped.

But he was beginning to be deeply concerned now over whether Marina Kyle had ever thought twice about him.

17

Three

As luck would have it, five days later, when no word had come from Mrs Santini, who had Denis Mallory's address, Ben Riggs drove up from Mission Street to see his friend on Montezuma Street.

Denis Mallory's rented room was at the back of the house, hardly big enough for his bed and a kitchen table and chair, the bathroom being down the dark hall. Ben caught him surrounded by, of all things, sketches of old British and French buildings, plus several of the Devonshire coastline and the moors.

Ben had a job for him, smallish but genuine.

"I got to talking to your friend, Larry Hoaglund," Ben explained. "We haven't found a permanent berth for you, but there's a small job that fits you."

Charity among friends, Denis thought but did not say so. He was grateful for their efforts. He laughed. "I'll probably grab it. Tell me more."

Ben shrugged. "The paper wants a sketch of our saintly new Mayor, old buddy."

"Friend or foe?" Denis asked.

"You know the *Journal*. Foe, of course. And a lot of humor. Not much money but it'll be talked about. The cartoon, I mean."

When Denis was silent, Ben pursued the matter.

"Well, what do you say? Or is there someone in high places you don't want to upset? You haven't been to see Jason Kyle yet, have you?" He noted the interest in Denis's eyes and asked, "What's the fatal charm?"

"Well, I've met the Kyle girl. If that counts."

18

"Nothing doing there. She's just come down with the flu. I heard it this a.m. But if you think she's changed her stripes . . ."

"You ought to know. You sent me there."

"Well, I'm damned. Then this sketch offer I brought you for the *Journal* is off. And I've climbed at least fifty steps getting up to this mausoleum!"

"Sorry I gave you this trip for nothing."

Ben Riggs waved away apologies. "And to show you I bear no grudges, my friend, I brought along a bottle – right off the boat – to stimulate you on your first *Journal* paycheck after two years."

They shared the gin Ben Riggs poured. Denis was a little ashamed of what he felt, like a schoolboy with a crush on the Kyle girl, and he still hadn't decided to tell Ben his interest in her was the real reason why he was holding out for the Kyle job. He knew the whole thing was idiotic. This was no time to throw away his immediate future on a highly dubious connection with the Kyle Baths.

He thanked Ben Riggs again once the drink was finished, and returned the bottle to him with the promise, "I'll let you know how things turn out, and next time, I promise, the bottle's on me."

"I'll keep that in mind, buddy."

Alone on the steps, Denis was aware that his landlady had begun to watch him from the front room with the scrim curtains discreetly pushed aside. He considered this a hint to be on his way, and made a fast bolt into the hall and back to his room.

Knowing what to expect of the deceptive sunny weather – the windy Golden Gate, he made a grab at his only English possession, a mackintosh.

The landlady, a rangy, toothy female, was lingering in the hall with its odor of spare ribs and sauerkraut – surprising for an Italian neighborhood.

"Going out to see the City, Mr Mallory?"

It always amused him to note that wherever he had gone in seafaring towns, "the City" was always their reference to San Francisco. He wondered if he would ever get to that point of adulation.

"That's right." He tipped two fingers to his forehead and then hurried down the long flight of front steps and off toward the Mission street car.

Was he going back there too soon? Would they think better of him if he didn't rush to chase them up? But he could always make a joke of it, saying he happened to be in the neighborhood. A little obvious, but he couldn't think of anything better at the moment. He didn't want Jason Kyle to think he was rushing things. On the other hand, if that nice Mrs Santini thought that, it might please her. He scarcely knew her but he felt already that they were friends.

After the transfers, he reached his destination across town and almost walked into someone in whom he had no interest whatever. Less than no interest, in fact. Blake Cavenaugh. The fellow was being very sociable with Mrs Santini at her box office window, where she was scrubbing the counter. She showed every sign of boredom and did not seem to hear many of his remarks.

"Well, it occurred to me," Cavenaugh said, "that with so many employees knocked out by the flu, that an extra girl might be useful. Her father asked me to speak to you."

"Not my business, Mr Cavenauagh. I don't hire and fire."

"Oh, come now, Rosie," he went on coaxingly. "You, of all people . . ."

Seeing her heavy frown, Denis reminded himself never to call her "Rosie".

She looked over Cavenaugh's head and nodded to Denis with a flattering attention that pleased him.

"Yes, Mr Mallory. You were expected. Do come around the chain . . . I'm sorry, Mr Cavenaugh. I'm afraid it's out of my hands now. Mr Mallory has been hired and it's his job as of today. Not that we are open yet, of course."

Blake Cavenaugh didn't seem the least surprised. He held out thin, somewhat bony, fingers.

"Good to hear it. Congratulations – er – what was the name again?"

"Mallory."

"Yes. Quite so."

Denis followed the cashier's directions, raised the chain, set it back in place with a heavy, thumping jangle. Not knowing quite what was expected of him from here on, he waited until she took his arm and they descended regally together. Marina's boyfriend was coming along behind them, not so much hurrying as making sure he didn't miss anything they said to each other.

Denis found himself on a lower level, just above the pool. Mrs Santini looked around, smiled and said, "I see we've lost our pursuer."

She was right. Wherever Cavenaugh might be, he had apparently lost interest in them.

Mrs Santini became a little freer, pointing out changes that might be made "when Miss Kyle is better".

Denis nodded and she surprised him suddenly by reminding him, "But I don't intend to go above Miss Kyle's authority. I merely hope she will be persuaded about eventual changes. I consider Miss Kyle my boss."

"I understand."

She looked at him, her eyes careful and observant.

"I hope you do. Nobody was ever so good to my husband and me years ago when he was ill. She was only a girl, but I'll never forget. Just about the last thing he said to me was to take care of Miss Marina. He was caretaker here clear back to when she was born to dear Mrs Kyle."

He touched her hand briefly. He did not usually feel this demonstrative. "I do understand, Mrs Santini. Would my word mean anything to you?"

She said, "Oh, yes. I believed you from the first. You have honest eyes."

He was embarrassed. Any compliments he received were not of that nature, but he was surprised to find he meant what he had said, and hoped she did too.

He glanced over at a room he recognized as Marina Kyle's beloved museum and, trying not to act like an author with his first sale, moved casually toward the miniature of Notre Dame Cathedral.

At the same time he was startled by the heavy echo of a door slamming behind a balcony halfway up the Golden Gate side of the building.

Mrs Santini swore in Italian.

He glanced at her, amused, but she made no apology.

"Those damned kids from this side of the marina neighborhood. They get in by one of the doors up there. It shouldn't be unlocked. Excuse me! I'll go and lock it."

"Shall I go?"

"No. But you might like to see where we've put your sketches."

Before he could thank her, she was off up the stairs to the next level. He pretended to have the most casual interest, though he couldn't help being curious, and after a minute or two he went to see whether his work had been exhibited at least halfway decently.

It was all of that. Embarrassingly prominent. But that didn't prevent his studying the sketches he had finished so quickly, at moments without much concentration. He wished he had taken more time with them, perhaps spent more time doing something creditable and less time giving his buddies a cheap sex thrill by sketching the prostitutes they saw on their leave in Paris.

He wondered if Mrs Santini had been reading his mind when she joined him suddenly.

"What did you think of Miss Kyle?"

"Very nice." He didn't want to overdo it.

She smiled, but her voice was firm. "Well, just remember. Be cautious with the old – Mr Kyle, but listen to Miss Kyle."

"I'll do that." He liked the idea very much.

Four

I t was more than two weeks before Denis saw the Kyle girl again.

Nor was he prepared when he did meet her. He was busy scrubbing up the displays on one of the balconies when a flurry of excitement made him look up toward the top of the main staircase.

Mrs Santini was waving a copy of the *Morning Examiner* and hurrying down the stairs to him.

"Read this, Mr Denis," she called. "Miss Kyle is up and out, good as new." Breathless, she thrust the paper into his dusty hands. It was folded to the "About the City" column and, to his annoyance, he took it with more haste than he would like to have shown.

She looked at him expectantly.

"See? The picture is fuzzy but anyone with her looks photographs well, no matter what."

It was true but, having heard no word directly from or about Marina, he did not want anyone, even his friend Rosa Santini, to know that he cared.

He could have kicked himself when he heard his own voice asking, though he knew, "Who's the fellow in the picture with her?"

Mrs Santini leaned forward, noting the news photo of the pair waltzing at the celebrated St Francis Hotel's afternoon Tea Dance.

"Oh, Blake Cavenaugh gets around. He owns the Western Pacific Steamship Line and the Cavenaugh Shipyards." She

23

added, studying the photo, "Cavenaugh and Miss Kyle have known each other for years. He and her father went to university together. I'm sure he wants to attach Kyle to his Cavenaugh empire through marriage to Miss Kyle. But he's going to be out of luck there."

The rich attract the rich, Denis thought cynically. So the guy could dance. Well, Denis considered himself a fair-to-middling dancer – which meant, slightly above average.

"Miss Kyle looks lovely," he remarked, careful not to be over-enthusiastic. "The flu doesn't seem to have hurt her at all."

"She does look fragile," Mrs Santini said. "But she's durable."

Durable or not, she looked like his type, even in an imperfect world. He returned the paper to Mrs Santini and went back to his cleaning.

Mrs Santini stooped to see what he was doing. He had been interrupted while scrubbing under the long row of seats but now he shook his cloth and grinned.

"I've never seen so damned much taffy. All sticky. They chew it and then kick it under the seats. It sticks on everything."

She laughed. "You're as bad as Miss Kyle. Janitors are hired for that." She hesitated before returning to her box office at the head of the stairs and pointed out the men working along the ends of the balconies.

"What do you think of the decorations a friend of Mr Kyle's made for the reopening of the bathhouse? The small local telephone company has merged with the city service. They took the tiny switchboard lights and strung them. They are going to light up the balconies and the rest Christmas-style. Along with rolls of red, white and blue crêpe paper."

He shrugged. "If the Lord and Master's friend did it, who am I to say no?"

She looked around. "Can we finish all this by opening day? That doesn't give us much time."

He raised up, bumped his head on the underside of a row of seats, and reminded her, "If no one else quits. Otherwise," he

24

reminded her with rueful humour, "you and I will be selling taffy, peanuts and ice cream up and down these balconies."

She remained good-humoured. "We'll be ready. At any rate, you and I will be."

He was more than a little sickened by his job. It wasn't quite what he had in mind when he joined the Kyles' temporary work force.

By lunchtime his appetite had been removed by his job. Since the ice catering service was late in arriving, he gave up and received from Mrs Santini a "frankfurter" – called a "hot dog" since the war began.

By two o'clock he was back discussing with a new cleaning woman the quality of towels, cloths and soap in the toilets. He had just finished this chore and decided the corners of this particular balcony needed more sweeping. Where the devil was the new janitor?

The sunlight across the balcony was suddenly cut off by two people, Marina Kyle and Blake Cavenaugh.

Cavenaugh was doing his best to assert his proprietorship over Marina. He also seemed to be spreading his friendly influence over everyone in sight. He immediately began to flatter Denis over his sketches. But of course, this was to please Marina, not the artist himself.

"So this is the artist, Marina. We must see more of his work. Congratulations, Mr . . ."

"Mallory," Marina said. She did remember Denis's name, which was better than nothing. She explained to Denis, "Blake here has an excellent little gallery on Sutter Street. I am hoping he will decide some of your work should be added to his fine collection."

Denis did not forget Cavenaugh's first indifference to his sketches, and he himself never thought they were professional, but he was more than pleased at Marina Kyle's interest in them.

Cavenaugh suggested, "I'm sure Miss Kyle would be willing to bring some over to me at the gallery some day; wouldn't you, hon?"

Hon! Denis almost wished the matter hadn't come up.

But Marina sounded sincere.

"I'd love to. Suppose we go up to Blake's place tomorrow, Denis. We'd better tell Rosa we are both going to be gone at the same time."

Denis was pleased at her addressing him by his first name. It wasn't much, but it was a start, and in front of Cavenaugh too.

"Good. That's settled," Cavenaugh cut in, taking Miss Kyle's arm. "Let's go and look at the sketches the young man has here in the Baths. I only saw two of them, but they were worthwhile. If you like Europe." He saw Marina glance at him and added, "And who doesn't?"

While they walked up the stairs, Marina agreed with Cavenaugh, and then smiled at Denis, as though she had done him a great favor, which, he realized, she had, in getting his sketches into the Cavenaugh Gallery.

On the ride home to her father's house on Cliffside Heights very little was said at first between Marina and Blake. This was often the case. He had been her father's college buddy and close friend before he and Jason ever talked about his possible marriage to Jason's daughter.

She shared her father's business with Blake but not their talk of her marriage. These business interests did not rouse any passion or excitement in her. Their physical relationship consisted of two false attempts at lovemaking, and his almost fatherly assumption that such matters could wait until "later", an idea with which she heartily agreed while promising nothing. She did not like to tell her father the truth, that she had no interest in marrying his closest friend and associate.

He had taught her a little about art, almost more than she needed to know. Though she had been unusually interested in the artist's work today, Cavenaugh had not even mentioned it. She said, finally, "Denis Mallory's sketches were really alive, weren't they? I could almost see London or Paris when I looked at them."

26

Cavenaugh smiled. "I'm afraid that's not art, my dear."

"What?"

His eyebrows raised.

"Now, don't get huffy, hon. You and I know good work when we see it. I assume you praised him because you need his help at the bathhouse. I'm perfectly willing to go along with you if you need him and feel he wouldn't come in without this absurd praise for his artwork. But you and I needn't fool ourselves. Your father would never do that."

"Well, my father did approve of—"

"For some reason of his own, I've no doubt."

To change the subject she said, "I feel I missed a lot while I was in the hospital. I'm way behind when it comes to balancing the books. And Father won't let me work on them yet. He keeps trying to spare me, as he says."

It annoyed her that Blake should be suddenly so interested in the bad driving of a woman in a sleek new Buick ahead of them that he asked her to repeat what she had said.

He chuckled. "Well, little girl, I wouldn't worry too much. Doesn't your father always know what he's doing?"

She shrugged. She didn't like being shunted off like this when, in a manner of speaking, the books had been her job for several years.

"It's getting pretty late and I want to check the bills for the reopening."

"I understand. You have a good head, my dear. But you must admit your father should have had a son to take some of his worries off his shoulders. It's unfair to expect a girl like you to do a man's work."

Once, it would have hurt to realize that she was only a poor substitute for a son, but by this time she was able to twist her warm lips a little and echo sarcastically, "What a shame!"

He laughed.

Her tone always escaped men. They figured it was just her acknowledgement of the truth.

He pulled up in front of the large, ground-level garage,

27

came around, got her out, and walked her up the stone steps to the first floor above the garage. He held his hand out for the key but found himself dismissed with her friendly apology.

"I have so much to do, Blake. With the opening so close and all . . . See you soon."

"Yes, of course. Good-night, hon."

He lowered his head. His lips faintly touched her cheek, then he walked down the steps again, but she saw that he was both puzzled and displeased.

She was sorry. However, it occurred to her that he took too much for granted. It wasn't just their disagreement over Denis Mallory's sketches. It was a feeling that he generally hadn't been very honest today and at other times. His attitude toward Mallory, for example, was pleasant, even friendly; but now, an hour later, she had caught him in a flat lie that he seemed to regard as normal. It was two-faced, and not for the first time. Did he conduct all his business that way? On other occasions she had made excuses, dismissed or pretended to ignore the dishonesty.

He was her father's closest associate and maybe set in his ways, but at times like this she didn't even like him.

She had half a notion to drive down town to the St Francis Hotel alone. She always found friends there and any number of Stanford graduates who would be glad to join her. Then, perhaps, they could all go somewhere for dinner, as they used to on Big Game Day, before graduation.

Why not?

She took a quick bath, wishing her father would let her get a shower put in her bathroom, then dressed and was making up when Jason Kyle knocked on her bedroom door. He was always careful to give her physical privacy, though he expected her thoughts to be guided by him.

She put her little silver mascara box back in her bureau drawer. He didn't approve of it. "Too trashy," he dismissed it with a disdain that many people found cutting and imperious.

"Yes, Father?"

"May I come in?"

"Of course." He always asked, but she liked the sense of privacy, since she had never been able to persuade him that she would prefer an apartment of her own.

He eyed her black-fringed new dinner dress and looked pleased.

"Then you are going out with Blake? When he didn't come in with you I thought you might have quarrelled."

"Not really. You don't quarrel with Blake. How could you? Isn't he always right?"

He smiled, evidently reading only praise in her remark.

"Quite true. Enormously helpful, if it does annoy me sometimes. I hope you two remain close."

"Close?" She tried not to put an inflection in the word, but he must have noticed something.

"That is to say, I hope you never trade his decency in for one of those gigolos who are so popular since the war. The city seems to be full of them these days."

She waved her silver-backed mirror to check her hair in its fairly modern tan-gold twist, but he was watching her face. She saw that he looked tired and a few belated wrinkles were beginning to be noticeable.

"Father, you worked far too hard while I was sick. I can take all those boring profit and loss figures off your hands now."

"Fairly soon, little girl. I don't want to rush your recovery. You know what those doctors said."

"Oh, don't be silly."

He gave her a chiding look but patted the back of her hand. "Well, we'll say no more about it for the moment. If you do see Blake tonight, tell him I'm still expecting a call about that preferred. He'll know."

"Preferred what?"

But he was already leaving the room. He smiled. "Well . . . I wasn't going to say . . . Your Christmas present. You do want

29

your very own sample radio in this room, don't you? It was going to be a surprise. You can get any station in the Union on it."

Curious. She could get any station she wanted on the radio she already had. She wondered if her father was working too hard since her illness. He always denied it, but it seemed likely.

He went out, closing the door behind him.

Puzzled, and not quite believing anything he said tonight, she put back her cosmetics and looked around the large, old-fashioned room that had been hers since childhood.

She had bought herself a new radio several months ago. What was this all about? She was reasonably satisfied with the radio she had chosen to replace the one that was broken. It didn't matter whether it went with the white bed, vanity dresser, and the long closet and highboy. And she had an old gramophone that she used more than her radio.

Hearing the foghorn of Mile Rock Light, she looked across the room to the long windows, through which she could see the occasional lights on the incoming fishing boats and the steamers from the Orient and Hawaii. She was no longer in the mood for the tea dance at the St Francis.

It was after seven when the Korean cook, Raymond Yee, carried Marina's dinner tray in himself, complaining all the way. He had been hired back in 1908 by Marina's mother and was considered by many San Franciscans the finest chef in California.

But a rich salary and Jason Kyle's praise before company did not salve his injured pride when – as now – he was forced to expend his considerable talents on a bowl of canned tomato soup, a pot of China tea, two slices of sourdough bread, and something in a closed tin box.

"All time you starve, Miss Marina," he greeted her as he began to set the tray on her dressing table. "That foolish pantry boy is right, one time. You eat this too." He tapped his fingernail on the tin box.

She laughed when she saw that it was a chocolate éclair, its top decorated with whipped cream. It looked good. She promised to eat it.

"You should eat with the master. It is bad to eat alone," he objected as he turned to leave.

"He eats too late. I want to finish Rosa's cash reports for the week."

As a matter of fact, her little dinner looked and smelled very appetizing. It also gave her more freedom to think about her father's uneasiness since she recovered from the flu.

What bothered him?

She had finished the soup, and one thick slice of bread, and was thinking about the éclair, when her father's phone rang somewhere in the house. If it was business, most of their associates would call her next and she waited.

As she expected, Gerda Ritter, the live-in housekeeper, knocked on her door shortly after.

"Miss Kyle, a gentleman wishes to speak to Mr Jason. But he isn't in. The caller said it was important. I gave him your number."

Almost instantly Marina's own phone rang and she called to the housekeeper, "There it is. I'll take it, Gerda. Thank you."

Probably Blake Cavenaugh about the deal Jason had mentioned. She was still a little irked by Cavenaugh's evasiveness over Denis Mallory's sketches earlier, but she reached for the phone receiver.

"Yes?"

"Miss Kyle? This is Denis Mallory."

Her fingers tightened on the receiver.

"I'm afraid there's trouble at the bathhouse. We've tried to contact Mr Kyle, but—"

"He isn't home. There was a business meeting."

"Can you come as soon as possible then? We've a fire here."

"What!"

"The fire department seems to be getting it under control, but—"

"Good God!" I'll be there. I'm hanging up."

He got in the words, "I'm told it's safe now. But we need instructions about the damage."

She heard no more. She hung up the receiver and hurriedly took out the first wrap she could reach in her closet.

Five

O nly minutes later she was driving round the cliffside and toward the Kyle bathhouse. She was relieved to see no flames lighting the night sky to the west, but there was smoke billowing up through at least one big glass pane in the roof, and the road past the Baths was crowded with cars, mostly two-seater roadsters, at least one horse and buggy team, and what appeared to be the entire San Francisco Fire Department.

Many firemen knew Marina and her father and in other circumstances she would have been delighted to see them. Now, however, she parked on the gravel near the entrance and was greeted by a fireman in water gear.

"All safe now, Miss Kyle. A couple of your employees are in there rescuing the stuff that got soaked with water. Several windows busted but no bones broken."

"Thank God for that!" She ran toward the staircase.

Everywhere below the level of the box office was so smoke-filled she and even the firemen had paroxysms of coughing.

The south wall halfway down was seared and many windows broken.

It was no life-and-death matter but Denis Mallory's sketches that Marina had liked so well were soggy, still dripping, and hopelessly ruined.

So much for Marina's worries about how she would explain to Denis Mallory that his sketches might not appear on Blake Cavenaugh's walls! But she was not in any way relieved over that.

She was still feeling her disappointment when Denis Mallory

appeared beside her, materializing out of the smoke. His clothing reeked of it.

"I'm afraid this whole end of the Baths will have to be renovated. Looks like much of it may have to be rebuilt as well. Hope you're insured."

She shook her head. "Never mind that. I hate to see your sketches wrecked."

He seemed surprised and looked into her eyes almost as if he didn't believe her. He said in an unexpectedly quiet voice, "That's very kind. No one else will miss them, believe me."

For a minute she was going to touch his smoke-stained shoulder in sympathy. Then she decided not to. He was curiously reserved with her. Surely, he wasn't afraid of her. It almost seemed that he didn't trust her friendliness.

She sighed but that was cut short by violent coughing.

"Well, shall we save whatever there is to save?" she asked.

But he was suddenly concerned with something more immediate. "The flu isn't anything to fool around with. You could get pneumonia."

She covered her mouth with her handkerchief. "Never mind that. How bad is the damage?"

"This side got it worst," he explained. "It was one of those weird accidents. The crêpe-paper streamers caught a breath of air from an open window somewhere along this part of the wall across the little lights. The lights were hot. That's about it."

Denis had turned to point out the lights and Marina gasped. "My God, your back's been scorched! Come with me."

Amid the screeching of wood elsewhere, as workers tore apart the useless damaged furniture, Marina led Denis into a little room used for first aid. Mrs Santini had arrived now and was there, doctoring a worker who had been cut by glass falling from the roof.

Denis was amused and pleased when Marina carefully removed the torn and burned strips of his shirt. She covered the seared flesh with salve; it made him wince but he lied that it didn't hurt.

Mrs Santini finished with her own patient and went out to discuss the technical aspects of the fire with the fire inspector and a representative of the insurance company.

Marina asked professionally, "How does your back feel?"

"Not bad. You have a great touch, Miss Kyle. A born healer."

She talked of his naked back as though it was an ordinary topic of conversation. Come to think of it, new male bathing trunks with no tops were now being worn in the baths.

But he was very much aware that this sudden and, in some ways, inexplicable attraction to Marina Kyle was about as useless as any he could possibly feel. People with that kind of money and power were not for him.

However, he hadn't yet found a way to avoid thinking about Marina, or about making love to her, for that matter. He still felt the overwhelming warmth of her hands on the flesh of his back. How long would it be before he could find her receptive to something more? And what could he offer if there was something more?

He wasn't even sure there would be "any more".

The burning patches on his back stung badly but he was trying to appear noble before Marina when a fireman called down the stairs, "Miss Kyle, your father's here; you're wanted."

Denis took Marina's arm and escorted her up the staircase.

Jason Kyle removed his daughter's arm from Denis and led her over to Mrs Santini's box office where the Fire Chief, surrounded by several firemen and two insurance inspectors, was waiting for her. Before they went into the little box office, Marina looked over her shoulder at Denis. "I'll see you later. We'll need your report, Denis."

Jason looked back. He didn't frown, but he was obviously puzzled that his daughter addressed the new Assistant Manager by his first name.

Then Jason called to him from the box office. "We need your report, Mallory. There is a good deal of red tape involved here."

"Really, Father!" Marina said sharply, but the imperious voice of Jason came again: "Mallory!"

Resenting everyone, Denis went over to the box office, careful to move at a moderate pace.

Six

T he Fire Chief had evidently gotten most of the evidence that concerned him and he was now examining the reports at Mrs Santini's counter.

One of the firemen was checking the reports of the three men who had strung the tiny lights and the crêpe-paper decorations. More than half were how water-soaked and the rest little more than ashes, some of which had raised havoc by flying around the bathhouse.

Jason pointed out, "We were told that those things were fireproof. You were here at the time, Mallory. Did they mention their being fireproof?"

"No, sir. I was told it was the management order. That was at mid-morning."

Jason Kyle waved a well-manicured hand impatiently.

"No matter. The decorations were a gift from a close friend and associate. According to a worker who was on the stairs at the time it started, we must blame the wind that broke that first pane of glass."

One of the insurance men nodded. "That's the story, Chief. The evidence seems to be all too clear. One of the fellows changing the crêpe stuff . . . he looked up and saw it start across the entire pool down there."

"And that meets with your observation, Mr . . ." – the Chief glanced at the paper in his hand – ". . . Mallory? You're new here; aren't you, sir?"

"Yes, sir," Denis said briefly, trying not to show any resentment.

"We owe Mr Mallory a great deal," Marina put in. "He was far more active than anyone else. He called the fire department and worked to clear out the debris, besides organizing the employees who were here, and still managed to call me. My father wasn't home."

The fireman put in, "Fellow kept using pool waters to stop the fire from spreading, and put out a lot of those blowing pieces of crêpe paper."

"They have it all down, my dear," Jason Kyle reminded her. "No one doubts that young Mallory did his part."

Compliments were nice but Denis wanted to get some place where those damned spots on his back could be salved. They burned now like fire.

"Seems pretty clear," the Chief agreed. "Of course, the insurance side of this mess is another matter. Mr Mallory's first report to us was very clear, and the others were helpful, but we may need a little more from the decorating people."

They argued among themselves for a few minutes. Denis wondered: Would they ever break up and let him go to a drug store? His fists hurt like hell when he clenched his fingers, and some cinders must have landed on the calf of his right leg. It felt like bad sunburn.

When they broke up ten or fifteen minutes later Marina offered Denis a ride home.

Almost in a panic Denis refused. It gave him the creeps to think of the elegant Marina Kyle going into the cabbage-smelling hallway of his rooming house.

"No, thanks. There's a drug store down the block where I live. I'll get fixed up there."

"Well, that settles that, gentlemen," Jason Kyle announced to the insurance men. "I'll see you all at your offices tomorrow. Still on Sutter Street, I suppose?"

"That's right, sir."

While the others left the crowded box office still discussing the fire, and Marina stopped to get Mrs Santini's view of the disaster, Denis went out across the road with his coat thrown over his good shoulder, wondering which bus would get him to his transfer point first.

He thought of calling a taxi or a jitney, which would be cheaper, but it would mean a long wait. Most drivers preferred to avoid the long hauls around the Golden Gate area. They could do much better downtown with shorter and more frequent runs. I need a car, damn it! he thought, but at the moment it was a dream. He was paid once a month and his second payday hadn't come yet. Worse! As he started to walk the long way toward the marina area, he realized something he had been too busy to think of before: he had probably lost his job. It would be weeks, maybe months before the Kyle bathhouse would be in business again.

The road tonight was much busier than usual. The fire apparatus was leaving, and cars, trucks and another horse and wagon were just beginning to pull out, but numerous cars were still parked along the cliff. Their owners stood on the cliff south of the Baths, analyzing the damage done to the south walls and several windows. The windows were nearly at water level, where, during the day, the rocks were covered with seagulls.

Denis was surprised to discover that among tonight's lesser disasters, he was hungry. He hadn't eaten since early afternoon and it was now nearly ten p.m.

Despite aches and pains, he decided to stop on Mission Street at a little diner that furnished many of his meals since his return from France. The diner's food wasn't up to Paris standards, but it was surprisingly tasty.

If he could just get a ride into town.

He had reached a corner where the road wandered off toward the millionaires' cove of Cliffside Estates when a car approached behind him, silhouetting him in its lights. He hoped the fellow would stop for him but he'd got used to how it was in France – there would be little hope for a free ride there.

The car's raucous horn signalled, either to get him out of the way or – was it possible? – to pick him up?

Good God! It was Marina Kyle, in what was almost universally called a "tin lizzie". Not at all the model to expect of

Jason Kyle's daughter. She called out in an unbelievably cheerful voice, "I thought it was you. Don't tell me you are out for more exercise. Hop up."

He would look like a bigger fool than ever if he refused her. She reached across the seat and opened the door on the passenger's side. He grinned, called, "Thanks. Much obliged," and, walking around the back of the car, got in the front seat beside her.

He hoped she wouldn't guess how good it felt just to be sitting down – or up – in this rattling little lizzie, and beside this particular girl.

"Still hurt?" she asked as she started along the marina road. The motor was running noisily. He was glad he didn't have to crank the car. He wasn't sure he could manage it at the moment.

"I feel a lot better now," he admitted.

"I'll bet!"

She looked over and smiled at him. Even in the starlight and his present condition, he found her smile looked enchanting and she didn't make the mistake of taking his admission as a compliment to her, although that too was on the fringe of his mind.

She added after a moment or two, "You're going to be sensible about this, I hope."

"Whatever it is, I don't feel in a fighting mood right now."

"Good. That will save time. You won't go to a hospital, I suppose."

"Lord, no! Do I look that bad off?"

She gave him a brief, amused inspection.

"You look tired and disgusted and a lot of other things, and you could possibly look bad – wicked, that is, but you don't look bad in the sense you mean. You probably need a good night's sleep and some kind of ointment. I did some Red Cross hospital work during the war and, I assure you, I'm quite capable of taking care of you."

He laughed at that, feeling better already. She had left several openings for him to take advantage of, but he suspected all the good feeling between them would disappear if he made any obvious advances. If she expected his advances, he would keep her guessing. Above all, he didn't want to lose her.

He was definitely encouraged by her next question, astonishing as it might be, coming from Jason Kyle's daughter.

"Are you married?"

Laughter prevented him from a resounding "no" but it was a very encouraging question. To keep the conversation on its present light-hearted level, he said, "Is that required for employment at the Kyle Bathhouse?"

"Baths," she corrected him. "I imagine you're like all these post-war heroes. You don't believe in marriage."

"For others? Great. For me, thank you, no! Not until I'm a millionaire. Which will be a long time. I learned that from my father's people. And I've no hunger for a family."

She was silent briefly and he wondered what she was thinking about. He couldn't imagine her life had been a happy one, led by a driven, ambitious man like her father. But she surprised him by saying wistfully, "I had a good childhood when Mother was alive. Father used to come home from the Baths at night, eat dinner with us, and then, an hour later, suddenly get up after reading the paper and say, 'Let's all go and get some ice cream,' and we all piled into the big Chevrolet, Mama and Father in front and our poodle and me in the back. It was heavenly."

He couldn't believe it but he took her word for it.

"Did you get the ice cream?"

She had left him mentally and was dreaming of all the times that were forever gone.

"Oh, sure. But it was the drive in the night that was so beautiful. All the tiny silver lights covering the hills and valleys of the city. Exactly like stars on a clear evening."

He was touched by her mood and her voice. It was almost as if she'd admitted him to a secret part of her. He reached out, covered her hand on the wheel with his, then said, "Ouch!" as his movement pulled the burns on his back and hand.

They both laughed and the spell was broken. Her dream of the past had been totally alien to him but, even while disturbing, it pleased him that she trusted him enough to confide it.

"Shall we go out to Valencia and turn into Mission?" she asked in a businesslike tone.

Oh, no!

"I wish you wouldn't trouble, Miss Kyle. I can get a street car either way and I'm mighty grateful to get this far."

She looked around, crossed Market Street, which was busy even at this time of day, and said calmly, "You needn't fuss about your rooming house. Rosa and her husband lived in rooming houses when I was little and visiting them was a terrific thrill, believe me."

She wouldn't know it, of course, but even this remark sounded condescending to his sensitive imagination.

"I couldn't hope to compete with Mrs Santini, I assure you. Anywhere along here will be a big help. Until I see you tomorrow morning?"

She reached over and he felt himself penned in lightly by one of her slim arms. "You'll see me right now, Mr Mallory. Now, sit back."

It was only later when he was alone in bed that he remembered this moment and wondered if she could be persistent and bossy like her father, after all.

She drove out to Mission Street and, to his surprise, stopped in front of a three-story corner building with one face on Geneva Avenue facing the car tracks, and one on a side street that was redolent of the odor of fermenting grapes.

As Denis sniffed the air, she grinned and nodded.

"The folks in this neighborhood make their own wine. Very much against the new Prohibition laws. But it is mighty good. Rosa Santini's doctor's office is in this corner building. When her husband was so sick, Dr Allegretti tended him. I know this district very well."

She parked in the alley beside the doctor's office building and had the good sense not to ask if Denis thought he could make it up three flights of wooden stairs. As a matter of fact, Denis found the going painful but performed very convincingly until they rounded the bannisters of the third floor, which he was secretly relieved to reach.

Marina made a racket knocking on the door and Denis knew if it had been he who was disturbed at about eleven p.m. he would wish the intruders to the devil, but she followed this up by calling, "Dr Allegretti, it's Marina Kyle. We need you."

This worked like a charm and the doctor, a chunky man with grizzled hair and a forbidding pince-nez, opened the door. He had a nice smile which softened the spectacles, but naturally he asked, "Miss Kyle! What could you be doing out in the Mission at this hour?"

"It's a friend of mine. He is our new assistant and we had a fire tonight."

"My Lord! A fire? Anyone hurt? I take it it's you, sir. Come in." He opened the door wide. Pipe smoke formed haloes around them and Denis found himself sneezing.

But the small room crowded with furniture was comfortably old and Marina pushed Denis into a well-worn leather chair, then begged his pardon if she had been rough.

"What's the nature of the injuries?" the doctor wanted to know. He knocked his pipe against a big, china bowl and started to his bathroom where he ran water and presumably scrubbed his hands, coming back with a clean, hemmed flour sack.

"It's burns," Marina explained. "We just need a little salve so he can sleep comfortably."

The doctor's still-reddish eyebrows raised and Marina added, "Alone, Doctor. The burns are between his shoulders and also on his right hand."

"Of course. Now, let's see. Do you want to leave the room, Miss Kyle? I'll have to remove the shirt . . . what's left of it."

"All right, my stuffy friend." Marina ran her fingers teasingly along the doctor's cheek and though the doctor didn't smile, he looked as though he would like to.

43

Denis put in, "Anything so long as you're quick about it, Doctor."

Dr Allegretti got bottles and powders out of a glass-enclosed china closet which probably had once seen a set of glassware or Victorian china. To please him, Marina wandered across the room on the threadbare carpet and pretended not to look at the patient.

Denis bent over while the doctor spread on a nineteenth-century salve and afterward insisted that Denis drink a solution of a powder which he'd dropped into a folded square of paper and then into a glass of water.

For the hand problem he loaned Denis a pair of surgical gloves after covering his fingers with a yellow salve and powder.

When they left Dr Allegretti, Denis was relieved that he could pay the doctor's fee. Marina wisely made no effort to fight for the privilege. Then they walked down the three flights of stairs, which Denis could navigate, feeling considerably better, though not good enough to let her see the dungeon he lived in.

He got his way when they reached the foot of the long staircase of his rooming house. She leaned across the seat and gave him her left hand which he took in his. But he couldn't stop there. This time, he didn't even ask himself if he was making a fool of himself. He reached out, with the injured hand as well, caught her around her slender waist and pulled her to him.

Her lips were warm, tender, totally irresistible to him. Even as his flesh first touched her, he recognized this as a mistake and God knew what it would lead to. He covered her mouth hotly, with a rising passion, and only let her go when she began to struggle.

To his astonishment she did not make the expected protest, hinting that he had somehow defiled her, but murmured, "I couldn't breathe. That's all."

"All!"

"Don't be silly. I didn't reject you, for heaven's sake."

He laughed at that, not quite knowing what to think, and kissed her on the nose.

Then he said, "You have an enchanting nose. See you tomorrow."

"And I'll see you tomorrow. Nose and all."

He went up the stairs, momentarily feeling no pain.

Just when he wanted to be alone to relive his questionable relationship with Marina Kyle, his landlady slithered out of her front room in her most officious manner.

"You had a call, Mr Mallory. Said he'd see you at the Baths tomorrow. Sounded important."

Doubtless Jason Kyle, with something unpleasant to say, like: "You're fired!" After all, he hadn't prevented the blaze.

He ignored the possible importance of the call. "Thank you. I'll see him tomorrow. There was a fire tonight and we were all rather busy."

"Suit yourself. But you know our policy, Mr Mallory. If you do return that call on this phone, it's five cents local."

He gave her a tight smile. "I will keep your policy in mind."

He went on to his back bedroom and, once inside, bolted the door. Except for his hour with Marina Kyle, it had been a lousy day, and tomorrow promised to be lousier, if that call was from Jason Kyle. He doubted the fire department or insurance people would call him at home. His report had been voluminous.

He sat down painfully hard and crawled under the old comforter.

In spite of the burned flesh, his dreams that night were full of Marina's kiss, and the touch of her flesh.

Seven

I n spite of the losses in the fire, Marina awoke happy and
ambitious to make use of the Kyles' bad luck.

She knew perfectly well that her little rendezvous with Denis
Mallory was irresponsible, but that was OK. A lot better than
sitting in the passenger seat of a car, nodding once in a while to
show she agreed with Blake Cavenaugh, and finding he was a
very convincing liar.

Denis hadn't said a word about the loss of his sketches, but
that only showed the kind of person he was. He might feel the
loss deeply.

She met her father at breakfast and found him much more
down in spirit than she had expected.

"Part of the Baths can be saved, can't they, Father? It certainly
wasn't a total loss. Besides, there is still the insurance."

He buttered his toast and agreed with her, but his attitude was
disturbingly hesitant.

"Naturally. The problem is . . ." He shrugged. "Some little
time ago we had some out of pocket expenses." She looked up,
surprised and he added, "It was while you were sick. Those
damnable expenses – you know how those things are. Special
nurses for you, and the specialists. And we've taken a dive. Even
the preferred, which is on margin."

She hardly understood any of this.

"But what preferred stock is this? I know we have common
stock in utilities, for one, but what's this, and when did it take a
dive?"

He reached for his butter knife again.

46

She reminded him, "You've already buttered the toast."

He set the knife down, ate the toast and wiped his fingertips on his napkin. He then looked at her.

"Cavenaugh Steamship Lines, my dear. You do remember. Or – perhaps it was when you were coming down with the flu." He added more warmly, "For heaven's sake, you can't be expected to remember everything. I think you've recovered a great deal. I've told Blake that. He's very close to you. Us, that is. Fortunately, there's nothing to worry us, allowing for our connections with Blake."

"I didn't know—" she began, then cut off the protest. She certainly didn't want to find herself among the bargaining chips in Blake Cavenaugh's stock deals. She was hurt that her father hadn't trusted her, but probably her illness had been to blame.

He evidently noted her shock and continued, "You don't realize, my dear." His smile was gentle. "Having a child in San Francisco's limelight is expensive. And especially with a serious illness, and all that entailed."

"Are things really that bad?"

"My dear child, these are matters for men. The subject is closed until next month. By that time, when the preferred has recovered, your annuities and the rest will be back in order again."

But why had it been necessary to borrow against her annuities in the first place? She couldn't believe he had spent it on her illness. And while they were at it, was it likely to be solved by a possible rise in Cavenaugh stocks on margin? To her it meant buying stocks on the principle that they would rise tomorrow. And those stocks were only purchased "on margin". Not owned in full. If the stocks didn't rise, or even fell, he would own nothing. Not even stocks which had gone down.

Before she and her father came to a serious argument over finances, a subject that had always been in his hands, she knew she would have to approach it very carefully. Besides the money, his pride was deeply involved.

She got up from the table, begging his pardon for her haste. "I

47

want to get over there and help Rosa. There's a lot to do. Denis did a good deal last night. He got himself burned rather badly doing it."

"Denis?" It appeared he would make some remark about this first name business, but he thought better of it. He went on amiably, "Try not to make Blake jealous, child. Remember how important he is to us."

That gave her more discomfort than ever.

He reached over and patted her fingers.

"Well, take care, my dear. I may be late. I have business to attend to. The insurance and all that."

He let her kiss him on the brow and went back to his coffee.

She left him and went out to her car. She employed no chauffeur. The more services she employed, the more tittle-tattle she had to listen to.

As she drove to the Baths, she thought about Blake. She had enjoyed a few brief romances in college without ever finding herself passionately in love. She wasn't sure she had known what it was like to feel a deep passion and was beginning to believe such feelings were beyond her. But she had been surprised by how deeply she resented Blake Cavenaugh's lie about Denis Mallory's sketches. It wasn't his indifference to the sketches, but the cold-blooded attempt to make Denis think he liked them. Was he always two-faced, even about his family stocks and properties? The sketches were only a small indication, but now her father was having money difficulties in which Cavenaugh was involved.

I was right not to fall in love with Blake like a fool, she reminded herself, especially when she could so easily fall in love with Denis Mallory. His talk of money and background didn't matter. Only his pride. And that applied to her father as well.

Her own money would certainly take care of them both. She could see that Denis had the kind of occupation that made him happy. A full-time artist. It wasn't as if she needed the various annuities. Her own estate was handled by her father. But much of the later profits had been earned by her. He had reminded her more than once that he would never withhold it from her without cause. As he'd added with an embarrassed laugh, "And you are the most sensible young lady in San Francisco. Don't we know that?" For the past few years she had thought she did.

She arrived at the Baths early but Rosa Santini was already there, studying endless, important lists as Denis brought them to her.

Marina was a little piqued by Denis Mallory's behavior. Respectful, friendly but formal, like a good employee, and Marina amended her conduct to suit the mood. She nodded and smiled at him but remarked to Rosa Santini, "Wonderful, the way our people showed up right on time, after that long siege last evening."

"Professional to the last," Mrs Santini said.

Marina did not miss the nuances there. She only half-ignored them. "Well, it's certainly a change after all we lost yesterday. Thanks be, the assessors are looking into it."

Behind them, Denis Mallory cleared his throat. "I'm afraid the losses are considerable. A lot of it is water damage and irreparable."

Rosa said, "They just poured it on in a flood, those firemen."

"We're mighty lucky we had them," Marina reminded her. "I'd not like to think where we'd be if it wasn't for them." She turned to Mallory. "Denis, why don't we examine the hopeful side of the damage, if any?"

"At your service."

He offered his left arm and they went down the stairs, avoiding the area where debris was still piled up. They passed the water-soaked little museum, which smelled unpleasantly of wet cloth, paper and all the torn, scattered contents of the room.

"It's sickening," Marina said. "Do you think you could replace your sketches?"

She thought Blake would love his reply.

"They were worthless anyway. I never was an artist."

"Oh, that's not true."

"Thanks. But it's true all the same. My only talent in that line is a kind of nasty little political sarcasm. It would be awful if I

49

happened to like one of our noble office-holders. I'd be out of a job in a flash."

"I don't believe that," she said after a pause. "Has Blake Cavenaugh been by today? Or mentioned your sketches?"

"Matter of fact, I found him here trying to open the padlocked door the workmen put up in the barrier you and I just went through."

She tried not to sound particularly interested.

"Did you let him in?"

"No. Told him I didn't have the key to the lock. He said he'd be back."

"Did he tell you why he wanted to get in?"

"Just curious about how much was saved, or so he said."

"And you didn't believe him."

He frowned, wondering what she was getting at.

"I never thought about it, frankly."

She stopped on one of the balconies and looked over the view before her, especially the big pool emptied by its use in the fire. She sighed.

Denis said guiltily, "We may have been wrong, but the few of us on duty were desperate. The flying bits of paper carried the fire to all those wooden seats on the south side, and the northern half of the place was damaged by the smoke and water as well."

"Good heavens! I'm not complaining. I only wish Father would put first things first. The Baths should have concerned him before anything else. Instead . . ."

He looked at her. "I thought he was talking insurance downtown this morning."

Much as she liked Denis, she hadn't meant to criticize her father.

"Of course. But there is more to it. I want to get on with repairs, get back to business. Not personal investments."

He was puzzled. "Well, isn't he?"

She suddenly turned indignant. "Naturally. But his finances are in serious trouble – Blake's involved, and I don't trust him."

"I wondered about that myself . . . I'll be damned! Speak of the devil!"

Made nervous by his exclamation, she looked up toward the street level at the top of the bathhouse. There was Blake Cavenaugh waving down to them.

She didn't want Denis Mallory mixed up in her private fears and doubtless thinking Jason was feeble-minded or something. She whispered, "Don't mention anything to Blake."

"No, but it seems to me, if you don't trust this bastard, you ought to keep him out of your business."

Men at the Baths didn't generally discuss "bastards" with her, but that was a small matter if Mallory was on her side and that of her father. She said hurriedly, "Just don't mention anything. He's Father's closest friend."

"I do understand you. I'm not a complete idiot. But if this fellow discusses anything you ought to know—"

"Of course he won't." She added in an edgy voice, "Then you must tell me, at once."

He grinned. "We understand each other." He took her hand in his.

They had only just released their touch when Blake Cavenaugh came jauntily down the stairs.

"Ah, Mallory. This is more like it. I'm in need of help. Someone who isn't known as part of the Cavenaugh Shipyards. What say?"

Marina stiffened. "I hate to remind you, Blake, but Mr Mallory is employed by Kyle Enterprises, and he is needed to give us his ideas on our future plans."

"Of course. Of course, hon." Blake Cavenaugh brushed her cheek with his lips but Denis noted that there was nothing sensuous about the gesture. The fellow might as well have been greeting old friend Jason. Blake then assured Marina, "But this won't take long, and it was Jason's suggestion. I need someone to run down the Peninsula for me." He looked around the ruined bathhouse. "Plans seem rather discouraging at this moment, wouldn't you say?"

"Depends on your plans," Denis put in.

Cavenaugh ignored this and especially Marina's small giggle. "How true! Wouldn't you say, Blake?"

"In the lap of the gods, seems to me. But that isn't answering my question. What do you say, Marina? I'll pay for his time, if that's what he's afraid of. Even artists have to eat."

Bristling, she looked at Denis and saw his expression: he was trying to tell her something.

He said easily, "Why not, Miss Kyle? It isn't as if we were accomplishing anything this way." He turned to Cavenaugh. "Now, what's your problem?"

As he turned, Denis offered Marina his hand again, his thumb pressing her knuckles. She couldn't mistake that it was a sign. She pretended petulance.

"Oh, well, do what you want. I suppose you think you men know best."

The two men went up the stairs, Denis looking back at her, but it was clear he felt Cavenaugh watching him and turned toward the street as Cavenaugh said something casual which Marina could see Denis answering with a shrug.

It was all a little odd: Blake's sudden anxiety to seek Denis Mallory's friendship.

Eight

B lake Cavenaugh had parked his Pierce Arrow directly outside the entrance to the Baths. A crowd was collecting around the big, impressive car, several years old, with the right-hand drive not yet changed to the American drive. This alone would have attracted an audience, especially teenagers and a few curious males. Instinctively, Denis associated the car with his two great-aunts. Would Cavenaugh want him to do the driving, appropriately serving the regal Cavenaugh?

But, apparently, the man was being democratic after all.

"Not this time, old man," he said as if reading Denis' mind. "This is just man to man, you might say. Marina is a darling but she does have elegant airs. However, I do think they are quite unnecessary in this case. No matter how decent Marina is about her position, she does love to advertise her superior status."

Such a long speech to tell Denis his company was far below hers! He saw through the ploy. But it did sting.

He settled himself with reasonable comfort on the left of the front seat and Blake Cavenaugh got in behind the wheel. Accompanied by a good deal of noise, yells and whistles, they drove off and headed toward town, then on to the highway out past the main cemeteries on the county's border. The morning light gleamed on the Pacific waters to the west and fields of green plants covered the area on the east side of the road.

Curious about the plants which looked vaguely familiar at this distance, Denis said, "They look like a garden border."

Cavenaugh chuckled. "Artichokes. It's a great, moist climate for them. When I was in college we used to drive out here after the Big Game and steal artichokes. Sometimes these days I take Marina. We're very close, naturally."

"Naturally. But a matter of curiosity: what are we doing out here in the mountains?"

"Hills, my boy," Cavenaugh said with some amusement. "You aren't a teetotaler, by any chance?"

What did that have to do with anything?

Denis said flatly, "Not that I know of. Are we here to steal artichokes?"

"No. I've finally gotten beyond that kid stuff. And I have several men who do my work for me. Artichokes not included. Sometimes we have a female – quite a dragon – who handles things. But it's rough getting employees you can trust these days. First the war and then the flu epidemic."

"And then I showed up. Lucky me."

"It's a job I may be offering," Cavenaugh reminded him. "And I'm afraid there won't be much of a job for you at the Baths. Not, at least, until matters get straightened out."

We're getting into something here, Denis told himself, pursuing the matter aloud. "I've begun to wonder if the old man is doing as well as we all thought."

Would Cavenaugh be foolish enough to give away his own part, if any, in the Kyle monetary problem?

He might not have been foolish but he was certainly cocky enough to betray a little of his own part in all this.

"He's not as young as he once was, and life has a way of catching up with these old silver-barons," Cavenaugh reminded Denis. "I was a freshman when he was a senior at Stanford," he explained. "So I guess I'm able to see his mistakes more clearly. We don't get any younger, you know."

And yet this two-faced rat thought it worth his while to keep the closest contact with his "great friend" and his great friend's daughter. What was it someone said: "You have to get close in order to knife a man."

This guy was bad enough, but the fact that he was closely allied to Marina Kyle was what really infuriated Denis. He began to hope he was right, that Cavenaugh was really up to something in enlisting him to join the Cavenaugh Crowd. If so, then this ride was more than just a chance to blacken the Kyles in Denis Mallory's eyes.

But in a way it was flattering. He must think Denis was actually a rival. It gave Denis a new view of himself. He had been thinking any serious relationship between him and Marina was impossible, but, obviously, Blake Cavenaugh didn't agree.

Of course, Cavenaugh must think Denis Mallory was a pretty venal bastard, but Cavanaugh probably judged everyone by himself. Besides, with Mallory's job hanging by a thread, thanks to the fire, he ought to be ripe for plucking. With sufficient payments as an inducement, Mallory could work both sides, reporting any of the Kyle movements to his Cavenaugh paymaster.

Charming.

Blake Cavenaugh kept to the highway with merely a glance down toward a miniature harbor with the morning waters rolling in. It seemed to be a fishing village. Appropriately enough, it was called Half Moon Bay.

Denis remembered writing a column long ago, with some rather absurd sketches, about a fishing village where a body had been washed ashore. Either a murder victim, a fisherman having accidently drowned, or someone involved in smuggling. As far as Denis could remember, no one had ever discovered how the body got there. Denis wondered, with a taste of dry humor, whether Cavenaugh wanted to remove him from the Kyle world the hard way.

"Know this part of the country very well?" Cavenaugh asked as they drove past another turn-off.

"There was a bit of smuggling here occasionally. Is that why I'm here now?"

Cavenaugh kept going, yet Denis was pretty sure that, for some reason, Half Moon Bay was his goal.

"Well, it's pretty important in bootlegging. They have quite a business here lately."

Denis couldn't help remarking, "That's just why none of the Krauts got me during the last couple of years. So I could become a rum-runner or whatever."

Cavenaugh grinned. "Not quite that bad. Their – shall we say – product – makes them friends of the Cavenaugh Shipyards. Of course, the business costs something after there's been a raid, but that's for the sake of appearances. After all, the Federal end of it costs more than the City and County."

"Federal!"

Cavenaugh pulled off into a shack at the left side of the road. It proved to be a garage of sorts. He sat there a minute watching Denis.

"First of all, old man, this is purely liquor for my friends and myself. Does that ease your conscience?"

Denis took a long breath. It occurred to him that this might be a frame-up to get him out of the way and especially from Marina. This would be a dandy way to get rid of Denis. Throw him to the government men.

As Denis considered his companion and went back over everything he recalled from when he wrote about Half Moon Bay, he remembered the cards in his wallet. One of them was a membership card for the *Journal*'s Goodfellow charity. It was outdated and meant little now, but it said he was an employee of the "*Evening Journal* – Beacon Light of the City", and it might do as a cover if he got in trouble.

Cavenaugh looked over at him. "My office got word the fish catch was in."

"Then what?"

"A fisherman named Bertuccio will meet us but he wants nothing to do with removing the – er – catch – so you and I will bring it up. Just enough to get my friends over the holidays."

Denis, concerned that he might be the patsy somewhere along the line said, "What do we say if Bertuccio turns out to be Federal?"

Cavenaugh waved away such an idea. "No problem. They're

paid plenty. No one is here when somebody from Cavenaugh Shipping is around. It's an understanding. Well, here goes." Knowing he was doing this under the amused eyes of a man he was fast learning to despise, Denis crossed the road after him, missed a speeding Ford by a hair, and went down with Cavenaugh toward the little town, not at all sure something very unpleasant wasn't being planned for him, such as being jailed for bootlegging. But he had gone this far and he was almost surprised to find Marina Kyle was worth going the rest of the way for.

He saw that they were headed for one of the grocery stores in the village. Outside and inside it was heavily draped with fishing tackle and anything likely to be of use to men of the sea or, in some cases, tourists. There was little here that appeared to be important to amateurs, who wouldn't know what to do with all this seafaring equipment.

Cavenaugh rapped his knuckles on the counter. A pretty Mexican girl came through a swinging door and stared at him and murmured in a soft, accented voice, "The *Señor* is not here, I think. He – he said he would go up the Peninsula. To San Francisco, I think."

Cavenaugh spoke smilingly, but with unmistakable force. "Find him. Tell him it's me. My secretary called an hour ago."

She was undeniably frightened, "I cannot, *Señor*. He is not—"

"Do it, my dear!"

Denis watched this mostly with distaste but also curiosity. Obviously, Cavenaugh expected his contact to be here, standing at attention. If it had been Denis, he would not have insisted on seeing Cavenaugh's contact. There was clearly something wrong here and Cavenaugh was apparently too used to having his own way. Since Denis himself might become involved, he advised Cavenaugh, "Best wait until another time."

Cavenaugh was used to having his own way but after looking at Denis a moment, he understood. "Well, we'll be back another time. No real hurry. But if that fish order is ruined, he'll pay for it, believe me."

He turned away from the counter, motioned to Denis, and started out the door. Having nothing better to do, Denis followed, pretending that he was just taking orders from his boss.

Cavenaugh had barely pushed open the door when it was thrust hard against him.

"What the devil are you doing?" Cavenaugh demanded. "Who are you?"

Even before the two officious-looking men showed their identification it was clear to Denis. Federal men must have been waiting for Cavenaugh and probably others. Cavenaugh resorted to haughty assurance.

"The ball for the Policemen's Widows' Charity certainly deserves refreshments. They're holding it the week before Christmas."

The two men looked at each other. The older and more authoritative of the two softened his demand, though he did not take his hand off Cavenaugh's arm.

"You have proof of all this, sir?"

"Certainly . . . I . . ." It was clear that he had none. He was still feeling through his vest pocket when Denis decided he would do better by saving the situation. Even if it did pull Cavenaugh's chestnuts out of the fire.

"Mr Cavenaugh," he began. The two Federal men and Cavenaugh turned to look at him. Denis went on like a good subordinate as he pulled out some cards from his own pocket. "My employer, the *Evening Journal*, is backing the charity banquet." He flashed the *Journal* charity card before both men at the same time. They tried to read it over his busy thumb and nodded.

"Good rag," the first of them agreed. "Their banquet last year was a swell public relations deal."

They began to discuss their own charity with Cavenaugh, who instantly reminded them of what Cavenaugh Shipping Corporation had done for them.

When the discussion ended, the men discovered "much to their surprise" that they had been invited to the *Journal*'s Charity Ball this year.

By the time Denis and Cavenaugh left the little shop with two big hemp bags of bottles, they were assured that this liquor wasn't nearly enough. "I know those *Journal* boys. They can drink us all under the table. When you order the next load, just explain about the benefit for the police widows. That'll do it."

Everybody laughed and Cavenaugh and Denis went their way up to the road.

"Good thinking on your part," Cavenaugh remarked as they stored the hemp bags away.

There was a little silence broken by Cavenaugh's proposition. "One of these days I really want to discuss your coming into the firm, Denis. Your quick thinking was admirable."

Now they were on a first name basis. Denis said, "Thanks," but didn't go on. Cavenaugh did, however.

"A bright fellow like you is wasted at Kyle's."

Denis pretended a liking for the idea but showed a modest hesitation about betraying his present employers. "I guess I could work both sides of the street. Tentatively, I don't want to leave them in the lurch."

"Oh, that's no problem. You'd be in an excellent position to let us know just – I mean to say, if Jason should try something against Cavenaugh Shipping, or our stocks, you would be in an excellent position. And it would be worth quite a sum to us."

"You are very generous," Denis lied.

Cavenaugh slapped Denis's knee in a friendly way. "We understand each other. Now, let's get back to town."

All the way back into San Francisco, with Cavenaugh pointing out how useful Mallory could be, and how he'd find himself a rich man one day, Denis kept smiling and nodding, but was very much involved with his own thoughts. Just how could what he had learned today be used to save the Kyles – one in particular – from being swallowed up by this shark?

Nine

With no one around the Baths to see her private feeling of loss, Marina wandered about the great building, picturing in her mind's eye the look of the place, trying to add up mentally the price of its repairs.

With the broken windows and ceiling the place was ice cold. The temperature was not helped by the chill wind whistling in from the Golden Gate. It was its enjoyable self in the spring and fall, but mid-winter did bring cold winds almost as bad as the foggy summer nights. The weather wasn't helped by the mournful sounds of Mile Rock Light close by.

Suddenly Marina heard a man's footsteps moving rapidly down the main staircase. Her heartbeat increased. It might be – surely, it was – Denis Mallory.

It wasn't, though. It was her father. He waved down to her, calling out in a voice that echoed as always through the hollow interior, "So here you are. We're needed to sign papers downtown. A great deal of technical rubbish, but they need it." As he reached her, he explained further, "There's been such a heavy loss, we need every cent we squeeze out of the insurance and whatnot." He chucked his bent forefinger under her chin and added jokingly, "There's nothing to worry about. Don't look like that. We'll soon have everything shipshape."

Her smile was weak. She knew her father pretty well and he seemed much too cheerful, considering the disaster last night.

She also admitted to herself that she was worried over Denis Mallory's disappearance with Blake. What was Blake's object in trying to win the friendship of a stranger without either money or influence – unless it was to provide himself with someone to spy on Jason Kyle and his monetary problems? He had shipyards full of employees who ran his errands as well as his companies, and shiploads of men who knew exactly how to handle the Cavenaugh affairs.

She followed her father up the stairs, trying to convince herself that in spite of the delay in Denis's return, he was undoubtedly learning something about Blake's interest in him, and in Jason Kyle's financial condition. The hints of Blake's possible dealings against her father sickened her. She had admired Cavenaugh for years and thought of him as a future husband. Never as a lover, but a man she could look up to and trust. Actually, a second father.

Now, her father's hints about money dealings with Blake, of which she had been unaware, made her worry about everyone – even Denis as Blake was in a position to tempt him to work against the Kyles. She had to believe in someone, but what was Blake up to, using Denis Mallory, a man he scarcely knew? She told herself she would soon know. It all depended on how much Denis told her about that ride to – wherever.

She stopped by Mrs Santini to tell her she would be back soon, in case "anyone" asked. Minutes later, beside her father as they drove downtown, she found herself staring at the back of the new chauffeur's head and remembering that he had been suggested to her father by Blake when their older chauffeur retired on some comfortable annuities. How handy those annuities were, just when Jason Kyle mentioned that his chauffeur was getting on in years and becoming crotchety!

Blake's suggested man, Sylvester, was more than a trifle homely. Make that ugly, with his bulbous nose – a "bourbon nose", Blake had called it, his close-set, pale eyes and his stocky build. But Sylvester was always obliging. Blake had pointed that out to Jason Kyle's amusement. With her recent mistrust of Blake Cavenaugh, Marina studied the chauffeur's slightly bulging red neck sceptically. She knew that her father and Blake often mentioned the close, dependable relationship between

Jason's daughter and the remarkably successful Blake Cave-naugh. Suppose Blake was trying to keep any young and attrac-tive males out of Marina's reach? Now, hardly knowing Denis Mallory, Blake was working the same trick to get Denis out of Marina's way. It would explain this suggested trip and probably a job-offering today. It might not be anything sinister at all. She hoped this was Blake's absurd plan. She didn't want to think he was trying to cheat her father. Still, since her suspicions had been aroused, she felt that Blake was now a man to watch.

Jason Kyle was definitely showing signs that he was not as confident as he was pretending to be. The nearer they approached the triangular bank building at a corner of Market Street, the more Marina noted a certain nervous excitement in her father.

Seeing her glance at him furtively now and then, he smiled and patted her hand. "You look depressed, my dear. Take my assurance. This business is actually to the Kyles' benefit. The banks have been extremely cooperative. The property is worth millions, on top of the insurance."

"Then why do we need to make deals with the bank?" she asked, even more worried when he frowned at the question.

He explained patiently, "You really can't be expected to understand all these complexities in a moment. It will take you years to handle these things yourself."

Myself? she thought. That stunned her, though she tried not to let him know it. For over three years, until her illness, she had run the Baths in his name. However, technically, he had con-tinued to handle payments and debts and when Rosa Santini sometimes questioned her about expenses that grew larger every quarter, Marina reminded her that Jason Kyle knew what he was doing. But did he? Or worse: was he himself responsible for expenses that had nothing to do with the Baths? And now he told her politely that it was none of her business. She'd never worked for a salary and still received what others would have called "an allowance". For the first time she asked herself, Should I find out if he is spending bathhouse profits on his risky gambles? Had Blake gotten him into competing with, or even being advised by

Blake? But the Cavenaughs bought and sold only on certainties, and they had been in the market for two generations. They seldom if ever let themselves be caught short.

She was too worried to do more than smile faintly when her father made a joke as they reached Market Street. "Here we are at the fountain of plenty, my dear. I hope this will restore your faith in your old father."

The elevator operator in the lobby of the bank building greeted the Kyles with enthusiasm. "My son-in-law wishes me to thank you, sir. That was a nice tip he got from you."

Jason laughed. "I wish I'd taken it myself." He must have noticed Marina's interest and he added, "Of course, I'm not much of a gambler."

The operator thanked Jason Kyle again for the "stock tip" and they all reached the second floor, which was devoted to official bank business. Jason walked into the secretarial outer staff room, then ahead to the various executive offices.

Marina stayed to speak with each of the young men and the elderly female who operated the switchboard. They all congratulated her on her recovery from the influenza and Miss Gissburg added, "Everything happens at once, doesn't it, Miss Kyle, first the flu, and then the market and now the fire at the Baths?"

"How true!" Marina crossed the elegant but faded carpet and passed the investments offices across from the sunny, corner office of the Second Vice-President. Through the investment officer's transom window she could hear the officer's jovial voice commiserating with her father. At any other time she would have knocked and called out. This time, she listened.

Her father did not answer the officer as she had expected, by laughing off the sympathy. He spoke lightly but with great care.

"As you must know, I am not a gambling man, but this puts me in an embarrassing position."

"Ah!" the other man said in a half-joking manner. "But we've had this conversation several times before, and I loathe a man who says, 'I told you so,' but frankly – need I say more?"

"I haven't come to discuss the errors of my ways, as you may imagine, old fellow," Jason Kyle put in as gently as he could without offending the officer.

"I understand, Jason. I think I may call you by your given name after all this time—"

"By all means," Jason Kyle said, putting as good a face on it as he could.

"Well, Jason, we all make mistakes. Worst are those in which we listen to the other fellow's "sure thing" gamble. But for this to follow so closely on those heavy losses . . . and, regrettably, last night's fire, it was worse than foolhardy to bank on those odds."

Her father's voice held an edge of panic. "But Vice-President van Turin, one of my closest friends, assured me over the phone that by the time my daughter and I came in, it would all be worked out."

"Not quite, Jason. As I understood it, the Vice-President asked you and Miss Kyle, whose annuities were involved, to come in and talk it over."

"That wasn't my understanding at all," Jason Kyle said stiffly. "I did wonder then why my daughter was included; since it is a mere matter of form. There would never be a shadow of doubt that my daughter invariably leaves such signatures to me. As the bank has always known, the family properties are mine and certainly may be used to – well, buttress the family holdings. My daughter is mere figurehead in the estate and would never dream of robbing me when I am in trouble."

"And Miss Kyle's work at the Baths for the past three years?"

"At the moment, Marina is an excellent – shall we call her a secretary? I am teaching her the ABCs of business. But strictly speaking, she can't even sign a . . . Where are you going?"

The investments officer pointed to the little window above the door. "To close the transom. Your credit would be disastrous if it got out that – well, I needn't pursue it. If only that fire hadn't occurred last night, you might—" The transom window closed.

Marina stepped back into the main office and leaned against the switchboard. Miss Gissburg reached out, touching Marina's

hand. "Don't worry, Miss Kyle. It all comes out in the wash."
She laughed wryly. "And there's always bankruptcy."
"Good God! Surely not that bad. We have good credit."
Desperate, Marina swung around toward the executive offices.
At the same time a light glowed on the switchboard and Miss
Gissburg got back to work. After giving the bank's name, she
said, "Miss Kyle, it's for you."
Jason Kyle, who had just come out of the office, clearly with his
mind on something more important, said, "I'll take it here." He and
Marina both reached out as Miss Gissburg hesitated between them.
Then she motioned to the nearest telephone and he took it up,
ordering indifferently, "Call me later. At my home."
Miss Gissburg took the phone and put the receiver back
behind Marina. The switchboard remained lighted.
Jason said, "We are leaving, Marina. Do come along. I have
an appointment with Blake."
Was he going to borrow from Blake Cavenaugh? Obviously
not for the first time. Or see if he could try somewhere else to
raise money on her own annuities? Was there anything else to
try? Had he always been so devious? He might at least have
discussed it with her. She would have given him every cent a few
days ago. But now . . .
Her mood did not lighten when he dismissed her feelings as
childish fears. It was his appalling dishonesty that had sickened
her. She doubted if she could ever trust him again.
"Don't look so serious, my dear," he said now. "You are being
absurd." He lowered his voice. "This little matter will be settled
in no time. Are you returning home with me?"
Behind him, the investment officer wished him, "Well, best of
luck, old man. This will all work itself out." He shook hands with
Jason and then with Marina and returned to his office.
Miss Gissburg looked from Marina to her father. "The call
was for you, Miss Kyle. It was about an appointment. They said
the – er – fitter would be leaving shortly."
There was no fitting. Marina said, "Father, I must have that
dress for the City Hall affair. You go on. I'll be home later."

"As you like." He gave her a nod and went out to the elevator. Almost before the corridor door was closed, Miss Gissburg handed Marina the telephone.

"That's an odd one," one of the clerks muttered to the other. Marina was too angry to care what they or anyone else thought. She took up the phone. Could it be Denis?

The voice was Rosa Santini, which encouraged her.

"Miss Kyle? Are you there?"

"Yes. What's the problem, Rosa?"

"I have a message from one of your old friends. You asked him to run an errand for you, down the Peninsula."

Marina's heartbeat quickened. Rosa thought of everything, including the fact that Jason might be listening.

"Yes, I understand. My old friend has returned. Good."

"Where can he meet you? Alone. Can you talk?"

It must be bad, all right. "Yes. What about the St Francis? Our accommodation suite. The dear old man should enjoy that."

Over the line Mrs Santini chuckled. "Understood. He doesn't want to be seen coming and going in the hotel. I'll give him one of my husband's jackets and a cap. Just a second. Hold on. Someone wants to say a word."

Feeling like a schoolgirl with her first crush, Marina said, "I'll wait."

Only a couple of seconds later she heard Denis Mallory's voice. Nothing ever sounded so good, if, of course, he was on her side. Rosa Santini behaved as if he was.

"Hello. Miss Kyle?"

Miss Kyle! Damn!

"Yes. Did you find out anything?"

"I did. It's as bad as you and I thought. I must see you. Soon as possible."

She explained about the St Francis suite that the Kyles kept for out-of-town visitors and tried to remain calm to the point of indifference. "Do hurry," she added.

"Believe me, I will. Mrs Santini is going to lend me her car. Got to go now. Goodbye, darling."

She was almost afraid to answer in kind. Something might happen to ruin everything. So she said lightly, "Same to you."

She went into the hall. When she was out of the elevator on the lobby floor, she hurried around the corner, signalled a cab and started off anxiously for the St Francis Hotel.

Ten

D enis Mallory drove Mrs Santini's Ford to a garage on Post Street suggested by Mrs Santini. Avoiding the elegant front entrance of the St Francis Hotel, he walked in off Post Street in the Santini jacket and cap. So far as he could tell, no one looked twice at him. Before he went overseas Denis might have been slightly self-conscious, but recent events had changed him. He despised the way Blake Cavenaugh had double-crossed the Kyles, and imagined he could use him as his tool.

At this hour, except for the elevator operator, he was alone in the elevator and relieved to be. All the way up to the fifth floor he was busy wondering about Marina's reaction when she heard what he had learned. Surely, Jason Kyle would end his dealings with Cavenaugh when he learned of the attempt to hire Denis away from the Kyles, obviously as a spy. Unless, of course, Marina really was in love with Blake Cavenaugh, and Denis refused to believe that.

He found the fifth-floor number Mrs Santini had given him and knocked, hoping for the best but not entirely sure.

There were movements inside, then silence. He slipped off his cap and, brushing the Santini jacket, knocked again, this time calling, "Message from Mrs Santini, ma'am."

That did it.

Marina Kyle opened the door a few inches, then smiled and pulled him inside. He reached behind him and locked the door with the apology: "Sorry. We don't need a lot of company."

"Never mind that. Come and sit down." She looked him up and down and then added, "I hope Rosa won't be offended if I say you look much handsomer than our old friend, Mr Santini."

He laughed, but kept his jacket on. "Never know when we'll have company."

She asked him to sit down near the side table and explained, "Dear Rosa called an old friend of hers at the hotel and saw to it that we had an ice chest ready for us. How early did you eat breakfast?"

"About six," he confessed. When she opened the chest and brought out one delicacy after another, placing them on plates, he could hardly resist reaching for, of all things, little toast points of caviar and an assortment of accompaniments.

"The toast is soggy," she admitted, "but as a man who hasn't eaten since six a.m., you shouldn't be fussy."

When he hesitated, she ordered him, "Dip in!"

He grinned and did so. There was more food than they could eat, along with . . .

"Good Lord! Is that champagne?"

"Of course. I am going to need some advice. I'm bribing you."

He took one of the tiny napkins, wiped his mouth, and then leaned over the food to kiss her warm lips. Beneath his own, her flesh trembled a little.

She seemed almost lost and then he smiled. He felt for her a deep and unexpected tenderness.

He asked, "Darling, are you still going to marry Cavenaugh?"

She confessed, "I never had another thought. I knew how happy it would make Father. They worked together on so many deals and they were both so good to me about explaining things in the business. And Blake and I seemed to fit – mentally, I guess." She flushed. "As friends. Our interests were the same. From the first time Father introduced us."

"But now?" he urged her hopefully.

"Well, now, Blake may be ruining my father."

"Do you think your father knows all Cavenaugh is up to?"

"He must. Father is so worried. I know he is. There are all the secret talks between him and Blake. And all this pushing for me to marry Blake."

He didn't want to throw more painful suspicions on her present mood and would have delayed telling her about his drive with Cavenaugh but her eyes narrowed and she pursued the matter.

"You haven't told me about Blake. What happened on your way down the Peninsula?"

He took her fingers in his again.

"It was sort of a half-offer of a job with the Cavenaugh Corporation." He added, to soothe her, "That was if the bathhouse thing fell through, which he seemed to—"

"To expect. Blake! My loyal hero!" she said, heavy with irony. "I might not believe that if I hadn't heard some news about Father at the bank. And it fits the way Father has been pushing me to marry Blake. He needs Blake's money and his influence."

"Did you mind so much?"

She laughed, on the edge of tears. "It wasn't very romantic, getting married to help Father's financial problems. But Blake had become almost like an old relative."

"But darling, hasn't love got anything to do with it?"

"Love? You mean sex? And – and passion?"

"Yes. I mean sex."

"I figured I wasn't very sexy." She looked up at him, trying to laugh. "Until – you know." Then in deep hurt and anger, she burst into tears, still laughing. "It's so silly. I've had sex before. But it wasn't – never mind!"

He pulled her to him, wiped her luminous eyes with a clean napkin.

Her tears gradually turned to laughter.

"What a dumb thing to do! I never cry. Well, hardly ever. For heaven's sake, let me have that damned napkin."

He laughed too, but tenderly. He confessed, "There have been very few loved ones in my life, but I can imagine crying at treachery. Seeing you this way is like a raw sore to me. Damn them!"

Her eyes widened. He added, "Then your father is betraying himself more than anyone else. Why?"

"Well, Father wanted to make big money. Like Blake does, so he evidently followed Blake's tactics. I suppose he eventually put up money from the Baths and some of my annuities. He counted on the banks today. Even his old friends refused him after the fire. Now, he's cut into all our assets. He never did that before. And it sounds to me as though Blake thinks you're the sort who's for sale and if he works it right, you'll tell him all that's going on at Kyle's."

"Possibly. He seems interested in grabbing off the Baths property."

She nodded. "He mentioned it to me once or twice. I think Father may have fallen for it. Taking over most of the property and putting in estates. Or elegant houses, like Pacific Heights and all that."

"Charming fellow."

"And my marriage to him would give him what he wants." She laughed again. "Not me! Oh, no! But the whole property. Father's not a young man, you know."

He looked at her. "Love or not, would you make a sacrifice like that to save your father?"

"Don't be silly. There's got to be another way."

He considered. "It might happen with anyone who married you, unless he signs an agreement that keeps the property in your hands. It's the only thing anyone in your position should do."

"That's ridiculous. If I had a better offer for my hand – so to speak – I'd get married tonight. Do I hear one?"

She was smiling now, but he ruined everything by shaking his head. "You know why I can't – until I'm somewhere on the level of the woman I marry."

"Who?"

"You know who. And even then we would have to agree that what was yours *was yours*."

"I'm willing," she said brightly.

He pushed the delicate wisps of hair away from her forehead and kissed her.

Then he walked slowly toward the crisp, golden afternoon

71

view of Union Square with its greenery, its busy pigeons and the surrounding tall buildings. He said abruptly, "Could you ever see yourself cutting away from Jason Kyle?"

She stared at him. "I couldn't actually betray him. He's all I have in the world. He means everything to—" She saw him looking at her. "There are different kinds of love."

He didn't argue with that but it seemed obvious to him that her devotion to her father exceeded her expressed feelings, if any, toward Blake Cavenaugh. By extension this could apply to any other man who loved her. Yet, there was passion between her and Denis now, and had been from the first. He wondered if he could ever overcome her need and dependence on her father and perhaps her father's need for her. He wanted desperately to make her turn that love to him.

He tried to smile. "Let's see if we can work out our problems between ourselves, without either the Kyle enterprises or Cavenaugh's millions."

She came to him, putting her arm gently in his and looking into his tense features. He couldn't resist the gesture and forgot their troubles for the moment.

He reminded her, "Sweetheart, we haven't seen the rest of your Queenly Quarters."

She played up to him. "And here we've been, wasting valuable time. Come along. Let me show you."

She took his arm again, pretended to enumerate every expensive item in the suite. Finishing the elegant salon, she showed him the way into the bedroom with its elaborate double bed, French dresser and lowboy on which sat a small but undeniably real radio set. He snapped it on and the room filled with the magic of the St Francis' own Art Hickman's orchestra playing downstairs.

She laughed on a note of tension as she joked, "Shall we dance?"

His arms closed around her. "Later."

He picked her up with an ease that made her heart beat rapidly and carried her over to the bed. He raised her unresisting body until she closed her eyes in ecstasy as she felt the warmth of his lips on hers, then their consuming power she had dreamed about last night.

She returned his kiss, trying to possess him as he possessed her, until his lips moved to her cheek and her forehead. She reached one hand out of the tight embrace, pulling his head to her, tousling his hair, which was in its usual unruly state.

She whispered sensual things she had never said aloud before. A minute later he was kneeling over her in bed, removing her flimsy, expensive blouse and skirt and she was reaching around his waist a little awkwardly.

They were joined so quickly, the pulse-pounding excitement of him within her, that she was afraid the thrill would disappear, but she found herself rising higher, to a peak of ecstasy she had never known before. The excitement did not drift away like the only half-achieved satisfaction she'd had in other and more tentative experiences.

When the breathless passion was finally drained by her effort to breathe, she knew that in moments she would want to show him, and be shown again, what real passion was. She could have laughed at the childish experiences she had known before she met Denis.

When he had surrendered her heated body to her and leaned over her, looking into her eyes, she moistened her lips and asked what he must regard as a stupid question with no known answer.

"Would you always love me like this?"

He was silent before admitting, "I thought I was in love once or twice before, but I know now this is real. I know it! I think I knew it the day I saw the beautiful cleaning woman."

He kissed her fingertip gently.

Then the idyl was broken.

There was the sound of a key being fumbled at the lock of the foyer beyond the salon. Marina sat up abruptly.

"Oh, God! That's my father!"

She brushed her skirt and fastened the pearl buttons of her georgette blouse. When she turned around, Denis looked reasonably proper and was just fastening Mr Santini's jacket. He looked at the foyer door, which closed again, slowly with an obvious attempt at silence.

"Is it . . . ?"

He was more disgusted than surprised. "Not your father. Anyway, he's gone now. But it was a man, and someone who has a connection with your father, as he had a key."

"Who – for heaven's sake?"

"Cavenaugh, obviously. The bastard wanted to see if you were here and up to no good."

Marina said flatly, "Well, he found out. But why did he run away?"

"Maybe he just wants to have proof to make trouble between you and your father."

"Well, I don't owe Blake anything. I certainly never said 'yes'." She added slowly, "And it works both ways. I guess that's the final proof for me. Against Blake, I mean."

He almost hoped she was right, but he said, "I can't blame him if he's jealous about you and me."

She laughed harshly. "Blake has never been jealous of my other boyfriends. He's too sure of himself. It's money. And his power over Father. That's where his jealousy is."

She reached out to him.

"Darling, there's only one way to defeat him."

He leaned over and kissed her forehead which was moist with her tension. "Shoot him?"

"No. We've got to get married. And the sooner the better."

"Marina, I told you—"

"Don't argue. We'll work it out."

He believed her because he wanted desperately to do so. In this moment, still under the influence of their lovemaking, he would not admit the doubts.

Eleven

"Why do I feel so relieved?" Marina asked as they walked arm in arm down Sutter Street to Grant Avenue and Chinatown.

Denis was afraid that when she realized she might lose both her beloved father and Cavenaugh, who had been her close companion, she would know that in many ways Denis was responsible. He asked himself if he could take the place of those two perhaps irreplaceable figures in her life. He tried to depend upon the truth.

"Because we are in love? That's my reason."

"Well, that too, of course, darling, but there's something else. For the first time in my life I feel free."

He laughed but there was more than humor in his thoughts. The last hours had gone so rapidly he was almost as concerned as he was happy. Money to support her was a big concern, but even more serious was the possibility that she had made up her mind on the spur of the moment, perhaps because of her resentment against the two men who had ruled her life.

During that sunny afternoon they strolled past the first of the Chinatown shops. These glittered with imported silks, from simple Chongsams to elaborate kimonos, as well as occasional shining ebony chests and jade ornaments. Further along, they passed the little restaurants that were Marina's goal.

Neither of them discussed their financial future.

"You think I know all about the fancy restaurants, don't you?" she challenged him. "Well, this little Chinese place was one of my favorites when I was a kid. I still love it."

He had been searching his brain for a fancy place that she would prefer but found that she was right about the restaurant and its food. Its type was being phased out nowadays. The booths were tiny private rooms just big enough for a table and two chairs, all surrounded by curtains and partitions separating the booths. The food was excellent but Denis kept telling himself that a girl who had grown up in the shadow of two millionaires was certainly beyond his reach, in spite of China-town.

He stopped drinking green tea long enough to say, "By the way, tomorrow I'm going to see a friend of mine – a terrific architect. I think you know – Larry Hoaglund. He planned and designed the new *Journal* building."

"Larry? I know him. Our banker, Al Freed, has been talking him up, trying to get him to design a house in the district above St Francis Wood as a wedding present for his daughter. Maybe Larry will create a house for us. Can I come with you?"

There was no use in telling her how expensive Larry Hoaglund houses were. He would worry about that tomorrow. After all, they had to get married first. And even that would take a great deal more money than he had ever come across.

When he left her at the Kyle home in Cliffside, he wondered if he ever would have enough to offer her a life in her father's league. But he was determined that she was the only woman for him.

They kissed each other and lingered warmly in each other's arms until a voice sounding as if it might be full of pebbles called up the steps to them. "What you doing up there?"

Marina laughed. "It's just Father's chauffeur. He has orders to see that I'm safely inside after anyone brings me home." She called out, "Just me, Sylvester. Good-night."

To Denis she whispered, "I'll meet you tomorrow. Say . . . ten thirty. Montgomery and Market corner."

He kissed her again, then asked, "Is that fellow only hired to keep off your unwanted suitors?"

"Sort of. He has an apartment off the garage. Don't forget.

Ten thirty. I won't be getting a chance to tell Blake our news until sometime tomorrow, so wish me luck."

"You know it, sweetheart." He kissed her hands as they came away from his neck. "I love you."

"Me, too. Don't worry now."

As he turned away and started down the steps, she called, "I wish you had a car, damn it!"

He waved and went out into the road, bundling up in the late Mr Santini's jacket and cap. He hoped that some day there would be a real life with this lovely and all too rare creature.

He wasted little time worrying about the Kyle chauffeur in the garage apartment behind him until he had walked around the cliffside road and taken the long stroll toward the cable car. By the time he discovered that someone else had chosen the same road out of the rather forbidding Cliffside area it was bitterly cold and he wished the late Mr Santini had dressed more heavily.

There was also something about the way his follower shrugged, as though getting his shoulders balanced, that told Denis the chauffeur, or whoever he was, intended to beat him up, or at the least knock him into the handy gutter. He sensed the fellow's approach by the thick scent of a popular talcum powder.

Very close. Timing his own move from long experience, Denis felt the chauffeur make his move but slipped out of his reach and cracked him across his neck.

The fellow lost his footing, tripped on the curb, and fell into the street on one knee, groaning.

He was still groaning when Denis returned to his fast pace, and reached the cable car turnaround.

By the time the car rattled down the Hyde Street Hill and had been swung around for passengers returning for the trip over Nob Hill to the St Francis Hotel and then Market Street, he knew the character was still following him. Doubtless, the chauffeur. Denis reached the car just as it was pulling back to the corner of Hyde Street and jumped aboard, fumbling for the change, to satisfy the conductor. When he looked back he could see his pursuer limping as he tried to run toward the cable car.

Denis laughed, went inside the car and sat down, exhilarated by his recent exercise.

It had been a relief to throw his pursuer off the track, especially if he had any connection with Blake Cavenaugh.

Marina hurried up to her own apartment, deliberately avoiding any of the household staff or her father, who was, luckily, still out. She used her own phone, listening at first to be sure no one in the house had cut into her call.

She was lucky to reach their architect friend, Larry Hoaglund, who had just come into his new Nob Hill apartment. He seemed glad, if surprised, to hear from her.

"Of course I can see you tomorrow, Miss Kyle. Well, I'll make time. How early? I'm seeing Denis Mallory at ten thirty or so."

She said nervously, "Quite a bit earlier. Actually, it's about Denis. A secret. Please say I can trust you."

Larry hesitated. "I think I'd better tell you – Denis is just about my best buddy, so I'd rather not discuss anything against him. You understand, I'm sure."

Her laugh was anxious. "It's really for him. You know how proud he is."

"God, yes! Well, how can I help him? Or you?"

"No one is to know anything about it. You see, we want to get married and I want him to have a decent job right away at what's left of the Kyle Baths."

Larry wanted to know why she couldn't arrange this herself, but understood when she reiterated the secrecy of her plan for the small, northern, rocky portion of the Baths.

"I want you to buy that remaining sector."

"Me!"

"Listen to me. Rosa Santini says one day Denis told her about a fabulous idea he had for the Kyle bathhouse. For us to turn it into cafés and gardens and whatnot. What pleased Rosa was that it was very like the idea her husband had a long time ago. A sidewalk café, perhaps, and all the rest of it – very Parisian."

"It might well work out. But my dear Miss Kyle, why do you

tell me? It would take money and a good decorator. Someone like—"

"Like you."

"But what has this to do with Denis or me? I like your idea, but I don't have that kind of money. Mine is tied up in housing above St Francis Wood."

Impatiently, she said, "I've got to have someone do this without having Father or Blake know where the money and arrangements came from."

Larry swallowed hard. Obviously, being human, he wanted very much to ask, "What's in it for me?" Instead, he asked, "You would like me to act as your front between the bank and your family?"

"Exactly. My credit is good. I have enough securities to back up my credit. But I want it kept strictly secret, not only from my father and Mr Cavenaugh but especially from Denis."

"Oh, yes. That would be a priority," Larry agreed. "I know the dear fellow. Proud to the limit. I take it also that my part in all this would be very active in the design and the rebuilding, and then I step aside and say, 'Here, old man. I'm feeling charitable. It's a success, so it's all yours.'".

She felt a hysterical desire to laugh but didn't.

"No. Once you put Denis in charge and things look like success, you have too much to do and can't handle it along with your more important business; so we buy you out. In the meanwhile, what you earn is your reward for all the work you do on it." There was a little silence and she went on rapidly, "Your salary during the time you work on it and it opens et cetera, will be enough to repay you for whatever you may lose on your own affairs. We can work that out later."

He chuckled. "You are a very trusting soul."

"No. I just want Denis to be happy."

"I wish I knew a female who would do that for me."

"I don't usually get cheated," she reminded him.

She thought: he's weakening. He'll see what a wonderful idea it is for Denis. And for Larry too, if he doesn't squander all his profits.

79

She heard him take a long, almost desperate breath.

"Well, it's a crazy idea, but it doesn't have to be a gigantic business to begin with. Who knows? It might even make us all a fortune. Are you sure you can count on the discretion of your bank people?"

"I know Al Freed well. I've known him practically all my life. He has hinted to me many times that I was being taken for a ride by – well, by others. He'd keep this business away from Blake and . . ." – *Father?* She couldn't admit that aloud – ". . . others."

He understood something else in her words. "I guess I'd better be on my best behavior too, but I can safely promise you that, honey."

Suddenly, she heard him suck in his breath and ask plaintively, "I wouldn't have to be the chef, would I?"

She was still laughing when she hung up.

She did not take his last words seriously but as she set the telephone back, he was saying, "Only you could get me tied up like this, sweetheart. I'll give it plenty of thought before I sleep but there's always the chance I'll wake up a millionaire."

She ignored that. His humor was always a little wild.

I knew that would do it, she thought. She could tell that he had liked her from the first – something else she'd better not tell darling Denis. She was proud of her manipulations. She was getting as good as her father and Blake.

This is going to really help Denis and we'll make our fortune together.

And their love had only begun. There would be so many more wonderful, passionate times like today at the St Francis.

How could I ever have thought I'd be happy with Blake? Not after my Denis, she told herself.

Twelve

L arry Hoaglund slapped Denison the back as he met him
 and Marina in the main floor lobby of his offices. The
architect announced in triumph, "I hope you're not going to be
too proud to accept a job. I need you, old boy. Don't fail me
now."

Marina clutched Denis's arm excitedly. "Oh, darling, it's
providence. What's the job?"

Larry opened his hands wide. "I've put in a bid and a modest
cash offer for that little tail-end of the Kyle bathhouse. Let the
big boys make millions on the major portion. All I want is the
little north corner. I'll even take the empty pool, to create
gardens. And the several balconies from the pool up can be a
balcony for a café, a higher one for something bigger, like
exhibits, and a bathing beauty contest. Maybe dance contests.
The tango is still good. Not to mention a new dance or whatever.
And – what do you say to a beer garden?"

Denis was bewildered. "What happened to your own profession? Not to mention Prohibition?"

Larry refused to be crushed. "We'll see to that problem when
we get to it. I'll confess it wasn't my idea at first. I got it from
your friend Rosa what's-her-name. Her husband had this notion
ages ago."

Marina turned to Denis. "He's right, now I think of it. Nobody would listen to him. But Rosa and I thought it was a great
idea. But I was pretty little then."

Denis cut into this daydreaming. "What's this got to do with
me? I do sketches. I'm no contractor. Or any of the rest of it."

Neither Larry nor Marina was downcast.

"But darling," she reminded him, "you never handled a bathhouse either."

The whole idea was so ridiculous Denis burst out laughing. When he could look at it more sensibly, he reminded them, "The Kyles won't permit it. Jason, anyway." He glanced at Marina. "That part is worth too much for what it would be worth to you."

Marina said suddenly, "No, it isn't. I just thought of something. Blake and Father believe the small north side is the very least important part. Blake wants to put in a fancy estate section toward the Presidio. A section like Seacliff or the Heights. Not houses built on rocks as they would be on the northeast side. He can't use Larry's part of the bathhouse because of the rocks."

"It doesn't matter anyway," Larry put in. "If I furnish the money, they'll be glad to get it. According to the bankers I've discussed it with, Cavenaugh needs the cash right now. He's got an enormous job ahead with those estates and all. With me, I've just got one place to put together. And the foundation for our entertainment center is already there."

"I hate to dampen your hopes," Denis put in sceptically, "but how are you going to give time to this fairytale and still build your elegant little Eastwood houses near St Francis Wood?"

Larry was nothing if not enthusiastic. "That's the beauty of it. I won't give up my own work. Once I get this place set up, and I can use a lot of what's already there, I'll hand over to a manager who knows cafés and all that Paris stuff. I'll see to the groundwork and someone who knows places from Paris to Coney Island, you might say, could—"

"From Paris to Coney Island," Denis stared at him and shook his head. "You've got one thing wrong. I was never in Coney Island in my life."

But when he looked at Marina she seemed to be growing more and more thrilled. "He's right, darling. He came to the right man. You!"

"My God!"

"Well, you could learn about it, to help an old pal like me. And you know a lot of chefs and sidewalk cafés and that sort of thing. We want it to have a flavor of sorts. Not like a California beach town."

Denis said, "Sounds like Playland at the Beach to me. And they go broke every few months."

"Oh, darling," Marina murmured, "don't be negative."

It was hard to resist that charming note in her voice. Larry even convinced himself. He added mischievously, "Maybe I should have bought the whole deal."

Marina was shocked. "Oh, no!"

Larry laughed. "Come on. I've already signed. They have my check. I've got to go through with it now. And you'll put me in one hell of a spot, buddy, if you don't help me out."

"According to what I heard from Father at breakfast," Marina put in, "Father owes so much to Blake, he'd do better in partnership with him. I said I didn't think so, but this idea of Larry's would get us out from under Blake."

Denis pointed out, "But if your father loses part of the Baths, its really part of your inheritance."

"Don't you think you're worth it?" Larry asked curiously.

"Certainly not. Ask me when I've made my own way and I may have a different answer."

"Well, I like that! If old Denis runs our place, won't we all profit too, ultimately?"

Both Marina and Denis laughed at that and Denis remarked, "I can see it now. We'll go broke in a week. Did she tell you we were getting married?"

"Certainly."

Denis shook his head. He felt as if he had never left war-torn France. His world was still upside down. "I'll never catch up," he sighed.

Marina pointed out, "All we need are the okays of Al Freed and the bank trustees. Nothing to it. Father needs the cash to buy in with Blake Cavenaugh."

Denis was still cynical. "Oh, if life were only so simple."

*   *   *

83

Virginia Coffman

In spite of his doubts, Denis found himself with Marina and Larry Hoaglund, half an hour later, waiting in Albert Freed's office of the Senior Loans Operation. There Freed's interest in his own daughter's wedding present, a new Hoaglund home in Woodside Park, almost took precedence over the affairs of the Kyles.

"My dear boy," Freed burst out after shaking hands with all present, "my girl has said it herself: she wanted nothing in life so much as a home by Larry Hoaglund. It will be her dream home for a dream wedding."

I hope the bridegroom shares the dream, Denis thought but merely obliged one and all with an inane smile.

Larry Hoaglund grinned and gave the banker an easy salute which was or was not an assent. The others in the room murmured congratulations to Larry but the tawny raised eyebrow Larry gave Denis told him that the wedding present deal had probably influenced Freed to support Larry's purchase of a piece of the Kyle property.

At that minute Jason Kyle walked in. Marina, who had been embittered about her father the night before, now moved over to Jason and greeted him with a brief kiss on the cheek. Jason nodded to Denis and Larry in his remote but reasonably polite manner and apologized to all present.

"Sorry I am late. There were business papers to sign, as you will appreciate. And I had my" – he ignored Marina and looked directly at the trust officer – "I had my new partner to consult. After a talk with my daughter at breakfast, I believe I made her see the advantages of selling the small northern sector of the property. My new partner did not intend to include that area in our plan for the Jason Estates."

This was the first anyone, including Marina, had heard of the name for the planned estates and she smiled, somewhat relieved. It put an end to the family corporation and exchanged Jason's daughter for Blake Cavenaugh as partner, but perhaps it would free Marina of her father's influence. Denis hoped Marina really was relieved by the change in her life, but he still wasn't sure.

Jason Kyle was amused and obviously proud that the naming of the Jason Estates had surprised them all.

"The main thing," he reminded them, and particularly Al Freed, "is that I am told the amount paid by Mr – er – Hoaglund will cover certain loans the bank holds against Kyle Baths. Is that true?" he asked Albert Freed.

Freed glanced at Hoaglund. "Certainly, the amount is correct. Young Hoaglund is aware that you retain the westerly half and the southern portion of the property. The dimensions are spelled out."

Larry was all smiles, Marina thought: as if he had nothing to lose. Which was true, thanks to her own deal with him. She was not sorry. She told herself it was the most important deal she would ever make.

Mr Freed beamed. "We'll just call in Miss Gissburg and one of our assistant trust officers to witness. Well, Jason, it looks as though your worries are over for the moment. Would you step forward with Mr Hoaglund and sign, and thirdly, Miss Kyle . . . Your signature, Jason, is good for your new partnership with Mr Cavenaugh."

"I understand," Jason said.

Marina said brightly, "I think it's great. Here we are, all happy. Even Blake. And I did so want the Kyle debts to be settled."

Denis thought Kyle was going to frown but the older man managed a smile. "Whatever makes my little girl happy," he said pleasantly to all present.

Marina took a deep breath. "So I guess I can announce our engagement soon." Before her father could open his mouth with what might or might not be pleasure, Marina added, "Well, here it is: it makes me happy to announce that Denis and I are going to be married very soon."

Denis didn't know which of them, he himself or Jason Kyle, was more astonished at this bold statement. Kyle's expression remained blank. Not that it mattered to Denis. He looked over at Marina, adoring her as she stared at him in triumph. He might have the job that would at least support them and apparently she was ready to live on his income, he told himself silently.

Bless her honest, straightforward heart!

No conniving Jason Kyle blood about his Marina.

Twelve

I t took Denis, Larry Hoaglund and even her father to convince Marina that the separation of the Kyle properties could not be accomplished overnight. Each day Marina went out to the ruined bathhouse and the cliffs around it.

Seeing the property as it would look under Larry Hoaglund's design and Denis's management, Marina spent time in Rosa Santini's company balancing books and pretending she saw the prospective development as an instant success. This persuasion was necessary with Mrs Santini, who liked the idea but suspected Blake Cavenaugh of biding his time before striking in some devious way.

Marina hadn't sought out Blake but tried not to avoid him on the rare occasions when their paths crossed. He seemed almost exactly as he had always been, calm and businesslike, perhaps more quiet than usual, but even that was typical of the man she had known. Rosa Santini remarked the day after the property boundaries were staked out, "He's a cool one. I'd like to know what he's really thinking."

"Probably thinking about the future success of his fancy new tract for the idle rich," Marina said, feeling it wasn't quite fair that after she had more or less jilted him, everyone was cynical about his new plans.

Rosa shrugged. "Maybe."

Marina laughed at the idea but later she thought about it. She had no right to be jealous. Her father was a free man. And she herself adored Denis. He was everything she might have dreamed of: a sensuous, quite perfect man. The only glitch was that she didn't entirely agree with Denis's pride, his ridiculous efforts to live within his means. Worse: he obviously expected her to live the same way. But there was the passionate sexual life they lived, and would live after their marriage.

This morning Denis had come to her father's house to pick her up in his rattling old second-hand Ford and drove her away like Prince Charming in a glass coach. He had to get back to Larry Hoaglund's plans for the development, but they stopped at what remained of the Kyle bathhouse. There, while they were bolted securely into the ladies' changing room, they had made love. Marina had never felt so daring.

How awful if she had never met Denis and had gone on to marry Blake! He wasn't that much younger than her father. He certainly never demonstrated any sexiness!

Rosa Santini stuck her pen in the inkwell and said, "Penny for your thoughts."

Marina took a deep breath. "I hope that architect hasn't gone in over his head."

Rosa started to say something, then just nodded.

Marina went on almost to herself: "For Denis there are so many memories tied to the idea of poverty. He said his family lived from payment to payment and mortgage to mortgage. Imagine! His mother's diamond ring was in the pawn shop as often as he could remember. He said it gave him chills to think I might end up like that if he wasn't able to support me."

"You won't, Miss Kyle." Rosa looked out the little back window of her box office and muttered, "Look who's down there on your father's side of the boundary. Counting the houses he's going to build, I'll bet!"

Marina looked down. The cashier pulled her back a few steps and added, "Don't let Cavenaugh see you."

Marina said, "I've got to tell him about my getting married."

"Mr Kyle's bound to have told him that," Mrs Santini pointed out.

"Tell who what?" Denis wanted to know.

Standing close behind Marina with one hand on her shoulder,

he looked down over her head at Blake Cavenaugh below on the windswept rocks.

Rosa Santini said philosophically, "If you all make a hit of this place, it doesn't matter what Cavenaugh wants."

Denis was encouraging. "That's the girl!" Then he told Marina, "Darling, if he's waiting for us to fail, he had better think twice."

Uncomfortably, Marina thought Blake might be much more confident than Denis suspected. Damn him! He had begun to frighten her. At least, his power worried her as it never had before.

Rosa Santini returned to the business at hand. "I've got to get the inventory ready – what there is left after the fire."

"Right," Marina said. "I'd like to go and have a look at the balcony up where we keep the door locked. I know it's not safe now but something could be made of it if we can lick the wind factor. Father had it made for his telescope, so he could look across to Marin County. That was ages ago."

"You know where that leaves me," Denis said. "I've got some things to check in the ladies' lounge and the gents' toilets."

"Well, after all, they are necessary," Marina teased him.

She blew a kiss to him and he went off between the semi-circular rows of seats now hopelessly burned and still, smelling of smoke. She watched him until the first ladies' changing room and conveniences swallowed him up beyond the alcove.

Marina was about to cross the area of the Baths now sold to Larry Hoaglund when her father called to her. "I see you're examining Hoaglund's new property. Thank God he didn't want our property, Blake's and mine. We've got big plans for the Jason Estates."

Relieved as she was to find her father happy, Marina was a little hurt to find out how easily she had been eased out of their new company. Not that she could blame her father – but it was a dampening truth to discover that her father had apparently never needed her in the business.

On the other hand, the guilt she felt in the loss of a piece of her father's property was nearly made up for by his secured part in the new Cavenaugh property called "Jason Estates".

"Well, Father, it seems everybody's happy then. I just want to see if we can make something out of that stupid little balcony out there over the cliffs. Want to investigate, Father?"

"I'm too old for gymnastics, my dear. And I might say, so are you."

"Rubbish. You can stand out on the rocks below and catch me if I fall."

"Let your Denis do it. He's around here somewhere."

He waved and went on.

Marina saw a shadow flash along the high walkway. Larry must have already ordered men in to repair what remained of the structure that had been saved in the fire. Or maybe someone was up there above her examining plans for Hoaglund. The area might be opened up to a strongly fortified view of the green Marin Highlands across the Golden Gate, along with Alcatraz Island and, nearer below the Baths, Mile Rock Light plus the choppy, sunlit waters of the Golden Gate itself.

She started around the lower balcony over the interior baths, found the staircase which was narrower than the big entrance staircase, and started up. The stairs, or better yet, an elevator could lead up to a high restaurant with that fabulous view. It would seem ridiculous to have an elevator like that, separated from the Golden Gate winds by nothing but glass. San Francisco could do it, with steel girders or whatever . . . Well, let Larry Hoaglund and the engineers figure that out.

She climbed more stairs. An elevator would certainly be an improvement. Even at a distance she heard the wind whistling around the balcony.

When she reached the balcony, she walked across to check the door. She tried the door knob and realized it was not locked, and the Yale lock was on the latch too.

Some of the young people from the marina area occasionally got outside. Once, there had been an expensive lawsuit when a boy from a local high school couldn't get back in and had to kneel and cling to the tiny platform until Rosa and the swing-shift man rescued him from what had been part of a fire escape blown away by the wind. It was extremely dangerous out there as the winds could easily be strong enough to push you over the edge and there was nothing to hold on to.

Marina was holding the door by the knob when a gust of wind suddenly tore the door open, leaving her out on the platform. She teetered on the edge, and as she turned to go back the door slammed shut. She pulled at the handle, but the door was locked . . . How could it be?

She cried out in blind desperation, "Denis! Help!"

A minute or two later, footsteps thundered on to the balcony. The door opened and Denis reached out, pulling Marina in with all his strength.

Marina shuddered, held tight against Denis.

"I don't understand," she said. "The door seemed to lock itself."

"It was the Yale that was locked – I suppose the catch must have slipped."

By this time Jason Kyle, and one of the men who had been tearing out the burned areas, arrived, and the matter ended. Denis was slamming the door shut again and the worker, at Jason's directions, went down to get material to seal the door.

Thirteen

Denis brought Marina down to the lowest balcony of the Baths and up the big staircase to Rosa Santini's office.

Hearing the story of the platform, Rosa remarked, chiefly to Marina, "I doubt if it was the intention, but your man is a hero, apparently." Then she tilted her head, indicating someone who had come up to the little group around Rosa's office. Marina looked over into Blake Cavenaugh's eyes as he gave them all his thin smile.

"What's this about heroes?" he asked.

Mrs Santini gave a cutting laugh, and Marina said with quiet triumph, "Denis Mallory here."

Blake blinked. "Well, you are a brave fellow." He looked over at the interior of the Baths. "Ah! Would that be the old fire escape?"

Marina caught the quick exchange of glances between Denis and Rosa as Denis went out to the curb to wait for Larry Hoaglund. For an instant she hadn't understood. She doubted their suspicions, whatever had happened. Though she thought it quite possible Blake wouldn't be sorry to have something happen to the "brave hero".

Then Rosa said brightly, "How clever of you, Mr Cavenaugh! You guessed right away where Miss Kyle almost got killed."

He was calm. It seemed inevitable. "I've told Jason a dozen times that he ought to have the platform torn down."

Marina's mind was on something extraneous. She thought it strange that she had never noticed before how chilly his pale eyes could be.

He cleared his throat. "Marina, my dear, Jason said you wanted to see me. But it occurs to me I haven't congratulated you on your engagement. We've been so busy, your father and I. I'm sure you understand."

"I know," she went on hurriedly. "I want to thank you for your help to Father, putting his name on the new tract, and all. I know you are bound to be a fantastic success."

"It's very promising. Let's hope he doesn't waste the profits. We don't want any gambling in the market."

How does he have the nerve to say that? Marina thought.

He went on. "But we will keep things on an even keel." He bestowed on her a sudden, benevolent smile. "Just as you will with your visionary soldier-boy."

She stiffened but assured him with pride, "I was always pretty good with our own stocks, as you must remember. Denis is an artist, not a stockbroker. He'll leave that side to me."

"Do you think so?" he asked pleasantly. "But of course, you know him so much better than I do."

She felt the cutting tone beneath his easy agreement, but didn't want to quarrel now, just as she had been leading up to an apology for her sudden engagement. She boasted with smiling confidence, "My Denis and Larry Hoaglund are very good friends. They worked together on the newspaper before the war. Larry didn't have two bits in those days, but he's certainly on his way now."

"On his way indeed," Blake agreed. "A natural friendship. Now, both have worked their way up to a rivalry with Cavenaugh and Kyle."

She hid her anger, saying brightly, "They will give Kyle and Cavenaugh a run for their money." All thoughts of an apology were dead. She laughed, pretended to blow a kiss to him and stepped out to the street to meet Larry Hoaglund, who had driven along the curb and was waving to her. She joined him as he got out of his car and asked her with amusement, "How are they taking it?"

"Lovely. You know what, Larry?"

"What? I'm all ears."

"Denis and I are going to get married as soon as possible and you're invited."

He grinned. "Just so long as I'm not the groom. I'm saving that for my old age."

Denis reached around her lissome waist, squeezing her. "Thanks for giving her up so nobly. I'll be glad to take her – if you've no objections."

Larry said, "She's got you hog-tied for the wedding band in the next few days. How's that for timing?"

For a moment she thought she ought to have talked the day over with Denis but after a moment he kissed the crown of her wind-blown head. "Why not? I've got to grab her before old Cavenaugh gets his ideas about her again. I'll be damned! He's still watching us."

"But he's still smiling too," Larry reminded them.

Denis closed his hand over her shoulder again.

"He's a busy little bee. I don't suppose he knew you were out on the platform."

Marina caught her breath. She didn't want to bring such a remote possibility into the open. "What's that supposed to be? A joke?"

"Maybe. But I don't think dear old Cavenaugh is too happy with us at the moment."

Larry laughed. "Did you straighten Marina's father out about your romantic plan?"

Denis shook his head. "Oh, no. I've already robbed him of his daughter."

Larry rolled his eyes. "Isn't love grand? Incidentally, where does the great event take place?"

"We haven't decided where yet. Some place where we were happiest. Where we enjoyed our first kiss? What do you say, darling?"

Marina was shocked but not quite sure how to take this.

"Why not? If that's where you've been happiest."

He appeared to hesitate. "I kissed you first at the foot of the front steps at my rooming house. That's a pleasant memory." He watched for Marina to react.

"Well, if that's your happiest moment."

Then he grinned and kissed her forehead. "Our happiest moment. Where were we really happy?"

She hugged him so hard he pretended to groan. Then she laughed. "You devil! You knew all the time where I wanted to be. In the St Francis Suite."

"You're a mind-reader, sweetheart. And since we want it as soon as possible, how about tomorrow – say around noon?"

She hugged his arm. "Oh, lovely, lovely. We'll have to work fast. The tickets and everything. I don't think my passport has run out yet. Father and I went to Mexico three years ago. I hope all those cafés won't expire before we get to Paris."

She started to add something but Denis said quietly, "We can't use Larry's money too freely. He offers a lot more than we should use. How would you like it if someone used your money for a honeymoon? We can borrow our ideas for the café where we find them."

She was frightened at how closely he might come to discussing the origin of the capital they were using.

Mrs Santini interrupted them, "Hey! What about the wedding? If I may be so bold?"

Marina ignored her, grinning. "Just so long as we honeymoon in Paris. We can be as careful as possible. We'll manage, and Larry has been awfully generous."

"That's my girl," Denis said and drew her to him. When he kissed her there were exaggerated sighs from Mrs Santini.

She murmured, "Ah, love! Love!"

Fourteen

B y the time Denis and Marina had finished the final legal
work for preparing the wedding, it was past the sunset of
their busiest day and they were barely finished packing, which,
according to Marina, was extremely simple.

She threw out an idea to Denis.

"I'll buy nice things on our honeymoon later. In New York or
even Paris. Who knows?"

"And how am I going to live up to your elegance? Can you
bear to visit just Paris this time?" He was only half joking.

She was anxious to oblige him. In view of her arrangement
with Larry Hoaglund over the financing of the café and gardens,
she was determined not to make trouble.

She agreed laughingly.

For Marina, her wedding and honeymoon were all so close to
her mind she could think of nothing else.

Almost all her life, money had appeared close at hand. Even
when her father's new gambling propensities took over, she had
known there would be money – there was what remained of the
securities left by her mother. But she did feel that the less said to
Denis about her mother's remaining estate, the better. There was
his infernal pride, which she admired, but when she and Denis
needed money, she wasn't above using it.

During the night before the wedding, she was so excited, so
filled with the ecstacy of an undreamed of happiness, she didn't
have time to concentrate on anything except the immediate joys
ahead.

She had been especially happy that evening when her father

said with a surprising warmth added to his elegant manner, "I hope to give you away, you know. I hope that suits you, my dear." He had hesitated a moment, then said with pride, "I have a little business with Jason Estates. Will you excuse me?"

Lying in bed that night she wondered a little why Denis always held her in his embrace so long. Her heart raced with excitement, and she could feel his deep response. But it was as if he hadn't all her faith in the time of love ahead of them.

No matter. She did sleep fitfully for what she realized would be the last time as a single woman in her father's house. And at least Blake Cavenaugh couldn't get the rest of Marina's securities. They would now belong to Denis and Marina, though of course a share would go to Larry Hoaglund for his part in the building of the cafés.

The day of the wedding was unusually warm, sunny, and cloudless. It seemed to fulfill all the promise she dreamed of.

With all that had been done the day before, Marina was surprised at how much must be done today. There was the matter of looking after the guests at the wedding – Judge Winterbourne, plus Jason Kyle and Rosa Santini, and any friends Denis might have. She doubted if Blake Cavenaugh would show up, though he had been invited. He probably would find some reasonable excuse to be away. Ben Riggs would be present with his wife, as well as the Assistant Manager of the St Francis and his daughter, and several members of her father's lodge.

It was after dark that evening when Mrs Santini told Marina that the bridegroom, waiting with Larry after an exchange of amenities with Jason Kyle, was looking a little anxiously toward the bedroom door and his prospective bride.

Marina took Rosa's hand with a nervous pinch.

"How do I look? I picked the outfit off the rack."

Mrs Santini tossed away that problem. "You never looked more stunning. That man of yours will adore you."

Marina hoped Rosa was right. There had been time only for a quick dash to the City of Paris Department Store's Special

Section for a wedding gown, and the straight dinner dress encrusted with seed pearls was simple. After Rosa's honest appraisal, she said hesitantly, "It really does look nice, doesn't it?"

"With that hair of yours down your back, and the little crown, it's sort of – well – angelic."

Marina laughed at this but then, anxious again, she begged, "When Denis came in, did he look happy?"

"All I can say is, it's a good thing old Cavenaugh won't see you."

"He's not here, I hope. Damn you! Don't joke. This is serious." Then she grabbed at Rosa. "We forgot the flowers."

"The place is full of them. I only hope nobody has allergies."

"Allergies! I need—"

"Never mind that. I'll fix you up."

Before Marina could say anything Rosa bounded out of the room and into the big living room/salon. Marina watched her go, her green, fringed dinner dress flaring as she ran.

How thankful Marina was that Denis and Rosa got on well! He must have led a bitter life to be so cynical and untrusting about most people. Dear Denis! He needed her love and trust.

Two or three minutes later Rosa hurried in with several rose buds which appeared to have been broken off from the big living-room decorations. Before Marina could stop her, she was winding stems and fern in a necklace and slipping it over Marina's head. No use warning Rosa not to knock off her little coronet. Rosa would know.

At any rate, the result, for some reason, suited the bride perfectly, stems and all.

"What did Denis look like? I mean, his expression?" asked Marina.

"Well, he kept looking toward the door here. Your father asked me if anything was wrong. He actually handed me this rose bud. I'm to wear it on my bosom, he said." She laughed. "I'm not the rose type. I see myself more as the crocus type."

That made Marina laugh too, although she was surprised that

her father had managed at this moment to pay attention to the decoration of the Maid of Honor.

Rosa Santini opened the door a few inches. "Ready?"

Marina swallowed hard and nodded.

Rosa Santini, who didn't seem afraid of anything, took her arm and the two women walked sedately to the door.

The Wedding March began on the suite's elegant grand piano and Jason Kyle, looking his handsome self, took Marina's arm.

Entering the big, crowded room, Marina got her first glimpse of the "few guests" invited. She hadn't thought there would be many more than ten – maybe a dozen at the most, but there must have been at least twenty-five to thirty. Several were hotel executives, three were from the tea-dance orchestra, aside from the bridegroom's few friends and Marina's doctor-friend from Geneva Avenue. There were two from the Mayor's office, the Chief of Police, and the rest seemed to be Jason Kyle's business associates.

It seemed to Marina that they looked deadly serious, but they all faded from Marina's view when she saw Denis. He wasn't smiling, like Larry Hoaglund, but his gaze was strictly confined to Marina – a tender, proud look. His eyes seemed to reveal more love, pride and devotion than anyone had ever devoted to her.

Her full lips, as tender in their smile as his, were answered with his own tenderness and she could ask herself now, Was anyone ever as happy as I am at this minute? Never!

The crowd parted, making way for her and Jason Kyle as they walked the length of the room to stand before Judge Winterbourne, whose back was to the fake fireplace, which had been piled high with winter blossoms and hothouse flowers. Jason stepped aside gracefully.

Denis took Marina's chill, nervous fingers, squeezed them and let them go, but his little gesture had been enough. She felt warmth surge through her body.

The service was short and simple. There seemed little about it that made her feel the religious significance mattered. But when

99

she and Denis exchanged vows, she knew their vows had been passionately sincere.

She made one mistake: when Judge Winterbourne asked her, "Will you take this man to be your lawfully wedded husband?" she answered, "I do," and then wondered if she should have said, "I will."

But no one seemed to notice, and when Denis slipped the ring on her finger, she felt the golden bond would bind them together for all time. They hadn't been able to find a suitable ring in the short time available and Rosa had suggested the yellow gold ring Denis wore, which had been in his family for generations and belonged to his father when his grandfather died early in the Boer war. It was Rosa who wrapped the ring shaft in pale silk thread and Denis's hand now slipped it over Marina's finger without its falling off.

Almost before they were ready for it, they were pronounced "man and wife" and everyone rushed to kiss both the bride and groom.

Denis had held Marina's nervous hands after slipping the ring on and was the first to kiss her. She heard his whisper then, close to her cheek. "Sweetheart, you know, don't you? You are my whole life."

She wasn't even sure anyone else would mean it, but she was certain he did. The others were drowning out anything else he might say, or she might answer, but she whispered, "Me, too," then she added, "I mean . . . You know what I mean."

The congratulations and well-wishing came much too soon – the guests got between her and Denis. Her father took her by the shoulders, pinching her flesh a little, and assuring her, "You know, dear child, all my thoughts are for your happiness."

She was touched and enormously pleased, though a tiny doubt made her wish he had included her new husband. But maybe she was asking too much. He was not a demonstrative man about emotions. At least he had come through with his good wishes.

He turned away and remarked on the decorations. The next

time Marina noticed him, he was chattering away to the bank officers about his own wedding to Marina's mother and how they had been divinely happy. Larry Hoaglund came up to them, interrupting Ben Riggs who was drinking bootleg gin, having refused the champagne. Ben was discussing Denis's previous job – what he called insulting the Mayor and City Hall with his cartoons. Larry, on the other hand, wanted to remind Denis of all the things he must check in Paris for a French café.

Miss Lupkin, another employee of the trust department in the bank, tittered loudly at something said to her, and then reminded Marina, "Honey, you going to cut the cake? I can't wait. It looks scrumptious."

Rosa Santini led Marina over to the long credenza where the seven-layer cake sat in all its glory. With Denis beside her, Marina did the honors, cutting the cake's thick white frosting, hesitating for a glance at Denis, hoping he'd understand. Then she presented a silver rose and a piece of cake that was chiefly frosting to her father. She was touched by the way Denis smiled and seemed to understand.

Jason accepted the silver plate graciously, inclined his head and stepped back. Marina gave the next to Denis, remarking as she looked up into his eyes, "Father used to say, 'You've got the biggest piece of cake.'"

He laughed, and murmured, "Don't be angry, darling," and had his revenge by accepting his cake and giving it to a deeply touched Rosa Santini, who added tears to the stiff silver rosette.

Afterward, when the chattering started again on a half dozen subjects, usually business, Denis reminded Marina in a low voice, "We'll have to be leaving soon if we want to catch the ferry across the Bay to the train."

She looked up and would have hugged him but he beat her to it, holding her tightly to him. She had nothing she could think of to say except the truth. "I love you so much. I never knew, not even an hour ago, I could be this happy."

But there were still the well-wishers who came up to them, talking about a thousand years of happiness, which even Marina could not top for wishes.

One of the well-wishers was her father, who immediately after took her aside as Larry and several others were showering Denis with their hopes and wishes.

"Always remember, Marina, your home is here, wherever you go or whatever happens. If you need me, I'll never fail you. Just remember that."

"I know, Father. I've always known. I don't like to leave you alone like this."

He seemed reasonably content. "I understand. But at least we've got Blake to count on. He told me that when we had lunch today. He means it. You mustn't mind his not showing up for the ceremony here. He felt pretty bad over losing you. I guess he just couldn't face the excitement."

"I can imagine."

He smiled, apparently ignoring anything sarcastic in her voice. "While you and Denis are gone, we are going to do wonders with Jason Estates."

"Yes, of course. I'm awfully proud of you."

He reminded her, "You remember what a long time we had getting you to understand double-entry bookkeeping? And so many other . . . But I don't want to detain you, dear. I think your Denis is signalling me. I do believe he is jealous of your loyalty to your old father."

"How silly! As if anything could weaken my love for him – or you," she lied brightly. But she wished he hadn't exaggerated her supposed girlhood failures with bookkeeping.

She nodded to Denis over the heads of several guests and turned to Mrs Santini, who followed her to the bedroom.

Marina hadn't had time to buy something glamorous for going away but made do with a lacy, feminine blouse and an oyster-grey suit with jewelled buttons. She would have preferred to wear her lovely negligee and hopped into that bed in the next room, but couldn't see herself wearing less than a heavy coat while crossing the chill waters of San Francisco Bay to the train on the Oakland Mole.

She came out of the dressing room to be greeted by the "oohs" and "aahs" of the crowd. Marina had one special target and Rosa Santini got the rose buds.

Then Denis took Marina's hand in his. There were remarks to him of "lucky devil" and Marina hoped he did not hear someone in the crowd murmur, "Marry the boss's daughter. That's the way." But her father heard, of course, and glanced over at her. She ignored this and kissed Denis beside her. The St Francis orchestra leader motioned to the female pianist at the grand piano, which, Marina observed, needed tuning. The pianist swung into a Strauss waltz.

Denis held out his arms. Marina went into them, and everyone backed off until the center of the floor was cleared. Marina was delighted by her bridegroom's ability to handle himself on the dance floor. He was so perfect in every way. She looked up, misty-eyed.

"I was never so happy. How can I ever be this happy again?"

He looked into her eyes. "If I have anything to do with it, you'll always be happy."

They had swung around the long room twice before others joined in.

Someone tapped Marina on the shoulder. She saw Denis's face before she looked around to see her father. Denis was not smiling.

Jason said, "Forgive me, dear. An important meeting. Write to me as soon as you change trains in Chicago. And New York, if you have time."

When he left them, Marina murmured to Denis, "At least Father didn't cause trouble at the ceremony. I hope he isn't going to join Blake Cavenaugh."

He smiled. "Don't worry. Your bank is still in charge of Larry's investment."

She said nervously, "Shouldn't we be on our way? It would be awful to miss the ferryboat."

He signalled the pianist and they wound up the waltz with a flourish.

It still took almost half an hour to say goodbye, thank everyone for the presents piled on the French dresser and bed in the next room, and hear all the good wishes plus the jokes.

Half the crowd followed them down to the lobby in the elevator and wished them well all over again along with kisses and hugs. Larry had insisted on driving them to the Ferry Building and Marina leaned far out of the back seat of Larry's Cadillac to blow kisses to the crowd.

As the car sped down Geary Street to Market, Marina looked out again. "I can see the Ferry Building in the distance. How about it, Larry?"

They had passed the Palace Hotel but Marina saw Denis look at his watch and she began to be more nervous. She felt his fingers warm on hers and was reassured, until she heard a peculiar sound somewhere in the car's engine. They were slowing to a stop.

"Good God!" Denis muttered.

Larry shook his head, looked back at Denis.

"I suppose this is a wedding joke," Marina said, trying not to be disgusted.

"Or a little post-wedding revenge by our friend Blake Cavenaugh," Denis suggested.

Larry shrugged. "I don't believe it. I know I had it checked this morning. We're out of gas."

Denis took a long breath, opened the door and got out in the middle of Market Street. He leaned back in, and put his hand out to Marina. "Sweetheart, are you game?"

"You bet!" He took her hand and she got out. She wasn't about to miss the ferryboat that would carry them to their honeymoon.

Knowing how cross her father always got when things went wrong, she was enormously relieved when Denis smiled at her. "It's only a few blocks. Can you run?"

"There's a streetcar back in the distance. But – come on. Race you to the Embarcadero."

"I'll flag down a car. Or a jitney," Larry promised.

"The main thing is to get our luggage there. Or – where are you?" Marina saw Denis already running, with a snap valise, plus Marina's twenty-nine-inch suitcase and Marina hurried along beside him with her vanity case.

Larry had gone out between the four car tracks on wide Market Street, and was frantically waving to a taxi.

Puffing, panting and laughing hysterically, Marina reached the Ferry Building with Denis. They dashed through the waiting room, now almost empty. The huge door to the wharf and gangplank was being pushed shut. Denis yelled and Marina screamed.

The door was stopped. They slid through to the wharf. Running down the dock, they got to the open gangplank of the white ferryboat just as the gangplank began to rise. Seconds after the bride and groom leaped on to the gangplank, the plank itself was moving upward.

Marina cried to a longshoreman, "We had to catch it. We're just married."

"Holy Smoke! And they're laughing," a sailor observed, shaking his head.

The newlyweds waved to the interested passengers on the main deck, as the ferryboat bumped its way from side to side, getting out into the evening waters of the San Francisco Bay.

The bride and groom were sure they had chosen right. They were nervous but wildly happy.

Fifteen

L ong afterward Marina insisted that their first arrival in Paris had exactly the feeling she wanted Denis and Larry to provide in their newly created sidewalk café. With its undeniable feeling of France, for her it conjured up the gardens to come, as all around her the busy city came to life.

Later in the day the Arc de Triomphe and the Louvre, looking very old and grey, and the River Seine, rapidly moving but rather dirty, were not as truly the Paris of her dreams. No. What they must have in their own Paris would be what she saw when they walked out of the Gare St-Lazare at dawn.

The Atlantic crossing had been delayed, causing the boat-train to pull into Paris hours late, though it was still barely sunrise. Instead of the mysterious night arrival she had expected, Marina was thrilled by the violent movement of a Paris dawn. Horses and wagons, noisy trucks and the popular and refurbished buses all circled the great station on their way to deliveries. On the sidewalks men with curved broomstraws much more ancient than the street brooms at home were sending the night's dirt into the gutter. Men on their way to early work kept crossing the ancient street in front of the funny, rattling taxi Denis had hired after he supervised the loading of the baggage on the taxi's roof.

It was hardly worth the money, Denis thought, to take a taxi for the small drive to the Hôtel Majestueux across from the fabulous opera house. However, it was obvious that Marina felt their arrival for the first time deserved such splendor.

Marina was so sure of their future that she had talked of very little else during the voyage over. Even during the unforgettable hours when their lovemaking fired them both with ecstasy, she would lie back against his breast and shoulder and murmur dreamily, "We really can make it last forever. I know we can." Keep that thought. "Ah! Here we are." They had pulled up in a half-circle driveway that was somewhat battered from heavy use after 1914. The taxi driver yawned, indicated that they had arrived and sat studying the busy streetsweepers in front of the café next door.

Denis was amused at having to wait for Marina with his hand outstretched while she stared with delight at the café, where chairs were being taken off tables and set in place, facing the two streets which seemed to fill with traffic within minutes.

"I love it. It's heavenly. Like a little toy city," Marina told Denis, clasping his outstretched hand.

By this time an elegant fellow they supposed to be from the management desk came down a few steps, inclined his head to them, and accepted Denis's introduction of Marina and himself with a politely regal air.

"Ah, monsieur. Madame. From – it is San Francisco, I believe," he announced, signalling a short, tough-looking little bellman. As the bellman reached for the baggage, the management's emissary remarked to Marina, "It has always been my desire to visit your fair city. You have a department store, I believe – the 'City of Paris'? – and other buildings dedicated to us. We are flattered."

Marina did not let this go unnoticed. She offered him her gloved hand. He surprised himself by putting his lips to her gloved knuckles while she told him in her sweetest manner, "And we have heard much about your lovely town. They say it is nearly as impressive as London and Berlin."

She felt her hand dropped, not rapidly but definitely. She grinned to herself while Denis gave orders to the little baggage clerk, and she started up the steps, into an elegant rotunda, to be joined at the manager's desk by Denis who wanted to laugh but refrained with an effort.

"We've started off right. Made a great hit with the haughty French."

She took his arm. "Well, darling, I am – who I am, after all. They must get used to me."

Denis did not argue over her manner. She was Jason Kyle's daughter and if it came to arrogance, she never let anyone forget it. His own anger too had always been aroused by superiority, though it would have to be considerably worse than the normal French attitude. He had never forgotten the days of his boyhood when he used to drop off his mother's wedding ring at the pawn shop for another loan. It was the only object of value they had and the pawnbroker's disdain made him bitterly resentful, but it seemed impossible that he could ever learn to be arrogant back. You had to be born to it. Or have a father like Jason Kyle, God forbid!

Marina ignored the presence of the elderly lift-operator when she told Denis minutes later in the velvet-padded elevator, "I had no idea they were so old-fashioned here."

"That's just class, darling. Don't you like it?" With a sinking feeling he thought of all their plans for a "Paris" sidewalk café and eventually a great restaurant, with enchanting touches, he hoped, of the fascinating city.

He still felt his disappointment by the time the bellman and the assistant manager, if that was his post, reached one of the bedrooms. He was sure, from the way she caught her breath in surprise, that she thought his tip had been too small. He added another ten francs, and could have kicked himself for it. The bellman departed, thanking him profusely, and the assistant manager was gone soon as well. Denis was embarrassed, but he laughed as though the tip had been unconsciously smaller than he intended.

When he and Marina were alone, he explained, "I can't help thinking that when I keep dishing out extra bills, it's really not my money but old Larry's."

She put her warm fingers over his. "We're setting out to make Larry Hoaglund rich, darling. He owes it to us."

He didn't see it that way but, theoretically, they were still on their honeymoon and he never intended to argue with her over her attitude to money. Still, he wasn't at all sure she was happy in this charming room. It was one of the best-known hotels in Paris and very historic, but obviously not up to what her father had led her to expect.

Damn Jason Kyle!

She apparently didn't read him as well as he read her, and while he was trying to put things to rights without offending her and her accursed father, he saw her eyes widen with excitement. "Come, quick! I want to show this to you. Look, darling!"

She nipped at his hand and attempted to lead him over to the French doors. "There. We can walk out on a tiny balcony a lot safer than our fire escape door at the baths! And you can see such a great view of Paris."

He found it touching as well as amusing when they found only one of them could stand on the so-called "balcony" at one time. And they would have to be extra careful not to lean too far over the age-blackened rail that protected them from the junction of two streets five floors below.

"I can see the opera house over around the corner," she said, hugging him, "and that street corner where the women sell violets. Real ones, aren't they?"

He promised they were, and pointed out the difference between the pale, exquisitely scented Parma violets and the deep wood violets. He was relieved that she saw something here that she could admire.

But then, looking back at their room she found the big brass bed which struck her as the last word in quaintness. This, however, had recommendations. She sat down on it and pronounced the springs "almost like home".

This, he hoped, was a compliment.

He rummaged through the largest suitcase on one of the two luggage rests and began to separate his property from hers. It was easy enough. He had all that he considered necessary for a few weeks of hard work looking up locations, ideas that would do well when properly adapted for Larry Hoagland's purposes.

It was an interesting job to him and made him think often of times during those nearly two years of his war. It was, or should be, a lot more interesting and certainly more pleasant than those war years. Friendships, and even love affairs, in those days had been geared to one thought. They were temporary.

Seeing him at his suitcase, Marina hurried to her own cases and began to unpack, shaking wrinkles out of expensive outfits. It had been thoughtful of Larry to send the heavy luggage first class in their own ship and then have it delivered to their Paris hotel even before the taxi arrived with Denis and Marina.

She'd finished putting her evening gowns and best San Francisco suits in the huge armoire as the hazy morning sun cut between the partially open drapes, which were faded but clean.

"We're missing the day," she reminded him. "We'd better get outside quick or we'll miss something."

He laughed, pleased by her enthusiasm. "Well, we can't have that. If you aren't tired. Any particular place in mind?"

"Everything but stuffy things like the Louvre Museum. We can save that for later. I know the little sketches you did are better than anything I can see elsewhere."

He thought this ridiculous compliment was laughable but it gave him pleasure, whether he believed it or not. "Say no more. We're off to scout around until you say, 'Stop!'"

She left the armoire and came over to swing her arms around his neck. "You're so good to me, darling." He kissed her nose, then her lips moved warmly to his and they felt joined "for life" as she told him when they freed themselves breathlessly.

As luck would have it, they were interrupted by a knock at the door and when Denis opened it a very young bellman held out a small silver tray on which there were two envelopes and several advertising cards. He remembered to tip and sent the boy away happy before examining the mail.

Marina looked over his shoulder. "How funny! You know everyone in Paris, but—"

"Not everyone, darling."

"But that's what's so odd. Both the letters are for me. Of course," she added casually, "one is from Father." She examined the other, also addressed to her. "I don't recognize that writing. Awful scrawl, isn't it?"

He glanced at it, puzzled. "Only Larry could write that badly. What the devil is he writing to you for?"

To his surprise on hearing this, she dismissed the matter. "Who cares? Tear it up and let's be on our way. Father has nothing to say in his letter. Just wishes us a happy honeymoon."

He shrugged, turned Larry's letter over and slit it open with his finger. "Must be news about the progress of things back home. I hope that damned Cavenaugh hasn't been causing more trouble."

"Do you think he might do something to hurt Father?"

"He'd be crazy if he did – it would jeopardize his own property." He gave her the opened letter from Larry without reading it. "Let's hear what his business is."

She took the letter, her fingers shaking a little, and explained to Denis with a nervous laugh, "He's just wishing us—" She read the first lines, looked up at him, waving the letter. "Ha! Here we were thinking the worst."

Dear old pal, and your lovely co-conspirator, all well here. The bank is pleased so far. Things coming along. My loan accepted.

I also put in for a little more, this time for the two new houses above the St Francis Wood district.

We have the first balcony nicely planned and the pool on our side drained.

I suspect Cavenaugh is green with envy. Their plans may take a lot longer. They've got more rock and wind than they bargained for.

I'm feeling so good I'd give a pretty penny to join you two and pick up some fresh ideas. But of course it's not my honeymoon.

Love to all, Larry.

111

"Good old Larry," Denis said as she handed him the letter. To his surprise she was frowning.

She saw his surprise and explained, "I don't like an outsider getting into our company."

He laughed and reminded her, "Well, strictly speaking, darling, it's *his* company."

He chucked her under the chin as she tore up the letter. He was amused by her desire not to let Larry Hoaglund gain an even greater percentage in their enterprise in spite of the fact that he had put up almost the entire amount.

"I do believe you're greedy," he pointed out.

She pushed him, showered bits of the letter over him and ordered him, "Hurry! We can't lose a minute. We may see wonders yet, darling."

Only half joking, he said, "I certainly hope so. I don't want you comparing our little honeymoon with some fancy affair in the far-distant future."

She shook her head. "Don't even hint at it. This marriage is forever." The possibility of anything else seemed to make her shiver. She reached in the armoire for a fur-collared woollen cape, then stared at him. "Denis, don't say things like that again. Promise me."

He agreed, finding her concern loving and endearing. He kissed her to seal the promise. He meant his part of the promise and devoutly hoped she would never have reason to change her feelings.

Minutes later they went down in the plush old elevator, slightly crowded between two American men still wearing doughboy caps. The ex-soldiers gave Marina a long look of approval. They exchanged glances and nodded to Denis, who grinned but was speculating on whether these doughboys had arrived a little late for the war or were just leftovers like Denis had been himself.

Though Marina smiled back at them, she was apparently anxious to show them her husband was no slacker. She remarked to him, sotto voce, "Darling, do you suppose they were in your company?"

"Not in my company. Could have been in the same battalion. More likely, just the same army."

She laughed but was satisfied. Meanwhile, the doughboys rushed past Marina and Denis, out of the elevator, through the rotunda, on their way to the joys of post-war Paris. Following them at a more moderate pace with Denis, Marina raised her pale eyebrows. "Great manners. Did you run into fellows like that?"

He laughed. "Seems to me there were a few. I'm not sure I wasn't one of them when I was in a hurry."

She punched his shoulder and they walked out on to the busy street. "I don't believe it . . . Oh, Denis, here we are. Where do we go first?"

"So, the Louvre's out. How about the Eiffel Tower – or is that too stuffy for you?"

She grinned. "I want to see the real Paris. After all, I had monuments in our little Kyle Museum at home."

"Are you hungry? This place over here is one of the most famous sidewalk cafés in the world."

"Do the French eat here?"

"Not the ones I knew. They couldn't afford it."

He had wanted to show her the glamorous heart of Paris, but was also relieved that for the moment her tastes were definitely more commonplace.

"I've got it: I read on the ship that everybody is pouring over to the Left Bank. Authors and artists and students."

"Great. Left Bank it is." He hailed a taxi in front of the hotel. It reminded her of the famous old taxi cabs that saved the Battle of the Marne. She asked if he had been in the battle and he was forced to point out that the battle involved the French Army and he hadn't been signed up in 1914.

Heroism was dismissed. "Anyway, let's skip the history," she said, "and look for the Left Bank."

He was surprised that she didn't tire as they strolled up the wide avenue de l'Opéra toward the long, grey length of the Louvre, which she ignored. She kept looking ahead, pointing out a poised and elegant poodle seated on his own chair beside his mistress at a sidewalk café, an organ grinder and his saucy monkey on a street corner, and finally the nearest Seine bridge leading to the place St-Michel and the Left Bank.

Thank God for monkeys and dogs! Denis thought. Whatever expectations Marina might have, she was now prepared to let the romance of the Left Bank burst upon her.

He pointed out a table full of obvious students, looking like Martians compared to the students at the Sorbonne before the war. They were wildly modern, even compared to the students Denis had consorted with when he first came to Paris almost two years ago.

It was Marina who noticed the girl. No! Make that a woman, probably somewhat older than Marina. Well into her mid-twenties – Denis's age.

"I think somebody is trying to get your attention," Marina told him, this time with no "darling" attached to her remark. He looked past the front row of students at their little round tables. Who the devil?

But the woman knew his first name. Formerly, her black hair had been wound in stiff rolls around her head. Now her hair was cut short and straight – almost doll-like. Her heavily made-up eyes accentuated what might be false eyelashes. They were too thick to be real. Well, real or false, they would win no prizes from Marina. She demanded in a slightly shrill voice unlike herself, "Is she real? Those eyelashes!"

The woman was somebody's friend but, as he recalled vaguely, she had been an annoyance even then. In answer to Marina's question, he said honestly, "I wouldn't know exactly. I've never examined the eyelashes. They look pretty fake from this angle. Her name is something like Ghislaine Yvette, or vice versa. Something like that."

Marina relaxed but still threw in a little sarcasm. "Well, darling, just don't get close enough that you can tell me whether she is real or fake."

He grinned, gave the woman in the café a salute with two

fingers, which Marina followed by her biggest wink and they walked on past the café with her hand locked in the crook of his elbow.

When they were on the tiny, quaint street that ran into St-Michel, Marina looked back but the woman had shrugged when her companions asked her who the "boyfriend" was and no more attention was paid to them. There were obviously plenty of males around.

"How about breakfast upstairs over that little café?" Denis suggested, pointing out an ancient, two-story building up a side-street. He had guessed right. She was thrilled by the quaintness of this quarter and the upstairs café.

They made their way through the ground floor, past a solid-looking female in black at an old-fashioned cash-register who looked at them in a businesslike way before motioning with one forefinger to the small, apron-wrapped male coming down from a twisted staircase leading to the upstairs region. All of this fascinated Marina and pleased Denis when he saw her reaction. He relaxed a little. With her new-rich background, she might have treated these little poverty-stricken places as if they were beneath the contempt of Jason Kyle's daughter. Denis recalled the upstairs café from when he and several other would-be artists had eaten here, and very little had changed in the last year and a half.

The waiter welcomed Denis with delight, especially after a look at Marina. "Married? That is good. Almost as good as to marry a French girl, but when I see the young lady here, I understand. Come. Follow me. I give you the table at the window. You may look out upon the place St-Michel."

The room was empty for the moment and he showed them to a table. While Marina examined the curious tablecloth with interest, the proprietor remarked to Denis, "You chose wisely, M'sieu Mallory. She is lovely." As Marina tried not to hear, he became even more effusive. "Many hearts must be broken when you snatched up that beauty, eh?"

Marina gazed innocently at the awning outside the window

while Denis assured him, "Believe me, Henri, I almost fought a duel with one fellow over my lovely wife. And he had her father on his side, too."

Marina closed her eyes and winced, not quite concealing her smile.

As for Denis, he wished his friend the proprietor would shut up. He wished he hadn't touched on the subject of Blake Cavenaugh. "That's enough of your chit-chat, Henri," he went on. "By the way, we haven't eaten since yesterday afternoon on board ship."

"*Hélas*, my friend, it is hours until our evening chef sees fit to show his gracious self. You know the temperament of these fellows."

Marina forestalled any idea of a heavy lunch or dinner at this hour. She cut in, "No, Denis. I want croissants and brioches, and coffee with a lot of hot milk in, and the blood-red oranges that everyone talks about in France."

"Sounds good to both of us."

Denis was about to pull out the rickety chair for his wife when the proprietor cried, "Just so, as you say!" He darted to beat Denis in pulling out the chair. At the same moment, from across the room with its ceiling no higher than an attic, both Marina and Denis heard very clearly a young female voice: "Monsieur Denis! You are returned alive, after all. *Le Bon Dieu*, he is looking good!"

Marina rolled her eyes and muttered, "Not another one!"

Sixteen

T he girl had just come up the stairs with a tray containing plates, paper napkins and two enormous cups steaming with coffee and boiling milk. The proprietor said loudly, "Odette, they are back again. The Yankees are back. Come and meet M'sieu Denis and his beautiful madame."

The waitress was hardly more than a girl. She contained herself very well, giving a little bob that just escaped being a curtsy, and Marina couldn't help admiring Denis for his poise in what she supposed must be an uneasy moment for him. He looked pleased, but not ecstatic, and said at once to Marina, "Darling, young Odette Pirie was a good friend to us when Joe Keller and I were invalided out at – whatever that place was called. Not too far from Rheims."

"I'm so glad to meet you, Miss Pirie," Marina said. "We all owe you very much for what you did."

She held out her hand and when Denis took the girl's tray, setting it on the table, the girl and Marina shook hands.

Odette Pirie was neither pretty nor flirtatious, but her brown eyes lighted warmly when she smiled at Marina.

"How good, Madame Mallory, that Monsieur Denis found someone worthy of him. My family all hoped it would be so. He was very good to us when the food was low. He and the other – doughboys, they called them, were clever about sneak— finding fruits and vegetables for my family, eh, Monsieur Denis?"

"Modesty forbids me to reply," Denis said and everyone laughed.

"She is a good worker too," the proprietor told them, getting down to business. "You must spend all your meals with us, M'sieu Denis. Our chef is a master at preparing *boeuf à la mode*, as good as it was in the days of Bonaparte and Danton."

Marina noticed that Denis seemed to hide a smile at this, but she allowed for a little exaggeration in the circumstances.

"I'm sure it is, monsieur," she told Monsieur Henri. "But in the meantime, I would love to sample your breakfast dishes, the croissants and also the brioches. Oh, and red orange juice."

Monsieur Henri was all apologies at this. "A pity, madame, but the juice you speak of, it has not arrived from Spain this . . ." He hesitated, then added, "This week. A pity. But our *jus d'orange* is like nectar of the gods, madame."

Nothing has changed, including Monsieur Henri, Denis thought and was relieved to see that the proprietor amused Marina as well.

The breakfast order seemed ordinary to Denis, but fortunately Marina said she loved it. The *jus d'orange* might be the wrong color, and to Denis it was not a breakfast beverage but, again, Marina expressed excitement over a real, genuine French breakfast "like the peasants have" and Denis did not argue. Aside from the slight anxiety he felt over how she would react to the things they did or ate that morning, he was enjoying himself.

To his surprise, Marina and Odette chatted away about Odette's memories of the war. The French girl enquired about how the war had affected Marina and her father in San Francisco. "It is so very exciting, your San Francisco. I think it must be the most romantic place in the world," she said.

Much as Denis liked San Francisco, this struck him as funny, coming from a young woman, hardly more than a girl, who lived in Paris. Maybe he could do something about this idea at home in the Bay Area. Let the San Franciscans know how romantic it was, and then point to Larry's café-restaurant with its charm and attractions as an example of Romantic San Francisco. He followed this with a mental note to ask Larry to "show" its romance. He wasn't sure of how this would be done but Larry, a worldly fellow, would probably have ideas.

Eventually, Monsieur Henri, having gone downstairs to supervise new customers, came back up and called Odette Pirie to her work. There being no one upstairs besides the Mallorys, this brought to an end the chatter between the women about what tourists should look for in Paris or, while they were about it, outside the city.

Denis had been surprised at how Marina had bristled at the arrival of Odette and at the woman in the café near the St-Michel bridge – he had been a trifle uneasy during their almost-meeting. He vaguely recalled her: Ghislaine, or something, and smelling to heaven of a cut-rate perfume peddled at cut-rate shops in the city. But she was apparently the kind that decent women feared as a rival. Curious how decent women guessed wrong about the Ghislaines of the world.

He hadn't seen a female in Paris so far who could ever compare with his own stunning Marina. Sometimes he wondered what she saw in him. It was, perhaps, a lack of vanity that gave him this thought, but all the same, he was never entirely sure their relationship would last.

She reached out and shook him playfully. "Darling, everyone's gone. Shall we be off too?"

He laughed lightly. "Why not? You know, sweetheart, we haven't seen Montmartre yet. Our little friend says they have fabulous paintings of Paris up there on what she calls 'the Butte'."

They went down the stairs, trying at first to go arm in arm, but there wasn't room. She went ahead of him, waving to Odette, who was looking uncomfortable as she avoided the teasing of half a dozen students crowded around an old table with its painted finish peeling off.

Marina nudged Denis. "What does that make you think of?"

"Well, they're pretty fresh."

"Oh, Denis, use your imagination."

He looked down into her eyes with their playful light. How enchanting she was!

"Keep the idea. Don't forget where we were."

She promised with her full lips parted.

He paid the bill, which had been written on the tablecloth they had used, the figures then torn off for presenting to the buxom cashier, which Marina thought was wonderfully quaint.

They went out to the street, now lively as if it were noonday. A taxi had just disgorged two tourists at the corner of the rue de la Huchette and Denis waved to the cabbie. They ran to the ancient cab, piled in, and the taxi rattled away toward the bridge. He knew where their hotel was but obviously wanted to take them on a tour of the city. It took a couple of minutes to argue him out of this idea, which Denis promised her would happen very soon. She laughed and huddled close. He held her to him, feeling the rapid beat of her heart, and kissed the crown of her head.

In the front seat the cab driver found all this romantic excitement less than amusing and they heard him mutter, "Tourists!"

But they didn't care. It was partly the truth, anyway. Surely, these times would remain with them forever, as Marina had insisted.

Five minutes later, when they reached the hotel and walked across the rotunda to the cushioned elevator, she looked up at him and he knew they shared this depth of feeling.

In their room, Denis took Marina in his arms and dropped her on to the big bed which had charmed her. She was thrilled by this behavior and held out her arms to welcome him. Before taking her up on her offer, he went over to the hall door, locked it, and came back demanding in an absentminded way, "Now, where did I leave off?"

"Coward!"

His kiss silenced any other objections he might have, if any. It was exciting and she loved it. And his passion grew more evident, as if he were hungry to taste her lips and then her throat. With her body still beneath his, he began to slip off her outer garments and even the small waist sash that was all the rage in those days. She wriggled out of the sash, her body shivering with excitement, their pulses pounding as he too undressed.

In those minutes they relived their first passionate love-making in the St Francis Hotel such a short a time ago. She had learned to use her hands and her bodily movements with a skill that he had taught her, at first gently, but then with a heated passion that grew with their growing knowledge of each others' bodies.

It was then that the door latch rattled and a female voice, somewhat irritated, called out in French, "Madame! Monsieur! Maid service."

"Damn!" Denis called out and moved away from Marina, tossing her fashionable new slip and suit skirt up over her body.

She laughed. "Let me help you, darling." She sat up and held bits of her clothing over her bare flesh.

The maid rattled the door again, then gave up and instead of using her pass-key, went away. Perhaps she realized they were newlyweds.

Marina watched Denis dressing. "Tell me, does this happen to you very often?"

That broke him up and as he laughed, he leant over her once more, his fingers brushing her eyelids gently before his lips lingered over her throat and breasts.

Belatedly, he answered her. "Not that I can remember. Anyway, I'm absolutely positive I've never known a vixen like you."

She started to say, "I certainly hope not," but it was hard to talk when his lips held her prisoner.

But the idyl would have to end. After the maid appeared again some time later and rattled her door keys as she tried to open the door, Marina reluctantly drew away and slipped on the delicate "teddies" she had bought for the honeymoon.

"No use, darling. We can't lie here forever. We simply must get to work."

He was surprised but delighted. "Sweetheart, I want to see an old chef I used to know when he was a bus-boy. He moved up fast. Rocco is a talented guy."

Her moist lips intrigued him as always, but what they said was disappointing. "I'm sure it's important, but what I need desperately are a few new – a very few, sweetheart – new clothes." She looked at him with longing. "You know I got hardly anything before our wedding."

"I know, but—"

"But you can't expect me to go about in Paris, of all places, with the rags I wore in San Francisco. Why, even Father noticed." She saw his eyes and murmured, "I'm sorry. I just can't lie to you, sweetheart. I love you too much for that."

He took a long breath. What a time to broach the subject that would always come between them as long as he had nothing and she remembered all too clearly that she was Jason Kyle's daughter!

"I suppose you intended to use your own money."

"As a matter of fact . . ." But she hadn't the nerve to go further on that score. She tried to get around it in a different way. "When you think about it, my own money in San Francisco is just going to waste – until we have a son of our own. Not that our son will need a lot of clothes. I mean, at first."

He smiled, but her eagerness hurt. He wanted so desperately to be the breadwinner; at least, to supercede her father in her eyes.

There were a couple of silent minutes. Then, with gentle care, she said, "We have more than enough money for our work on Larry's plans. And he certainly doesn't want me to look like a drab little California Nothing."

"You would never look like a nothing."

"In your eyes, maybe, because you love me. But we want these Parisians to know our business is going to be a success. Not a cheap little – oh, darling, you know what I mean."

He looked around the room, heard the noisy traffic outside the long windows, and shrugged. "There's something in what you say."

She hugged him so hard he grunted but he managed to kiss her cheek, which was the closest piece of her lovely flesh that he could reach.

"All right. But none of your own money, darling. We are earning what Larry paid us, and that will have to do. I'm not about to let the Kyle money support my wife."

"No, master," she said demurely, and then brightened. "Now, I'm going to buy my clothes. Your little friend Odette told me about a great couturier, off the place Vendôme, I think she said. It might be just the thing. And I'll have fun walking there. It's not far, and I want to get a feel of Paris."

"Yes, darling. Just don't spend too much. Remember, it's not really our money. I'm only the manager. I may not even be that if I don't make good."

"You know perfectly well you're going to be the great success of San Francisco. And I'm not the only one who thinks so. Rosa Santini told me so at the Baths."

He finished dressing while he made a joke of her compliment. "My mother used to call that kind of remark 'taffy'."

They were both in excellent spirits when they left the hotel half an hour later. Denis insisted on walking with her to the couturier's shop near the elegant Hôtel Ritz and reminding her just how she should return on the rue de la Paix to the boulevard des Capucines where she would see their hotel within a block or two.

She gave him a mischievous look. "Oh, why aren't we staying at the Ritz? They say it's so awfully – well – Ritzy."

He stopped as they were crossing the boulevard. "I hope you don't mean that."

She was amused at how quickly she could upset him. "Darling, a joke. Only a joke. Besides, it doesn't sound like fun at all."

"I wouldn't know."

He took her arm and walked her rapidly across the boulevard. She was already pointing out various cafés that attracted her, but they were not the famed and expensive ones. That was a relief.

Still, it was all-important to him not to disappoint her. She deserved the best – including her very natural desire to buy Paris fashions; she certainly couldn't be blamed for that. He only hoped, and found himself close to prayer, that she wouldn't go overboard for them. If so, it would be not only a sign of the future, but also difficult to explain to Larry, since Denis himself had neither drawn nor earned a salary yet. And it was difficult to know why he should earn money on this post until he proved his worth to Larry, who had been more than generous putting up the expenses for the trip.

Denis kissed her goodbye, made her promise not to venture beyond the exact streets they had walked through, and was careful not to ask her to be careful of what she spent.

She read his mind, however, and as she kissed and then hugged him, Marina promised, unprompted, "You haven't married an awful spendthrift female, and I'll prove it to you."

He walked on toward the rue du Faubourg-St-Honoré and the restaurant that he recalled being across from the grounds of the Elysées Palace. The restaurant, with its familiar deep forecourt full of tables and chairs, remained where he remembered it and he reached for the latch to enter. Although the door was unlocked it was too early for lunch and the staff, two of whom were setting out glasses and napkins, paid no attention to him.

He asked one of the busy, elderly men if the chef, Rocco, was about. The grizzled waiter pointed a bony shoulder across the formal restaurant to the kitchen beyond. Nothing had changed. Denis smiled to himself and crossed to the kitchen where his friend Rocco, a jovial-looking Florentine, was tasting a bit of rabbit he had fished out of an interesting pot.

"Smells like your delicious *lapin sauté-chasseur*, your form of it, that is," Denis greeted him.

Rocco dropped his fork into the pot, grinned at Denis and gave him an exuberant hug. "I've expected you since your letter arrived, my friend. Come. Sit down near the stove where you can smell my concoction."

When they were seated on high stools Denis looked around the aged kitchen, sniffing pleasurably. "If I could bottle the odor of your cooking, Rocco, I could make my fortune."

"*Eh, bien*, thank my first sous-chef. Superb. Mr Chong. I merely took it from there. Tell me, are you come to Paris to help me out? I could use you." He sighed. "The war took every decent waiter in Paris, leaving me the ancient dregs. You were a handy fellow that time you helped me serve those hungry Yankees of yours."

"Sorry, Rocco. I'm working for a fellow in San Francisco. At least, I hope I am."

"Ah! A maître d'. Perfect. You have just the reserve necessary. With a little sprinkling of a smile. So Frisco has confessed at last that it is really Parisian at heart."

Denis winced. "Not 'Frisco, old fellow. You know better than that. Anyway, I'm not the elegant front man. Larry calls me the 'manager' for the moment. I may not last."

Rocco waved away such possibilities. "Your letter said your bride was with you. Business and pleasure at the same time, eh?"

"You'll meet her soon. She is the most beautiful woman I've ever seen." Seeing Rocco's toothy laugh, he added, "I mean, in every way. The minute I saw her, she was everything I've ever dreamed of."

"*En effet*, perfect."

"Steady on – that's going a bit too far!"

He had expected his friend to have some fun over his marriage but Rocco only nodded wisely.

"Now then, to business. You do not waste your exciting honeymoon in Paris just to pay your respects to old Rocco."

Denis looked around the smoky kitchen toward the dining room. "My boss is making over a bathhouse."

"A bathhouse!"

"Well, after a fire he bought a piece of it. The ceiling is moveable, of glass, or will be. And I remembered your place here: the forecourt with its tables and chairs under an open sky."

Rocco reminded him, "Only when we have good weather. Not always."

"Well, in our case, a glass roof to keep out the fog, or the rain on occasions. What do you say?"

"Sounds great. Especially as your employer has the freedom of a flexible ceiling, one might say . . . But why do we not discuss this with your employer, this Hoaglund?"

Denis stared at him. "How do you know his name?"

"That? Oh, it is of the most simple. I have had a letter from this Hoaglund. He was more confiding in his letter than you, my friend. He seemed to know you would visit me."

"Of course. I told him I wanted your advice."

"Just so. And he will be happy to meet and discuss the restaurant with you and – I flatter myself – me."

"What? From San Francisco?"

Rocco corrected him patiently. "No, no. When he comes to Paris. In a little over three weeks, I believe he said. He will be your shipmate on your return to the States next month."

Denis managed to control his feelings. Much as Rocco liked Denis, he might easily give Larry a hint that he would not be welcome to join Marina and Denis, not only in Paris but on board ship for the rest of their honeymoon. Was it worth calling off the deal through some personal pique of his own? Further, Denis had used money belonging to his employer and that would certainly put him in Larry's debt.

There was also the great disappointment he knew Marina would feel. It looked as though he would have to pocket his pride in order to pay Larry back. Once that was done, Denis felt that he might be in a position to seek another job and get rid of this anchor around his neck. But he knew what it would mean to Marina and that weighed as heavily as any part of this unpleasantness.

Seventeen

By the time Denis left Rocco's restaurant, filled with advice from his good-natured friend, and having tried to record it with a number of rapid sketches, he had made up his mind to stick to his part in the restaurant-café. But when he had earned what he considered he had spent on this honeymoon, he would see about another job. Maybe a fairly careful lifestyle would become acceptable to Marina. She knew how things were and, bless her, she would be reasonable once she got used to it.

Meanwhile, as Denis strolled along the rue de Rivoli and turned off toward the place Vendôme, he hurried his steps a little, hoping to catch Marina at the dress shop. But he was a little annoyed when the staff, led by a lean, haughty female of middle years assured him that no one recalled Madame – what was the name? Ah, but of course! Madame Mallory . . . He went out, slamming the glass door, and determined that Marina should lord it over acquaintances in San Francisco, quietly sporting her new clothes, which others must certainly recognize as Parisian.

By the time he came in sight of their hotel and started to cross the busy boulevard, he stopped suddenly by a stall of flowers, and picked out two bouquets of exquisite wood violets and had a more faded but infinitely more gloriously scented bouquet of Parma violets placed between them.

Then he crossed the street, beginning to forget business troubles and remember once more that he – lucky dog! – had actually won the most enchanting woman in the world.

He arrived in the hotel's semicircular drive just as a cabbie, a bearded Russian emigré, was helping Marina unload her boxes, packages and string sacks from the roof of his taxi. When he was relieved by Denis, he grinned, accepted a bundle of paper francs and, with a salute to Denis and his wife, sailed off, to be swallowed by the crowded thoroughfare. He hadn't said "thank you" in any language but at least he was friendly.

Marina, after thanking Denis for the violets, and being kissed by him, laughingly explained her fascination with the cabbie. "Oh, darling, you would have loved him. He spent the whole time telling me a Russian joke. He was delightful. Honest!"

Picking up some of her purchases, and being aided by a baggage handler who came out of the hotel's rotunda at a decent but not inordinate pace, Denis went up the steps with Marina. He agreed about the Russian. "Some of them had a rough time getting out of Russia but they are fun. Drink a lot, those I've met, but on the whole, they certainly add to the color of the city."

"You see, sweetheart? You and I agree on everything."

Marina kissed Denis on the ear. Passersby proved indifferent to this demonstration, a point she noticed with a trifling surprise.

Turning his own bundles over to a bellman inside the hotel, Denis kissed her in return, and then looked into her eyes momentarily. "I've missed you like mad. Did you like the shopping? Did you have a good time?"

She was delighted. "I'm glad you missed me. And believe it or not, I've been a very good girl. As careful with my purchases as – as you would approve of."

"Were you?" He found her concern especially endearing. "I hope you didn't overdo the carefulness. I want you to be happy, sweetheart."

She scoffed at this. "I did it partly for you, but not altogether. I must be honest. I hated the first shop. They were worse than patronizing. They acted as if I were beneath them. Me! Jason Kyle's daughter. So I went around the corner on to the rue St-Honoré. That's where the wagons used to carry all the poor victims to the guillotine. Isn't that awful?"

He laughed. "And you liked it?"

"Well, there were some absolutely scrumptious shops. Reserved sales people like the other one, but nicer. I saved a lot of money. And best of all, some things don't even have to be altered." She made a charming face at him. "They said I had a perfect figure. So, few alterations."

"I could have told them you were perfect."

They were both happy. In the elevator he looked at her reflection in the mirror. Yes, he thought, not for the first time: I'm a lucky fellow.

Wondering if she would be glad or sorry to see Larry Hoaglund as a part of their honeymoon, he said, "You finished shopping sooner than I expected."

"That's really the nice part," she reminded him enthusiastically. "I think San Francisco has just as much to offer as they do here." He was amused at this reaction, typical of his wife and so many other natives of the city by the Golden Gate.

By the time they entered their large, comfortable room and saw the westerly sun shining in from between hotels across the nearest streets, Marina could hardly wait to show Denis what she had bought.

He dropped packages, boxes and bags on the bed, which had been made up in their absence. Marina meanwhile excitedly ordered the bellman to spread out the boxes he had carried and he placed them beside hers on the bed.

Denis had made up his mind not to be ill-natured, no matter what the clothes had cost, but from the triumphant way she held up the various pieces he began to understand that she had actually economized in some way and was expecting he would be pleased.

He was. Everything was in in the latest fashion: a long-waisted, beaded gown; a sporty tennis outfit – "for a girl who never learned to play the game," she admitted, partly boastful. "And a suit I love. Sort of aquamarine with those pretty little imitation diamond buttons. And a cape that matches my hair, they said. Not one of them is a fancy designer gown. Well, I didn't think I should overdo it, so that's about it, except for pumps and lots of silk stockings." She looked at him soulfully. "That doesn't shock you, does it, darling?"

"Not at all. I think they suit you wonderfully." He kissed her on the bridge of her nose. "But there's one objection."

She was alarmed. "But I thought I – what is it?"

His smile reassured her. "Nobody will believe these aren't Paris Originals."

"Beast!" But she was delighted and he reached for her, swinging her, swinging her around a few yards while she laughed. Then, remembering the bit of news he had for her and not sure how she would take it, he said casually, "You don't dislike Larry Hoaglund, do you, darling?"

She was surprised at the change of subject. "Of course not. Why would I? In a manner of speaking, he's the boss."

"Our boss."

She shrugged. "Only for a little while. We'll make so much money we won't need him any more. And I'm sure he'll want to sell to us in the end. Why?"

"Because he has decided we may have too much fun alone. He's coming over for our last ten days. He wants to return with us on the same ship."

Slowly, she drew away from him. "But it's our honeymoon."

He studied her face. "You really don't like him, do you?"

"That's silly," she protested. "Of course I do. I just think three on a honeymoon are one too many."

"But it's a little difficult to forbid him when he's paying for it."

"No, he isn't – I mean – we're working over here for him. Earning our salary." She saw that he was puzzled and reminded him after a moment's uneasiness, "I just don't think he belongs on our honeymoon. It's so unromantic."

He laughed at that. "Well, I promise to make up for it by being twice as romantic. How's that?"

It was apparently enough. She reached for him and he received her in his arms, relieved that their problem was over.

He was not surprised when, some time later, his lively wife

yawned, reminded him that she was more tired than she had thought, and went to sleep on the bed, against his shoulder.

Half sitting, half lying beside her and studying the quaintness of the big, high-ceilinged room, he wondered how he could possibly have earned her love.

He was awakened several hours later by Marina, leaning on her elbows and staring down into his face.

"Darling, what's up the hill where that new white building is with all the domes and things? I got a glimpse of it today when I was returning from the shop."

He gathered his wits. "Are you talking about Sacré-Cœur? Very fancy and controversial. I sold half a dozen sketches of it a couple of years ago. Do you like it? Some don't."

"Well, I do. Let's have dinner there. And if I'm not mistaken, we'd get a dandy view of the city from those steps."

He chucked her under the chin with his forefinger curved. "You'll get a view, my darling, but I'm afraid you'll starve to death if you go there expecting a Paris feast. That's a pretty well-known church: the Basilica of Sacré-Cœur . . . Would you like to eat dinner up in Montmartre?"

"Love to." She hugged him, then jumped down off the bed and rustled around, searching for an appropriate outfit, not too showy, but nice enough to dazzle the natives.

"Not too dressy, darling," he warned her.

"Why's that? Are those the slums of Paris?"

"No, but Pigalle is near the foot of the Butte – that's Montmartre. And the Pigalle district is another matter."

They could leave Pigalle for another time when she would talk him into a "short" visit there, but she was in a hurry to see the famous Montmartre Butte, beginning with the Basilica of Sacré-Cœur, which Marina found awe-inspiring. With this in mind they took a cab to an area just below the Butte, and walked to the center of the place du Tertre in the heart of Montmartre.

Surrounding the place du Tertre, the cafés were very much back at business after the shabby days and nights at the end of the war. Denis didn't want to disappoint her, but admitted he thought it the center of trashy tourist Paris, though he soon saw that this was crushing to all her romantic hopes.

Since the winter air was clear but biting cold, Denis suggested they have dinner inside one of the cafés but Marina looked over longingly at the center of the busy, noisy, place du Tertre, so he gave in. They settled themselves at the last free table following the departure of several writers still arguing over a painting they had seen on sale down the curving, aged street behind them.

They had no sooner settled themselves when Marina looked around the square with interest, and nudged Denis. "I think you're being summoned . . . *sweetheart*."

He didn't like the way she used the endearment and turned around to see a female making kissing signs at him from beyond the barrier around their café. She was a total stranger, blonde, fortyish, her obviously dyed hair cut very short in the latest bob. He looked at Marina. "Shall I call her over? Or, may we have our dinner first and afterward join her in the place Pigalle?"

She frowned at the woman. "How awful! I thought they'd look more glamorous. Don't bother to call her over."

He laughed, reached for her hand and kissed it. She gave him an affectionate smile.

"She's gone. We scared her off," he said. The whole thing was ridiculous, though he did wonder if there were many more whores lurking nearby.

Marina turned her attention back to him after watching the woman attack another male across the square. "I'm afraid you've lost out. She's going off with some old duffer who just came out of that café down the street." She pretended to brighten with a new idea. "Maybe we could add a few of her type to Larry's restaurant back home."

"I can imagine. Darling, there are laws in our neck of the woods."

"And none in Paris?"

"Not that anyone notices."

The waiter had come up and they both ordered. Marina surprised Denis by ordering an incredibly thin but still rare steak with what she called "heavenly French fries", which he pointed out she could get at home. He added, however, "Make mine the same," and ordered the *vin ordinaire* of the house. Then he jotted down a few notes and sketched the scene around them, to her great interest.

"Be sure to sketch your Pigalle friend," she advised him with amusement.

He promised to do so but folded up the little graph notebook and put it away, anxious to help Marina enjoy herself.

When they had finished dinner, drinking a toast to the future, he walked with her under the dim lamplights down to the place Pigalle that fascinated her. It was exactly what he had expected but in spite of his description it was disappointing to her.

"They're so – well, not as thrilling as I expected."

He promised her, "Never mind. I'll try and act so romantic you won't miss Pigalle."

"Heaven forbid!"

She was glad when they found a taxi and were soon on their way back to their hotel room.

In spite of her disappointment over the "wicked excitement" of Montmartre, she was soon delighted to find herself in the big brass bed with Denis and learning more about what she called "French love" on their first night in Paris.

Denis was awakened a little after five in the morning by a knock on the door and a youthful bellman's voice.

"Monsieur – Madame. Message."

Denis got into his robe, took a couple of franc bills out of his billfold on the credenza and went to the door. By the time he had paid the boy and closed the door with the cablegram in his hand, Marina was awake, blinking.

"What is it? Not about Father!"

"No. Not about your father. It's Larry, the damned fool, telling us all is well! At five a.m."

"What? Let me see."

She took the cable and read it aloud: "Sealed up south walls. All well. Enemy now separated a quarter-mile from us. Congratulations. Larry."

"Poor Father," Marina murmured and gave the cable back to Denis.

Eighteen

During the magic weeks that followed their arrival, the glories of a Paris reviving after the war surpassed what Denis had hoped Marina would share with him. She soon embraced Parisian life, and easily won over Denis's friends.

Then the honeymoon came to an end quite unexpectedly, just as they had finished borrowing ideas from France and were expecting to spend the last few days before Larry's unwanted arrival with Denis showing Marina the rest of the Ile de France. She was more impressed by the Barbizon countryside than Versailles and Fontainebleau, both of which she dismissed, to the shock of the guides, as "boring". "Poor old Alcatraz is more interesting," she told Denis and said she would rather ride in the rattling, bouncing buses or the famous Paris metro than drag her feet around Versailles' long halls.

It was on the last two of their free days before the arrival in Paris of Larry Hoaglund's boat-train that a small disaster struck. They had enjoyed a romantic dinner in Denis's favorite restaurant, the Grand Vefour, for which he had taken care to save money, and only minutes after they left to hail a taxi, Marina found herself forcing back an upset stomach.

They reached their hotel room shortly after and her nervous bridegroom was about to send for a doctor, but Marina came out of the bathroom a few minutes later, insisting she felt fine. She had no more trouble that night and Denis cancelled the call, but it was not the last time she was in trouble.

The next day she couldn't enjoy her beloved croissant and coffee, and by the time they were on their way up the Champs-

Virginia Coffman

Elysées an hour later, she complained of cramps and Denis insisted on getting help from the druggist on a corner in sight of the distant Arc de Triomphe.

Marina laughed at her husband's anxiety and explained that they didn't want to ruin their honeymoon. The Frenchman grimaced. "It happens, madame. At the least it is well for the child that it will have good, very solid parents. In these wild days, one cannot always make guarantee of such a necessity."

Denis, meanwhile, was watching Marina's face with trepidation.

"Darling, it's wonderful. Monsieur here is right. It isn't as if we weren't looking forward to it."

Smiling, he drew her to him. "We've got many months for that. We'll be starting home in a week."

"True." She turned slightly and kissed his cheek. "I wonder what we'll call him."

The druggist grinned at their conversation. He cut in. "But, madame, what if she is a young female, as lovely as madame."

"My sentiments exactly," Denis agreed.

She nodded and having received an antidote to her stomach problems, they went out on the Champs-Elysées.

In no time, they were arguing in a friendly way over the name of a child who wouldn't be arriving for three-quarters of a year. After a few minutes Marina suggested hesitantly, "I don't suppose you'd stand for the name 'Jason' if it's a boy."

Anything but that! After a few seconds he had an idea. "My mother's maiden name was Dina Gregg. If she's a girl, how about Dina?"

She made a face, then begged his pardon, amending it to "Greg" with one "g".

They tried out the name on each other, then she said it louder and several passersby looked around.

"I like it."

He hugged her to him. He was suddenly more delighted than he had ever thought possible. The idea of giving their child the name of Denis's mother might wash out all his mother's life of

136

unhappiness. As for his own wife, Denis had never loved any human being as he loved this honest, beloved woman who had married him.

He wanted to spare her too much exercise and, finding a cab at its stand, he signalled it and they rode out through the Bois de Boulogne, with its stark tree limbs against a wintry blue sky.

Sitting huddled against him, she murmured with a pretense of sadness: "I was wrong when I said how happy I was."

"What?!"

"At our wedding." She grinned mischievously. "I'm even happier now."

They both enjoyed her little joke and decided the only bad thing ahead was the impending arrival of Larry Hoaglund. But Denis reminded her, "We really owe him a lot. All this that we've had these last few weeks we owe to old Larry. I've got to work hard paying the old boy back as soon as we can possibly get things going."

But Marina was singularly ungrateful and said only, "I wish he'd stayed away entirely."

She was right, of course. Larry was a nuisance. It would have been a lot more romantic sailing home without good old Larry.

Denis didn't want to act like a typical father-to-be, but from the time they left the druggist's shop with its green light, he had one thought: to be sure Marina was well taken care of until the birth of young Greg, or whatever Marina would accept as a name. Jason? Good God! Anything but that.

During all the time he had known Marina he had been haunted by her father's name and his constant presence. Denis refused to believe his feeling against her father was based on plain jealousy of the man's influence on Marina.

However, on this particular day he was glad to gratify Marina when she saw a new and unusual camera in a window on the avenue de l'Opéra.

They went in to examine it as a present. The camera took pictures that were postcard size and the large, black-and-white subjects in the pictures were crystal clear.

"The baby ought to love it when she can carry it," Denis agreed while the salesman and Marina discussed all the intricacies of the Eastman Kodak.

"She?" Marina echoed. "This is a coming-home present for Father," she insisted.

It was on the tip of his tongue to make some objection, polite but a definite hint. Then he realized this was no time to argue, but he felt a peculiar little pinch of regret for the unborn child, wondering if the child would always come after Marina's father.

By the time they were ready to go out to dinner that night, Denis had decided it was rather silly to resent giving a present to Jason, who must be lonely. There were hundreds of presents coming to the little unborn child, in all likelihood, within the next few months.

That night they enjoyed what they called their "farewell evening" together, knowing Larry Hoaglund would arrive on the boat-train the following day. Since they'd expected that Larry's few days in Paris would be busy, Marina and Denis had tried to crowd everything into those days and nights they'd enjoyed for nearly a month.

As it turned out, however, Larry seemed perfectly satisfied with all the ideas, sketches and plans that Denis had gathered up for his approval, except the tentative name suggestions. He'd simply skip any reference to Paris.

To Denis's surprise and puzzlement Larry addressed Marina especially and, for the first time in their relationship, Denis was just a little jealous, wondering if possibly Larry was beginning to see Marina's charm as more than a mere partnership with her husband. But this was absurd. Why wouldn't Larry find Marina attractive? Any man would. Denis was annoyed by his brief suspicion.

Larry was all enthusiasm, however, when he discussed their future plans. "You'll see," he promised them. "All that you two wrote about can be used. Even if we don't hit on the Paris idea as much. I was talking to someone the other day and it just occurred to me that we have a lot of San Francisco to sell along the Golden

Gate. Anyway, we are still putting all your ideas to use. I tell you, it's almost enough to make me give up those gorgeous houses above St Francis Wood and plunge into saloon-tending." He looked over his whisky glass in the hotel's rotunda room. For some reason he had caused Marina annoyance and Denis had to remind her that she had said last night she was tired of Europe and anxious to get home.

Backtracking, Larry grinned. "Only fooling. I wouldn't take over your jobs, kids. I've got too much to do with my own affairs."

Denis put in thoughtfully, "You're right about not putting too much weight on the European aspect. There's the Prohibition problem, and we don't want the government after us, God knows."

"That occurred to me too. Matter of fact, I got to thinking about it on the way over," Larry put in. "We keep the look of the place with a Paris touch. All those sketches you sent, Denis, about the galleries, for instance. Great stuff. But we don't want to lean too heavy on the saloon look. They're sure to keep an eye on us for that."

"How is Blake doing?" Marina asked. "I mean, is his estates thing going to be too close to your place?"

Larry finished his whisky, then waved the empty glass around to emphasize his amusement. "No, they're facing the Pacific. He's having trouble with the falling rocks, the slides, all that. He finally figured out he had to plant a lot of that grey-green vegetation to hold things together. I'll bet he wishes now he owned our half of the cliffside area. We planted first thing we did. Got the idea from Sutro Baths and maybe the Cliff House."

"Well, Cavenaugh is no fool," Denis remarked. He ordered another round of whisky, and then asked Marina, "Will you have another, darling?"

But she was going to see the hotel doctor in the morning and he was relieved when she refused lightly.

Larry guessed why she was being careful and said suddenly, "I envy you two. I've been through two weddings and innumerable marriages by buddies and I've never seen a happy one." He added quickly, "So this is a first."

"Why did you spend all that money and come over?" Marina asked bluntly. "Don't you trust us? And you say now, we shouldn't lean too heavily on the French atmosphere."

He gave a sheepish grin. "Well, to tell the truth, it wasn't actually my money."

Marina was staring at him. He went on and shocked her almost as much as if he had mentioned her name.

"This'll really knock you down, kids. It was none other than Marina's father. Jason wanted to be sure you were OK. That's all. I went second class, incidentally."

Denis said, "Well, I'll be damned!" but didn't like to say any more in front of Larry.

Marina had quite a different reaction. She softened. "Father did that? Well, bless him! He really did care about our honeymoon."

"I think he was lonesome," Larry explained. "He does nothing but talk about you two."

"Two?" Denis asked, but Marina put her hand on his and he felt that whatever he wanted to say would have to wait.

Larry shrugged. "Well, he's been hounding me about the project. Asking if I received any messages from you. But it's my belief he's being eased out of Cavenaugh's project and he's got nothing else to do. Anyway, he offered a name for our project – 'Golden Gateway'. How does that strike you? I thought it wasn't too bad."

Marina looked almost sheepishly at Denis. "It does seem to fit better than . . . Well, better."

There was very little Denis could say except that he didn't like it, and he knew his main reason was because it came from Jason Kyle. After all, the project wasn't his, and Larry seemed to like it. "It's your money," he said finally. "We're only your hired hands."

"Oh, darling," Marina said coaxingly, "it doesn't matter, does it? I rather like it, but I may be prejudiced. So what is Blake doing to Father?" she asked sharply.

"Like I say, he's been just about eased out of Cavenaugh's affairs. Bleed 'em dry and throw them away, that's Cavenaugh's racket."

Denis couldn't help saying, "What a bastard!" even though his feelings for Marina's father weren't exactly pristine and pure.

But as they discussed the subject, Denis couldn't help feeling a little prick of triumph if, in the long run, he and Marina eventually had to support the man who was still a supreme influence in Marina's life.

"If he breaks from Blake, he's bound to be on our side," Marina said.

Denis reached for her hand, his thumb stroking her knuckles. "All the friends we can get may be valuable."

Marina was looking at him tenderly.

"Darling, thanks for that! You made me awfully happy. We don't have to be bosom buddies with Father, but if he breaks with Blake—"

"Or vice versa," Larry put in, giving voice to their thought.

She tried to ignore that.

"Oh, God!" she cried.

Before either man could get to his feet, she pushed her chair back and hurried across the rotunda to the restroom.

Larry stared, wide-eyed, as Denis went after her. Larry called to him, laughing. "One of the hazards of marriage, old boy!"

Denis didn't hear him. His vagrant thoughts about Jason Kyle's influence were gone. His concern now was for his wife's health and this new, warm pride.

A son, Greg. Or a daughter. He didn't care. He had lived a very solitary boyhood with two unfortunate people who were never happy in their poverty-stricken marriage. Now, for the first time, he knew what it was to love and be loved by his wife, who was everything, and soon his daughter – or son – who would be a piece of this beloved woman.

Nineteen

T he Overland Limited pulled on to the Oakland Mole and Marina clutched Denis's arm excitedly.

"Home again, thank heaven. There's the dear old white ferryboat waiting for us. Just one little ferry ride and we're back in the City."

Denis loved her enthusiasm even if it did belittle their honeymoon somewhat. He smiled but reminded her, "A lot of work ahead. I'll admit I'm anxious to get at it, but you, poor darling, are going to take it easy for eight months or so. No running around climbing the stairs and wandering out on that damned fire escape, or lookout. Whatever you call it."

"I promise, master," she said demurely, but he knew her too well now to believe that any more than he believed in the "master" part.

Waiting behind them for the porter to set up the stool for their descent to the train shed, Larry put in, "Most of the skeletal changes are done by now, but when it comes to the employment department, that's you, buddy."

"What you say goes," Marina confirmed, hugging Denis's arm. "Just don't leave out Rosa Santini. We couldn't get along without her."

Larry said, "Hmm," which was just a bit doubtful but before he could explain what that meant, Denis said emphatically, "Rosa comes with the business, or no business. She's the first friend I had the day I met you, darling."

For just a few seconds Marina hesitated, then laughed. "Let's not get too enthusiastic."

Any time she showed jealousy, Denis was amused and pleased, but he was careful to turn his head and kiss his wife's cheek as a reassurance. He didn't want Mrs Santini to get in his wife's bad graces. The woman was a friend, but better than that, he felt her loyalty to Marina and to him was genuine.

The porter had put his stool down and raised one hand to help Marina down the steep steps. She looked at Denis before descending.

"Tip?" she whispered.

It was one of her few qualities that annoyed him but there seemed to be nothing he could do to stop her. It always made him think she was insinuating that he was cheap or that he didn't know enough to tip the fellow. He nodded to her, hoping he had answered her question, followed her down the steps to the dock floor.

A minute later he was nudged aside by Jason Kyle looking his elegant self as he embraced his daughter and kissed her lightly on the forehead. He murmured something about missing her and then turned politely to Denis and Larry Hoaglund.

"Welcome home, gentlemen. The City missed you. You'll be happy to know there is a good deal of talk about Mr Hoaglund's project."

Larry beamed. "Fine. The more the better. Have you inspected it lately, sir?"

Jason took a moment to warn his daughter, "Watch this crowd, my dear. They all want to go on board the ferry first. Not that I can blame them." As they crossed the big gangplank, pushed and shoved by other hurrying passengers carrying their bags, he answered Larry: "I've given myself a little tour now and again. Of course," he added, "when I received the cable from Mr Hoaglund yesterday about the promised addition to our family, I realized that there must be larger plans. Your home, for instance. You'll need more money from – somewhere."

"Larry told you about the baby?" Marina asked, trying to hide her feelings. She had felt Denis's hand tighten on her arm and knew he was angry that Larry had been the one to break the news.

Larry looked flustered. "It was such exciting news, I thought Mr Kyle should be the first to know. I'm awfully sorry. I didn't know it was a secret."

"Secret!" Denis repeated. He and Marina exchanged looks. She pulled her thoughts together. "Well, it's done now. But I wanted to be the one to tell you, Father."

Jason seemed to think the matter of telling him had now been settled. "Of course, we can't be too careful these days. Every worker since the war seems to think we owe them a living. But I must say, your people have done famously." He laughed a trifle selfconsciously. "You've got my friend Cavenaugh mighty jealous. He didn't allow for so much expense and time on the damned rocky cliffs that everyone thnks are so scenic."

Marina and Denis exchanged glances. She said, "Oh, Father, does that mean you are suffering financially too?"

"Suffering? Well, when you gamble, you must be prepared to pay the piper, my dear. But as for me, I'll come about very shortly." He cleared his throat. "And I may tell you in confidence, Mr Hoaglund, Blake is prepared to pay upwards of half a million dollars to add your little café – what is the newest name? – 'Golden Gateway' – to Jason Estates. Not, I'm sorry to say, that my own share in Jason Estates is much more than nil at this moment."

"I think you ought to know, Father. Denis and I are investing all our time and labor in that place."

"But my dear, I was speaking to Mr Hoaglund about the matter," Jason reminded her smoothly. "And I hope you aren't investing quite all your time in the little project. Surely, the most important matter will be your child. I know Denis won't want you to spend a lot of time at this Gateway place."

"Don't be silly, Father. I intend to spend all my time up until the baby comes being at the Gateway and offering my help where it's wanted."

Jason took this calmly. "I imagine the owner of the Golden Gateway will have something to say about your presence in your condition, even if your husband doesn't."

Denis interrupted this all-knowing comment. "That is decidedly between my wife and me. Or had you forgotten?"

As they were jostled on to the ferryboat, Jason persisted: "But at least the owner of the Gateway has something to say, eh, Hoaglund?"

"He'd better not!" Marina snapped so cuttingly she astonished Denis.

As for Larry Hoaglund, he had the good sense to end the conversation by saying, "It will be entirely up to Mrs Mallory, sir."

Marina smiled on a note of triumph. She couldn't remember when she and those who supported her side in a matter had the last word against her formidable father.

When the big, broad-beamed white ferryboat pulled out from the Oakland Mole Marina and Denis made their way out to the bow, and she apologized to Denis for her father's interference. But on her way she obviously sympathized with Jason Kyle. "He wants us to stay at the house until we find an apartment. Poor Father! I've no doubt his share of the Jason Estates is going to be more 'nil' than even he thinks. What on earth is he going to live on?"

Denis sighed. "Surely, he didn't owe everything to Cavenaugh. He must have something left after the sale of the bathhouse."

She shook her head. "There is some reason why he wants Larry to sell out to Blake, and I think Blake has promised Father a piece of the Gateway, probably tacked on to what Father never did receive from the Jason Estates deal. I'm sure Blake just wrote off anything Father might get from that deal, saying it was gone before anything could be done about it. You know: expenses. That can cover everything."

Denis reminded her, "Blake isn't going to give him a pleasant smile. By this time, I think we know Cavenaugh pretty well."

She agreed ruefully. "But I see it coming. What can we do?"

It was perfectly simple to Denis. "Just persuade Larry not to sell."

To his surprise she waved away Larry's possible sale with one hand in the chill wind that swept over the boat deck.

"That's the easy part. But it's Father's future I'm concerned about."

He wanted to say, "The hell with Jason Kyle," but he knew better. He remembered all too well his concern about his own parents and the necessity to see that they were supported.

She suggested cheerfully, "I suppose we could use Larry to employ Jason in some way. And doing so, we could wean him away from Blake."

He laughed. "I doubt if Jason would be willing to become a maître d'."

Reluctantly, she nodded.

He looked back into the interior of the ferryboat where half a dozen people were at the soft drinks counter ordering what were now called "hot dogs".

Denis called her attention to Jason and Larry. "Your father's been talking to Larry. That's why Jason held back. Wanted to get him alone."

"Let them talk. Larry will never sell to Blake."

That was good to hear. He only hoped she would stick to her guns. He didn't want to argue with her or cause any friction that might upset her now.

Denis had already suspected what was coming. At the moment they would live at the Kyle House on the Golden Gate Heights. Denis had no objection to dining at Jason Kyle's home now and then. After all, until recently it had been his wife's home as well. But he had no intention of living there permanently. Anyway, it was a relief that Marina agreed to let him pay monthly rent to her father at a reasonable rate – she was probably keen that her father would get some money out of it. And, as Marina had pointed out on board ship during her first hints on the matter, the Kyle housekeeper was trustworthy. She could ensure the right nurse was chosen to take care of the baby in case, as Marina pointed out casually, "You and I have to be away from home sometimes."

He didn't argue. She had just gotten over a nasty fainting spell which scared him, though the ship's doctor assured him that she was in excellent condition, and spending a few months at the Kyle home was little enough to pay for her health. So Denis agreed, and Marina relaxed.

Once they reached the Ferry Building Jason pointed out that his own car and a new chauffeur were waiting for them outside.

Denis remembered the dark street some months ago, and the chauffeur recommended by Blake Cavenaugh who had tried to waylay him. Had Jason realized finally that the chauffeur had been in Jason's service as one of Cavenaugh's informants?

As it turned out, the chauffeur was temporarily Jason Kyle himself.

Meanwhile, Marina was pointing out excitedly, "I know that boy in your front seat. Isn't he Rosa Santini's nephew? Hello, Nick! I haven't seen you in ages."

The boy, about nine or so, looked up from a pamphlet and grinned at her. "Hi, Miss Marina. Mr Jason has taken me on. Sort of temporary."

Jason saw that he had pleased his daughter. "The boy is just in training, so to speak. Do you like the idea?"

Marina, torn between pleasure and worry, said, "Good heavens, Nick! Aren't you rather young to be learning to drive? You can't be over nine or so."

Jason pointed out, "Rosa's sister-in-law asked if young Nick could work weekends as a bus-boy. Rosa has supported the boy's mother since the father died during the flu epidemic. I thought I'd try him out around our home for a little while. Run errands and that sort of thing."

Marina was touched. "Father, that was wonderful of you, if you don't work him too hard."

Nick Santini interrupted firmly. "We ain't after charity, ma'am. I reckon you know that. And I have a kind of thing I'm working on to save money for, so it's real fun, far as I can see."

"Good boy." Jason ruffled up the boy's hair. "He'll do. Keeps me from being lonesome, too. And incidentally, it keeps him out of Blake's hands."

Denis could see that Marina was touched by the boy's ambition and her father's kindness. It was clear that she didn't ask herself who would pay the boy for his help. But Denis had two thoughts about the matter. The mention of Blake Cavenaugh aroused his suspicions. Had the boy been sent Jason's way to find out if Jason was betraying any of Cavenaugh's deals? Then, too, if Jason really was broke, how would he pay the boy – if he did so, of course?

Assuming he had the money, Denis would certainly pay to help Rosa Santini's family, but he couldn't allow Jason to wheedle out money from his daughter . . . But it was really not his affair. And all considered, he liked the boy.

They all piled into the car. Larry offered to sit in the front and drive, giving Nick Santini pointers on the way, he promised.

"Not driving the way you do sometimes," Denis reminded him.

With a look at his daughter, Jason suggested they all stop by "home" and have a thimbleful of the genuine Scotch he had ordered in from his bootlegger. Larry was about to agree enthusiastically, but Marina, after a glance at Denis, refused.

"First of all, we want to see our precious Golden Gateway." She knew Denis must be anxious to see it and her own curiosity was aroused as well. Larry was just a trifle less thrilled over the idea, but Marina understood all too well that he couldn't forget: the place actually belonged to Marina and Denis.

They went directly out past the marina area with its many new houses and the tempting little improvised yacht harbor, and past the Presidio with the new "Golden Gateway" looming between the highway and the Golden Gate cliffside. Seeing it now, even from the outside, Marina understood why Blake Cavenaugh would now like to add it to the Jason Estates. Building on the estates had evidently barely started. Between the few cliff-hanging skeletons of buildings and the new Golden Gateway, there was at least a mile of hillside newly planted in vegetation to hold the cliffs.

When they arrived at the Golden Gateway, Marina took the boy, Nick, under her wing, beckoned Denis to join them, and let him lead the way with an impressive jingle of keys, while Jason Kyle casually sauntered along at the end of the procession. The new bathhouse had been so revitalized, one would hardly recall the original glass-enclosed, barnlike structure. Three-quarters of the bathhouse had been torn down and new walls put in so that the new restaurant and café were moderately expansive, but far from the huge, hollow place they all remembered.

Larry pointed out the reinforced glass ceiling that would be a feature on starry nights for the expensive restaurant upstairs opening on to a romantic balcony. This looked down on the "outdoor café", which Larry pointed out had a garden blooming all year and a little, semicircular pool, where – it was hoped – small coins might be thrown. For charity, of course.

As Larry pointed out, "Since San Francisco uses silver a lot more than paper money, we ought to do well for the widows and orphans."

There was little that either Marina or Denis could say. It was amazing how much of the bathhouse could be saved for the Golden Gateway. They investigated the presently empty café and restaurant and seemed to see the furnishings, exteriors and interiors, as if they were present and finished.

Marina echoed Denis's excitement when she watched him anxiously, pointing out where all the furniture and hangings would be. "Darling, it's thrilling, isn't it?" she wanted to know.

With his arm warmly drawing her close, he nodded and explained in a low voice, hoping neither Larry nor Jason Kyle would hear, "It seems unreal. I mean, that we – no. That I should be involved in this."

She was startled, even uneasy, which surprised him. "Don't be silly. It's *your* dream. You sketched so many of these things in Paris. See? Larry's definitely used the ones you sent. There's one there. And that one of the café terrace – see the upper level where the elegant restaurant will be? I loved your sketch. But it looks even better when you see it on the balcony in front of the dining room."

While Nick frowned and looked away, Denis kissed Marina and didn't mind that their companions and the watchman saw them.

He had learned long ago to be a pessimist, but he felt different now. Thanks to his beloved Marina's hopes and wishes for him, he knew it could all come true. He had one more wish, even more important: that their child would be well and healthy and have a life full of happiness. If she was a girl, let her not be like the other "Greg", his mother.

Twenty

Denis spent the months before their daughter's birth working early and late, overseeing the builders and doing far more physical labor than Marina had expected. He pointed out that if he oversaw things himself, he would know they were done properly. Larry Hoaglund seemed to appreciate this, because he went about his own business – the homes above St Francis Wood – and had a curious lack of interest in the Golden Gateway.

Denis did his best not to neglect Marina, welcoming her to the Gateway whenever she wanted to drive out with him and give her own opinion on everything in sight. When he hinted that the owner, Larry, might disagree, she laughed and said simply, "He'd better not!"

Nevertheless, his instincts told him that the only way to hold on to this lovely creature who had agreed to marry him was to have tangible assets. Money. Property. Pride.

One night after an excellent but quick dinner he planned to hurry back to the Gateway for his usual review of the day's progress. He was reluctant to leave the dinner supervised by the Kyles' superb Korean chef, but work came first. As he explained to Marina, he would only take an hour and then hurry back. He was concerned about the none-too-expert gardeners chosen by Larry for the garden and rivulet in front of the "French Café" on the lower floor.

He was hurrying down to the terrace in front of the Kyle garage when he was called by Jason Kyle, a trifle more personal than usual. "I say, my boy, must you leave my girl alone every night? She's so desperate, she has taken to playing mah-jong with the housekeeper."

Denis knew perfectly well that his father-in-law was right, though he resented being reminded. The fellow acted as if his paternal duties included advice to husbands.

However, he tried to keep the peace, for Marina's sake. "Sorry. It's a little something that has to be done. And by the way, I discussed this with her. I'll be back in an hour."

He went down the outside steps and got into his secondhand Buick parked in front of the house.

He drove out to the Golden Gateway where he was a good deal surprised to find young Nick Santini hard at work cleaning up what remained of the flowers that had been put in front of the French Café on the ground floor. The gardeners had left things in a real mess. Nick was embarrassed and held out a bundle of moist flowers uneasily. "They just left this stuff behind 'em, sir."

"I can imagine. I see they're on their way to sign out right now. Anyway, it was very good of you, Nick." He took them from the boy, adding, "I'll speak to Rosa. I mean, your Aunt Rosa. I'd like to see you employed here for a couple of hours a day. Not to interfere with your schooling, but otherwise . . ." He smiled, offered his free hand to Nick who wiped his palm on his knee pants and then shook his employer's hand.

"Thanks, mister. I can help Ma and Aunt Rosa. I still figure I can save a little something later on, but it's good to help Ma when I can."

There was something Denis especially liked about the boy. He remembered all too well the feeling he himself had developed early, that his money, however little, was needed by the women-folk at home.

"What are you saving for?" he asked the boy with interest. "A scooter? Skates?"

"No, sir. Something kind of silly, I reckon. At least, that's what they call it in my class. Nothing important."

Denis knew the symptoms all too well, including the pride with which the boy said now, "I got a lot to do first. 'Scuse me, sir, but

I best be off now. I've got a few things to do around the apartment."

He started off toward the new, narrower but much handier staircase.

"Here. Wait, Nick. I'll drive you. You can save a little money. Always take advantage of a free offer."

Nick blinked and then grinned. He didn't thank Denis but he obviously appreciated the offer.

He waited in his Aunt Rosa's little office until Denis had settled with the gardeners, who were up on the highway level getting into their two Fords. What surprised Denis most was not their resentment at being fired after the fourth or fifth time they had botched a job but what they said afterward. One of them claimed he would see to it that the owner, Larry Hoaglund, kept them on.

Denis, coming out to the curb behind them, heard the other gardener stop his buddy from going to Larry Hoaglund. "Forget it. Hoaglund will do nothing. You won't get anywhere with that bastard." They got into their cars and rattled off.

It was clear that Larry had lost interest in the Golden Gateway. Strictly speaking, Larry could afford to lose interest. His work on the estates and the beautifully created private homes of San Francisco were making him rich. The question was, why had he decided to take on the creation of Golden Gateway in the first place?

Probably, like many other men of talent and money, he wanted more challenges. Once he'd begun to work on the creation of the Gateway while Marina and Denis were on their combined honeymoon and investigation of what Paris had to offer for ideas, he'd realized the Gateway bored him.

"Well, it doesn't bore me," Denis muttered aloud, to the puzzlement of Nick Santini.

Denis found out that Nick and his widowed mother lived in an area Denis particularly liked: the North Beach Italian section.

The boy explained with some pride, "We only have one room now. When Pa died we had two, besides the kitchen and all. Pa

153

made wine in the cellar. Our wine was awfully good but Ma wouldn't let me drink it."

"No, that I understand," Denis said. "But all the same, a lot of people think a little home-made wine is good for you. When my parents moved west from New York, my father drank a lot of . . . He liked it very much. I used to 'rush the growler' for wine, not beer or whatever. So you live in North Beach. Can you see Washington Park from there?"

"Yeah. We think it's better than Golden Gate Park. That's for the rest of the city. But the one we can look down at right from our front window belongs to us folks."

"You're absolutely right." Denis glanced at his wristwatch, a gold-plated souvenir from fellow doughboys in France. "Wow! We've got to hurry. I told my bride I'd be back in an hour."

"You'll make it, mister. You drive fast but careful . . . Miss Marina sure is pretty."

"She sure is!"

They drove rapidly around the cliffs and over past Fisherman's Wharf toward one of the cable car turn-arounds. In a few minutes, while Nick looked out at the twinkling white lights that spread over the city's many hills, they reached Columbus Avenue, the main artery for Chinatown and the Italian quarter called North Beach.

Nick sat up. "Did you know our people stopped the earthquake and fire along here, sir?"

"I do. How did they do it?" he asked, though he knew.

Obviously, Nick was anxious to tell him. "With barrels of wine. We were some clever, don't you think?"

Denis laughed. "I certainly do. If I ever build a house it's going to be in this general area. With lots of barrels in the cellar. Of course, that would only stop a fire, not a 'quake."

Nick stiffened proudly. "We'll think of some way."

"I'm sure you will."

By this time they were nearing the park which was the soul of the district. Nick started pointing out the rooming houses lining the steep little streets that led up the hills above the park. He wriggled proudly. "There. The next street over. Our little street goes right to the top of the hill. That's us."

Denis looked around at Columbus Avenue, which cut across the area. The street was still busy with the walking traffic and autos, though many areas were shrouded in darkness between small cafés and just opening nightclubs.

Following Nick's directions past still busy Washington Square to the little streets that climbed the hills to the east, Denis let Nick out in front of his doorsteps. Then, still puzzled by something the boy had said, he changed the subject. "You spoke of saving money for something after you have given your earnings to your mother. What do you want that badly?"

Nick shook his head as he got out of the car. "They don't have 'em here yet."

"Good Lord! What could they be?"

"Nothing. Everybody thinks I'm crazy. But I'll get one yet, and not from charity."

Nick started up the steps, then stopped. "I'm going to take pictures. I'm going to be famous."

"Wonderful!" Denis admired his ambition. "Why won't you take a gift if someone wants to help you?"

"Because it wouldn't be mine, don't you see? And the camera I want takes pictures of scenes and people you send away to your folks and all. You can't get that kind right now. But you wait and see – they're going to be here pretty soon. Some other cities have one. Or maybe more." He went on, turning suddenly and came back down a couple of steps. "If I got one from somebody else, it wouldn't be all my work, and I want it to be just my camera and my pictures. You know. They give prizes for good ones. Pictures, I mean."

He went on into the house, slamming the door. The dim hall light went on, and the boy was gone. Denis started the motor, swung out from the curb, and was soon on his way back to his father-in-law's house.

He pulled up on the terrace of the Kyle house and would have gone into the garage, but it was filled. He recognized his wife's

Ford and Jason's car beside it, but for a minute he couldn't place the third one. It was glistening and new, a red sedan.

Then he realized he had seen it once when Larry zoomed up to the Golden Gateway recently and announced that he had given himself a present. It was the only time he had been at the Gateway in at least ten days. This suited Denis who enjoyed working on his own on the final touches of the café and its surroundings.

Curious about his visit this evening and a little uneasy, in case he wanted a lot of changes, Denis left his car and went on up to the front door. The minute he opened the door he heard the swinging "Castle Walk" playing on Jason's new Victrola. This was punctuated by laughter, male and female and then Jason's remark, "Nicely done, Marina. I'm impressed. You are still light on your feet, but remember your condition."

"Father! For heaven's sake!" But Marina did sound out of breath and that thought annoyed Denis as much as the sight of Larry Hoaglund removing his arm from around Marina's waist.

But as Denis came into the big living room overlooking the Golden Gate and the distant hilly slopes of Marin County, he reminded himself that none of this would very likely have happened if he had been here. It had been stupid. Of course, Jason had been right. He should not have left her alone.

It was a little late to realize this now, so he controlled his sullen jealousy and managed to smile for everyone, especially his wife. When he took her hands, drawing her to him, and kissed her, ignoring the interested observation of the other two men, Marina's pleasure pleased him enough to overcome his jealousy.

Fortunately, either Marina or possibly her father had seen to it that she didn't drink any of Jason's bootleg gin, as she pointed out to Denis when she saw his glance at the half-empty glasses beside the two men.

With Denis's arm around her, Marina explained happily, "Darling, Larry says the bank, or at least the Trust Department boys, are awfully pleased. They talked to us – to Larry, that is – of what a handsome investment the Golden Gateway looks like.

156

Golden Gate People

On the sly, they advise us not to sell out, or let Larry sell out, on the deal."

Jason cut in with friendly interest. "I've had suspicions along that line. I mean – Blake thinks he got the worst of the deal when he took the south three-quarters of the Baths." He added modestly, "I must confess, I more or less hinted to Blake that such was the case. Well, he didn't see fit to take my advice months ago; so he just might have lost his chance. Not that I have anything to say on the matter officially."

Larry and Denis looked at each other, but Denis could see that Larry was willing to give Jason credit for being right – for once. It would mean, as Denis suspected, that Jason would now undeniably do much better to join what might well be the "winners" in this deal, whom even the banks scented as a success.

"Oh, let's not be tiresome," Marina interrupted. "Father, would you mind putting that next record on our Victrola?" She turned to Denis who was holding out his arms.

With her body warm and close to him, he counselled her, "No more dancing tonight, sweetheart."

She laughed. "All right. We won't dance now, but we'll make up for it later."

"Later, sweetheart. I promise." He kissed her cheek and then her full, always inviting lips. He was no longer embarrassed by the knowledge that both Jason Kyle and Larry were taking an interest in this demonstration of their love.

But once the record began to play, Denis and Marina were enchanted by the memory the music evoked. He whispered, "Remember?"

"Oh, darling, I do! The Bois in Paris, the accordionist. And the sassy little monkey tipping his hat when I tossed him a five-franc piece."

They looked at each other. He asked, "Are you thinking what I'm thinking?"

Excitedly, she took up the thought. "The café at the Gateway. It's a natural. There could be an accordionist during the busy hours."

157

When they looked back at the men, they found Larry reasonably pleased, and Marina's father, after a hesitation, somewhat enthusiastic. "It may be rather a silly business, but I wouldn't be surprised if it made a real spark with the females. Very romantic, you know."

Belatedly, Larry agreed. It wasn't that he hadn't thought of it as a good idea in the first place, Denis thought. He simply didn't have the enthusiasm one might expect of a major investor. At any rate, Denis and Marina were more than a little excited.

And of course, her father's enjoyment of the idea made Marina doubly convinced that they were on to a brilliant idea. About the time the record ended, she murmured to Denis, "As long as Blake has cheated Father of his investment. Father is entitled to invest in Larry's little Golden Gateway."

At the moment Denis couldn't think of a way to keep him out. It didn't belong to any of them but to Larry. He could only hope Larry would realize the risk of getting Jason involved when he had recently lost the entire Kyle Baths!

But of one thing Denis was sure. The accordion idea suited him and Marina. It might be too sentimental, too much a female touch, but it was perfect for the "sidewalk" café idea.

Twenty-One

L ess than three months before Greg Mallory was born, Denis and Marina agreed on an accordionist, after their third attempt at finding one, only a matter of days before the opening of the already talked about "Golden Gateway".

"No monkey comes with this accordionist, of course," Marina told Denis sadly. Then, with a twinkle, she reminded him of what he already knew. "But the accordionist alone is enough. If we waited any longer, our own son and the accordionist would arrive at the same time."

It wasn't the music that had proved the problem, but the nature of the accordionist; though he would probably be among children on occasion, they didn't want anyone too Santa-Clausy, or too charming. He should be edgy, crabby, and yet have a likable quality that popped out just when his audience thought he would go into a rage. They'd finally found a fiftyish fellow who drank a lot. But beggars can't be choosers.

Denis shrugged as he chose French chairs and tables for the front of the café facing the rivulet and garden. "All the same, he is a terrific player for the type we need. Gets along with the people, and all that."

She was being careful of her movements now but, eyeing him nervously, she hugged him, with care. "Darling, you really are happy, aren't you?"

He was just as careful with her but managed to lean over what she called "our Greg" as he kissed her. "I know I shouldn't say it, sweetheart. It's bad luck."

"What, for heaven's sake?" she asked, alarmed.

"I'm absolutely, positively happy. In fact, I could never be happier in my life. It isn't possible. How did I get so lucky?"

She was wearing flat shoes as she stood on tiptoe to kiss him on the nose. "Are you really? No matter what? I mean, even if I wasn't perfect?"

"How silly you are! But I love you for it."

They were interrupted by her father, who had driven in from the Golden Gateway with a report that the place was being swamped by curiosity-seekers and ought to be cleared out.

"What are they doing there?" Denis wanted to know, his tender mood with Marina completely gone. Still trying to be gentle, he removed his hands from her warmth and beauty. He had been out at the Gateway for twelve hours but he saw that he must go back to sort out this new trouble.

"They're probably just prowling around. I noticed they seem fascinated by the interior. Maybe because we've kept them out. It looks terrific now that, except for these little tables and chairs, the furnishings are practically all in place. I suppose Larry must intend to open before the month is out? Blake has been over there. Likes what he sees, I suspect."

"Has he paid you any of your profits from Jason Estates, Father?" Marina wanted to know.

Jason grimaced. "I've been told they went back into the firm. My contract stipulates a share of net profits."

"Oh, Father! He should have paid you on the gross profits. It should have been in the contract."

But seeing that she had humiliated him in front of her husband, she maded a gesture of sweeping away such trivialities.

"Darling," she said to Denis, "let's go out and see what's going on."

"Honey, the doctor said—" Denis began but Marina waved this away. He decided not to argue over the matter.

Half an hour later, in a fetching maternity cloak against the lashing wind off the Gate, Marina watched Denis pull around to the parking spot in front of her and before he could get out, she'd nudged her way into the front seat beside him. He reached for her, brought her closer and settled her in what she claimed was perfect comfort.

He put one arm around her and they drove out past Fisherman's Wharf, the marina and the Presidio to the highway in front of the Golden Gateway.

Marina had been here only one day in the last two weeks and she saw now that with all the subdued lighting and shaded lamps, the place was even more impressive.

"Look!" She pinched at Denis's coat sleeve. "There go a couple trying to get around the saw-horses and the chain. Uh-oh! Rosa has seen them. She'll stop them. I hope she doesn't discourage potential customers."

"Not in this case," Denis assured her. "She's too good a business woman. See?"

Sure enough. Rosa had gone up to the pair, who looked like tourists, middle-aged, the lady shivering a little, and neither of them prepared for the onslaught of cold summer nights.

With his arm around Marina's shoulder, Denis reminded her, "Let me know if you get cold."

"Don't be silly. I was born here, honey. I know what to dress for in July."

He grinned at her possessive pride in her city, no matter what its weather might be like, but he took care to keep his arm around her shoulders like a shawl.

Rosa heard their footsteps on the gravel and called to them. "These nice people are Mr and Mrs Samuel Pebmarsh of Afton, Iowa. They've heard of what's going on here. Folks, these are two of the managers, Marina and Denis Mallory."

Mrs Pebmarsh was enthusiastic. "How nice to meet you! My hubby told me there was an old bathhouse here, but I like this better. Is it possible – I don't suppose you'd let us get a peek at the inside?"

With a side-glance at the Mallorys, Rosa murmured, "Well now, seeing you're from that grand state of Iowa, I think we might . . . What do you say, Mr Denis? Miss Marina?"

Marina nudged Denis. "Be nice, darling."

Denis rose to the occasion. "Since you're from Iowa, where all that terrific corn grows, the least we can do is to show you around."

Everyone but Mr Pebmarsh was pleased. That gentleman was heard to say, "All right. We'll go afterward to Sutro Baths and see a real bathhouse." No one paid any attention to him and he followed along, more or less under the momentum of his companions.

To her embarrassment Marina found herself under the kindly administrations of Mrs Pebmarsh who joined her, leaving Denis the task of interesting the grumpy Mr Pebmarsh as they descended the new staircase.

"My dear," the good lady began, just above a whisper, "do you think it wise to go down these stairs in your delicate condition?"

"It's the only way I know of to get down to the French Café," Marina said, trying not to put an edge of sweet sarcasm on the words.

"Oh, true. I mean no offense. But as I've had five of my own, I can't help feeling a concern for new young mothers. This is your first, of course?"

Marina said it was and quickly changed the subject, pointing out the fresh flower beds ready for tomorrow's planting.

"Charming. Charming. But as I was saying, I hope your doctor can be counted on."

"My doctor and the midwife should know."

"Well, that ought to be satisfactory. Then you are having the child in your own home? Excellent. My dear, I do not trust all these unknown hospitals, the strange nurses, and the rest." She sighed with relief. "So now we can enjoy ourselves. That café – it is a café? – is utterly charming. Over beyond the flower beds. Good heavens! Is that an accordion I hear somewhere?"

"Rehearsing, I'm afraid," Denis called back to them. "Shall I tell him to wait until we are gone?"

"No, no." Before Mr Pebmarsh could express an opinion, his wife clapped her hands and looked around in her enthusiasm for the unseen musician. "I haven't heard one for ages. Samuel, remember the one we heard in Chicago on our honeymoon? You were so taken with it."

Mr Pebmarsh corrected her. "I considered it a trifle better than the jazz we hear everywhere these days."

Marina was feeling tired and a little bored with trying to make conversation. She wanted to sit down, but she smiled weakly. "Denis, why don't we introduce Bernard – that's our accordionist, Mr Pebmarsh – and I'll just sit down a minute." Denis was ready to lift her or do something else drastic, but she waved him away. "Go get Bernard, dear, and if he is ornery, sock him in the jaw for me."

Everyone laughed and luckily it calmed her worried husband.

"I'll get him. Mrs Pebmarsh, and you, sir, would you mind sitting by my wife for a minute or two?"

Mrs Pebmarsh fluttered delightedly, though her husband rolled his eyes heavenward at the over-anxious husband. But he conceded to Denis, "They do insist on doing things they shouldn't."

Denis frowned. "Yes, and she only just recovered from the flu a few months ago, and this is our first child. I'm afraid Marina isn't as robust as she might be."

When Marina scoffed at this he went striding off in a hurry to keep her from getting too worked up.

When he reached the Café's kitchen, he found it crowded with half a dozen teenagers dancing to the music of Bernard's accordion. Bernard's music didn't fit the dancing which was half-tango and then some version of the Charleston. Denis looked around, worried and angry, only to find Rosa Santini at his side. "They won't hurt. They spread the word. It's good business."

The young dancers had seen Denis and Rosa now and, one by one, they wound down like collapsing toys. "We were only kidding, mister," one of the most active young dancers apologized. "No harm done."

Denis motioned to the accordionist. "Will you come over

toward that group by the stairs? The ladies want to hear your playing."

The group of teenagers broke up and tagged along the outside rim of the balcony. Bernard and his instrument went to the waiting group along the balcony where the sidewalk café diners would soon – Denis hoped – be equally pleased. Bernard played for them and it worked out all right, to Denis's enormous relief. He had been half afraid his wife would want to get up and dance to the music.

"All right, honey?" he asked Marina and repeated the question, feeling like an idiot in his nervousness.

She lifted his hand and coat-sleeve and touched her cheek with them. "Yes, darling. But make sure you never laugh again at an expectant father."

"I promise!" He kissed her, ignoring the snickers and giggles from their young audience.

Meanwhile, Rosa leaned over to them. "The ice cream was delivered along with the ice. Maybe, as they leave, we could give them each a lump of ice cream in a cone."

"And have them riot every time they don't get one free?" Marina asked, but she looked into Denis's eyes and softened. "You know, I think you'd like a cone yourself."

Sheepishly, he acknowledged that he was thirsty for just such a treat.

Rosa sighed and laughed, then told everyone to line up on the stairs *going out*. They would all get their cones. She winked at Marina. "And both of you."

Mr Pebmarsh surprised everybody by chiming in, "A cone eaten on a summer night. Puts me in mind of my boyhood." He addressed Rosa. "Can we get in line, miss?"

"You bet, mister."

The younger group shuffled around, kidding about obeying instructions, and finally formed some kind of line on the staircase. They were laughing, jeering, pushing, but goodnatured. Bernard's stern features broke into a little grin and his long mustache rippled up and down with what Marina decided was pride or pleasure. Perhaps both. In any case, he began to play while Rosa went back to the pantry beyond the Café kitchen and Marina nudged Denis. "Go and help her, darling. I'm not made of ice cream – I won't melt."

"I'll be sure she is all right," Mrs Pebmarsh promised while her husband climbed to the top of the line on the stairs, to Marina's amusement. Denis, obeying his wife's order, went to the kitchen to lend Rosa a hand.

He reached for an ice pick, chipped off some ice cream and managed to fill cones with it as fast as Rosa handed them to him. If he hadn't been so concerned about Marina, he would have felt like a boy again, remembering rare moments in his childhood when his father had brought home ice cream for the family.

The young visitors behaved reasonably well, though a couple of the boys aimed bits of melting ice cream at each other. One lump went down the front of a girl's gym blouse, accompanied by her excited screeches, though she'd obviously enjoyed the Golden Gateway. Marina was doubtful.

"As long as it doesn't mean a swarm of kids wanting free ice cream every day."

But Rosa took exception to this. "You never wanted ice cream and couldn't afford it, Miss Marina," and Denis silently agreed with her.

The little party ended in a matter of minutes with one of the boys chasing two girls down the highway, using little balls of melting ice cream as weapons.

Rosa yelled after them, "No tricks when the place is open for business, kids. The cops will be around. Just remember."

Most of them looked back, and at least two gave her a salute. "OK, ma'am."

In a few more minutes they had all scattered and even the Pebmarshes were saying "good-night" and thanking the Mallorys. Denis and Rosa cleared up the mess and were congratulating each other on the success of the friendly policy when Marina called to Denis from her chair on the outer rim of the balcony. "Darling, are you through there?"

He and Rosa exchanged glances. He tossed a dish towel into the sink and went to Marina. There was no mistake. She was looking pale and in pain. Over his shoulder he called to Rosa as he picked up his wife; "Hurry! What's the nearest hospital?"

But Marina insisted, "No. Home."

Rosa was beside them in seconds as Denis started to carry Marina up the stairs to the highway. "Is it the pains, Miss Marina?"

"No. Just discomfort. 'Night, Rosa."

As Denis carried Marina out on to the pebbled walk, he ordered Rosa, "Call Dr Chalmers. You have his home and office numbers."

In his arms, Marina breathed a little easier. "False alarm, darling. But let's get home anyway."

He settled her into his car close beside him as Rosa came running out to the curb. "He's coming. He's always been afraid of Mr Kyle."

"Thank God he's coming anyway," Denis muttered, though Marina, with her cheek against his shoulder, said sternly, "Don't be silly. I've never been better."

He took off at considerable speed, hardly relieved by Marina's assurances that she was fine. They reached the Kyle house almost in a race with Dr Chalmers and half an hour later Denis was happy to receive the doctor's guarantee that Marina had been right. She now felt fine and they needn't worry for at least a few weeks.

Denis was wiping sweat off his face when he found himself being in sympathy with Jason Kyle for one of the first times in his life.

The older man shook his head over his own concern and, having walked up and down the big living room for the last half hour, told Denis, "Her mother was like that. Narrow in the hips. It was nerve-wracking when Marina was born. But look at her now. On second thoughts, skip that. I'm afraid life is full of these crises."

"Good God! I hope not." Denis took out his pocket handkerchief and wiped his forehead again. More to be sociable than out of real interest at the moment, he asked, "How are you and Blake Cavenaugh getting along?"

Jason walked over to the long windows, staring across at the dark hills across the Golden Gate. "I like what you and Hoaglund have done to my bathhouse. It was time for a change. The city is ready for something else and, for once, I think Blake guessed wrong. I have a little left, minor stocks, some dividends. I've been thinking . . ."

Surprised and ever suspicious of his father-in-law, Denis grunted and Jason, after glancing at him, said no more.

Denis was wondering if Blake Cavenaugh had put him up to this. He couldn't shake off his mistrust.

Twenty-Two

G reg Mallory was born in the best of San Francisco seasons. No clammy foggy nights, no rainy, if invigorating spring days, no winter with its sunny but windy weather. Early autumn was young Greg's time and this satisfied both her parents, once Marina decided she would "accept" a daughter after all.

On top of this momentary disappointment, she felt that the whole thing had been a conspiracy to keep her from attending the opening of the Golden Gateway's French Café. This occurred on a night when she was ordered to remain in bed, though Greg did not actually arrive for almost a month after that.

There was nothing fancy about the opening. That would be saved, Denis hoped, for the future opening of the elegant restaurant that would hold sway with its plush furnishings high above the French Café, and opening on a balcony of its own.

But the fact that Marina would be able to attend the opening of this future triumph did not make up for her missing the French Café's lively, informal night.

The small but real accomplishment of the French Café's opening was spoilt for Denis when Marina still complained about missing it weeks later. Denis had tried to cheer her up by staying with her that evening, letting Rosa Santini, Larry and even Jason Kyle describe the success of the little opening, which appealed to the public for its reasonable prices and its "fun feeling", as the newspapers described it.

Nothing, including the opening, could possibly mean as much to Denis as the arrival of little, solemn Greg Marina Mallory with her ever-searching hazel eyes. Curiously enough, Marina's father took a fancy to her. The man hadn't appreciated his own daughter and Marina, in turn, always felt there was something inferior in being a female.

In late November, when Greg Mallory was almost three months old, Denis found a way to make up to Marina for what she had missed while she was being so ridiculously coddled, as she called it. He approached it gently in a devious fashion as she got ready to visit the Golden Gateway for the third time since Greg's birth. The fact that business at the charming little French Café was doing surprisingly well gave Denis his opening.

"Larry's been talking about some fancy plan for a maître d' in the French Café. I suppose it might give a little class to it but, for a sidewalk café, it seems snobbish unless we have someone specially suited. A male I think would be awfully pretentious. OK when we get the upper balcony done, but—"

Her eyes brightened. "It's a great idea. It should be a female." She looked at him. He could almost read her lovely eyes. She shrugged. "Well, who would you have in mind?"

He took the leap. "You. Starting Christmas, maybe."

Her mouth spread in a heavenly smile. "Really? You really thought of me?"

"I don't know what Larry will say, but he's never around enough to care."

"Oh, never mind Larry." She raised her voice. "Who cares what he thinks?"

He was puzzled. "Has he offended you or something?"

He knew his own feelings about her. She was one in a million. Any man would be an idiot if he didn't want her. But he trusted her. He had never had any cause to think she was anything but honest with him.

She said, "I know he's your friend. I'm sorry I said anything."

"Honey, this isn't like you. Larry got us into this business. We owe him a lot. But if he's been making passes at you, or cheating us on our salary or something – just tell me. The hell with the business!"

"You don't understand. We don't owe him anything. I mean,

169

not after all you and I have done with the French Café. And he certainly hasn't been making passes. He knows he wouldn't dare. He owes . . ." She reframed her protest: "Darling, would you go and see if the nurse needs anything for the baby while we visit the Gateway."

He kissed her, bothered by the troubled look she had.

What ailed her? Why did she have it in for Larry? He felt that he had missed something along the way and didn't know what it was. He was still annoyed over Larry's possible flirtation with her. He knew Larry worked fast with other women, and he had been fool enough to believe that Larry would keep his hands off the wife of a friend. Maybe he wouldn't.

Young Greg was already used to her nurse, Nella Calley, the Kyle housekeeper's sister. She was pleasant but firm and, to Denis's relief, was neither too brusque nor too likely to spoil Greg. For a baby so young, Greg was remarkably curious about everything she appeared to see. Denis had supposed that, like a puppy or a kitten, she didn't become quite normal until she was at least several months old, but Greg seemed different. Neither beautiful like her mother nor troublesomely mischievous, she was, as Denis described her, really unusual. Not the ordinary child at all and fascinated by the world.

Everybody usually nodded understandingly at this and perhaps smiled behind his back, but he could afford to overlook this amusement at his expense. He could even overlook a more serious matter: Greg was almost immediately fond of her grandfather, Jason.

Poor mite. She had no way of knowing that her grandfather had almost ruined the life of her mother because he'd wanted a boy and had to make do with a female.

After Marina's seclusion before her daughter's birth, Denis was more proud than ever of her looks and loved to show her off to the world. He still couldn't believe she had chosen him.

As Marina had predicted, Larry Hoaglund thought the idea of her as a hostess at the French Café was great; in fact, he tended to approve all the suggested plans of Marina and Denis with a casual wave of the hand. "To tell the truth, right now there's nothing in my mind but the new tract spreading into the Richmond. Nice, middle-class homes with a distant view of the Pacific."

"When it's not foggy," Marina put in.

"Listen. These are San Franciscans. They don't mind such trivialities."

And he went on talking enthusiastically about how the nearby Golden Gate Park helped to make the whole neighborhood of his new tract special, in spite of being row on row of new houses over what once were sand dunes.

By Christmas time Marina had had designed for special evenings a sensuously cut toe-length gown of moss-green silk cut on the bias and clinging to her slender form as far as her newly fashionable high-heeled pumps. She wore a fringed torero jacket which matched the gown and Rosa said, not necessarily in approval, only Miss Marina could get away with it.

Blake Cavenaugh, though invited to the Christmas party, had sent a brisk refusal, saying work was proceeding so fast on his estates that he couldn't afford to take out time for anything.

Everything went well with the Christmas Party – until the disaster between little Greg, who had been taken into her grandfather Jason's arms, and the big Christmas tree on the balcony above the garden.

"Isn't it amazing the way the baby takes to Father?" Marina remarked to Denis.

He hadn't noticed. He had been busy seating the Mayor, several City Hall officials, the Chief of Police and the Fire Chief with their wives, and hadn't noticed what was beginning to look like a steady habit. It annoyed him, an emotion he realized was born of jealousy, and it took a little doing for him to reply.

"He gives her so many gifts, no wonder. The little mite is only human."

"Thank you."

He looked surprised and she added, "For not being jealous."

Jason Kyle had been using the new camera Marina brought

171

him from Paris, and Denis was glad to see that Nick Santini, seated nearby with his mother, had bought a camera of his own, though not the fancy one which his raise in salary at Denis's instructions had been meant to cover. It was a little box affair that couldn't compare with Jason's camera, but it clearly served the boy's purposes. Jason had been snapping everything in sight, hardly bothering to pose his subjects, before he took up the baby in his lap. Nick, on the contrary, seemed to have a deep interest in the technical aspects of every picture he took.

Denis had been so busy lately he hadn't had time to pay much attention to the interrelationships of the people he knew, but he was glad to see that his daughter liked the boy. As Nick passed the baby, trying to focus on the best angle for a shot of the well-lighted Christmas tree, Greg reached out across Jason's arm, calling to Nick apparently in her own unintelligible language.

Nick looked over at her, made a waggling motion with his finger and, on the spur of the moment, snapped a picture of her. She giggled at this attention, and Nick went along the balcony to get some shots of the bright decor in the rest of the Golden Gateway. It would be worthless, Denis knew. The boy's camera would never take pictures in the dark interior beyond the decorations.

Greg turned her attention to her mother, who was standing for the moment beside Jason. Greg held her arms out to Marina, who leaned over and kissed her. Then the child pointed to the shining ornaments on the tree and made noises which made Denis smile tenderly though he had only a general idea of what she was trying to say. The child leaned out from her grandfather's arms, her grasping little fingers almost touching a small red ornament which gave her back a reflection of her face. She was now the object of attention from those nearby, who found her effort to reach the red ornament amusing.

Then, so slowly no one was aware of it at first, she closed her fingers around the little red ball. She pulled at the ball, which came off the tree and in her palm. She was surprised and stared at it, fascinated, closing her fingers on it tightly.

Then the excitement began. Someone cried, "She'll cut herself." Someone else warned, "It will break in her fingers . . ."

Too late, both Marina and Denis reached for the child. Marina lifted her out of the arms of the still puzzled Jason.

By this time the child had borrowed the tension and fright of the grown-ups and, upon noticing a trickle of blood along the hollow of her palm, she let the first tears gather at the corners of her eyes. She still hadn't moaned or protested, but she held up the hand with the now broken bits of stained glass gathered in her palm.

Marina was horrified. "Oh, God! The poor little lamb!"

Jason sat there speechless, alarmed but anxious to do something and not sure what would be best. Denis pulled his thoughts together. He looked around, remembered the doctor at the Mayor's table and called to him.

Meanwhile, half the room was drawn to this little drama. Some of the guests at the tables were standing up to catch a glimpse of the drama's little star. There were "Oh!"'s "Poor little tyke!"'s and one or two indignant "What the devil?"'s.

Dr McChesney, a slightly heavy, mature and competent-looking man, came at once. To the enormous relief of Denis and Marina, he said calmly in a businesslike voice, "Don't move her hand. Just let me see . . . Yes. A splinter of glass is caught in the flesh. No more. Do you have any first-aid equipment?"

Impotent anger gripped Denis. Why hadn't he thought of the full first-aid equipment? He had gauze, bandages and a salve but nothing intricate like miniature scissors or tweezers. He didn't know really what was required.

But as he started to speak, Jason Kyle looked in on this consultation. "Blake Cavenaugh has all that equipment, in case of accident. His men are working on the Jason Estates, a few hundred yards along the cliffside. Blake is working tonight. I saw the lights. Less than a quarter mile. I'll go."

Everybody, even the little victim, looked over at Jason respectfully. Jason started around the balcony to a small emergency door below the balconies. But as Denis started to follow him anxiously, Dr McChesney caught him back.

"Better stay here, Denny. The little girl may panic if anyone else leaves. The thing is to keep her calm and reassured . . . Now, missy, that's a very pretty hand. What say we admire it together?" Over her head and her puzzled eyes, he ordered, "Somebody get some alcohol." He added firmly, "Not liquor."

While everybody talked in a hushed voice over the child's head, Greg sniffed, appeared to swallow her tears, and decided that being the center of attention had its interesting side. Marina looked across at Denis.

In a nervous voice she murmured, "She will be all right, won't she? I mean, no blood poison."

This alarmed Denis. "Good God! There's no danger of—?"

"Quiet!" the doctor ordered, indicating the child's head which bobbed up at the concern in her father's voice.

Everyone immediately descended to funereal calm, and in the background several people began to relate tales of horror involving their own children.

Young Nick Santini came a little closer with his box camera and Greg reached for it. He held it before her, clicked something on the box and she watched, fascinated. The slow tears had stopped falling while she watched him.

Two shadowy figures came through the low side door across the unused area of the building's interior which was dramatically shrouded with velour and Christmas decorations.

The two men hurried across to the balcony of the French Café, one of them looking like Santa Claus, with a heavy box lashed to his back. Seeing the men, several patrons hurriedly emptied into the stream beside them the contents of the cough medicine bottles they had brought to spice up their cocoa, coffee, tea or Coca-Cola.

With his mind on the more crucial matters Denis still thought wryly, There's going to be a lot of cleaning up of our little stream tomorrow, just in case the Prohibition forces pop in.

Blake Cavenaugh was the man with the loaded wooden box

and Denis had never been so glad to see him. As Blake opened the box to show Dr McChesney, Jason explained, "Blake insisted on coming himself. He wanted to help, you know."

The doctor was arranging the old-fashioned cutting table in the brightly lit kitchen, on which to set Greg like a little princess, as he said. From Blake's box he took out gauze, alcohol and tape and some tiny, sharp objects that shone in the light. No one wanted to think of that babyish hand at the mercy of the scissors and knives, but thanks to the doctor's soothing voice, she found it all fascinating.

The doctor adjusted his spectacles, told everyone to give him elbow room and in a matter of minutes, hardly more than seconds, he had removed the glass splinter. In another couple of minutes the tiny rivulet of blood had gone and although Greg's tears began to gather again, she laughed at Nick, who had made a ridiculous face at her. Nick's mother looked proudly at Rosa Santini. It was the first time she had seemed to enjoy herself all evening. Clearly, the two sisters-in-law were not bosom friends.

"Thank God," Marina murmured, reaching over to lock her fingers in Denis's. "Poor little mite. This is a lesson to me. I'm not going to allow her to be taken to this place again until she's older."

"Here is Blake," Jason suggested to Denis. "You will want to thank the good fellow."

Denis shook Cavenaugh's hand, assuring him, "We can never thank you enough. You've done us an enormous service, believe me."

Blake replied with a modest smile. "My pleasure, I'm sure."

Women became busy trying to fuss over the heroine of this disaster but Denis was as anxious as Marina to get their daughter back home. As soon as Dr McChesney gave the word, Denis made his excuses to the crowd, promising to return immediately, and he and Marina left the French Café. The place was still buzzing with involved tales of other children, generally their own, who had faced "danger" when barely out of the cradle.

175

Jason started after them but explained at the top of the stairs, "I may as well remain, represent the family, as a matter of fact. You won't believe this but Blake had a check made out and was waiting to give it to me. My long overdue first dividends towards the purchase price of the property."

In much better spirits, now that Greg showed signs of falling asleep sucking her thumb, Marina was delighted at her father's news. "Do tell Blake how we appreciate what he did tonight. He may have saved our poor little lamb from blood poisoning or something."

Denis was every bit as relieved as his wife was.

Jason was in an excellent mood, armed with the peace-offering and the knowledge that they were in Blake Cavenaugh's debt – a matter which did not overwhelm Denis, in spite of his gratitude.

Twenty-Three

The Golden Gateway really took off during its first year, and as Denis and Marina left for the French Café early one afternoon the following fall, they discussed asking Larry what he thought of breakfast parties to take up the business that came in mid-morning. People arrived trying to find breakfast before they went further around the cliffs to Sutro Baths or eventually the Great Highway along the cold, rolling Pacific Coast. They were both keen on the idea, though Marina reminded him that they couldn't work twenty-four hours a day and it would mean getting another staff for morning work.

As they were leaving the driveway of her father's house and Denis once again reminded her that he could soon afford a house just for "the family", she reminded him for the twentieth time that Jason *was* family.

At that moment they met Jason driving toward the garage. Jason, leaping out of his car like a teenager, laughed and offered them a Jumping Jack he had gotten from a shoe store and he came to their car door, highly satisfied with himself.

Damn! thought Denis. Why didn't I get something like that?

It was ridiculous and he was annoyed at his own jealousy, but it did seem strange that this man who had never shown an unselfish interest in his own daughter should know how to win over his grandchild.

"See? I got it free at the shoe store. The little princess will love it."

"She will, Father," Marina called. "You'll find her in the playroom with Miss Calley. Do be nice to Miss Calley. She

177

knows we don't want to spoil the baby."

"Don't give it a thought. I'll be my charming self," and he went up the steps into the house.

Marina was amused as usual and glanced at Denis. "Father means well, dear."

"I wish he had meant as well to you," Denis said and they drove out to the highway.

By the time they reached the Golden Gateway and pulled up at the busy front of the building Marina said, "Looks like you needn't worry about the Café's success. See that line, and they're barely open. Poor Rosa! She'll be swamped showing them all down to the Café. And the kids too. From the high school."

"Are they behaving?"

"Looks like it. Rosa could always handle them, and she had some rough ones in the bathhouse days. She's ushering some of the older crowd down the stairs. What a girl!"

"Worth her weight in gold," he agreed as he parked the car at the curb and went around to help her out.

Rosa didn't come back to them until she had shown some of the patrons the direction along the balcony to the French Café. The women were giggling and pointing first to the blue sky overhead and then the welcome tables and chairs overlooking the stream that ran through the garden.

"How's business?" Denis asked her when she reached them.

"Great," Rosa said, obviously with pleasure, but Denis thought there was something on her mind, and he started to bring it up, but Rosa seemed to change the subject. "However, we do need someone down here to lead people to their tables and all that business. I've got my accounts to take care of. I'm a bookkeeper. Not a fool maître d'. Besides, there's all that standing up to do. I prefer sitting down."

Denis promised, "We can solve that problem. At least, whenever our daughter can spare her, now and then. Marina's agreed to be our maître d'. Probably just on special nights, isn't that right, darling?"

"Who knows? We'll work it out. I don't want to miss anything though. I'd rather make it a steady . . ." She saw them both staring at her, and she added, "We're bound to work it out."

Bernard had begun a little French tune and was wandering between the tables. Somewhat to Denis's surprise, several of the men, though none of the four from the local high school, nudged Bernard and stuck a dime or even a quarter in his pocket. He didn't refuse it but merely gave them a nod.

The high-school group seemed to be behaving. The boys would whisper in the girls' ears and the girls would squeal, but gradually they settled back and concentrated on their sandwiches and bottles of purple Delaware Punch, which, along with root beer and Coca-Cola were their favorites.

Rosa Santini started back up what to what she now called her "Office", since she no longer sold tickets but was the official bookkeeper. On her way up she stopped briefly by Denis and remarked, "I'd like to see one of you for a minute later, Mr Denis," and then she went on.

"Busy as a beaver," Marina taunted Denis. "I see somebody over in that corner. A nice old spinster, used to teach me mathematics in junior high school. I was hopeless. You run up and take care of Rosa. She's so damned conscientious . . . Hi, Miss Skinner. Haven't seen you for ages."

Denis let her go because there appeared to be no way to stop her from hurrying here and there. He called after her, "Don't leave here until I get back, darling."

She jeered in fun at his concern, "No, master, I'll be good."

He was still smiling when he reached Rosa Santini at the top of the stairs and walked over to her office with her. This boxy affair still overlooked the highway and, in the other direction, the partially completed estates under the large sign:

BLAKE CAVENAUGH PRESENTS
THE NEWEST IN MAGNIFICENT
ESTATE HOMES OVERLOOKING
THE GOLDEN GATE.
WATCH THEM RISE!
Jason Estates

Denis remarked, "Could he have gotten Jason's name any smaller?"

Rosa laughed without humor. "God knows what he'll do if he gets hold of Larry Hoaglund's place here."

"You think he actually wants to run a couple of restaurants, besides all those fancy, cliff-hugging houses?"

"Who knows? Stranger things have happened."

Rosa unlocked the door and he followed her into the tight little office, prompting her, "Now, what's all this about? You said you wanted to see us. You sounded – well, a bit on the spooked side."

"I am. I just want to know where I – hell! – where I stand with Hoaglund."

"Good Lord! Is it money? You of all people! You can write your own ticket. You know that. You have charge of the payroll."

"Don't be insulting. It isn't that at all."

"Well then, what is it?"

She motioned him to take a stool and reached under the counter, bringing up an ancient ledger that looked as if it had been used before the war and probably had been.

"I can't explain all the short-cuts I have made for ages in my accounts. You'll have to take my word they're honest."

"I'll take your word, Rosa. I'd sooner doubt myself. A lot sooner. Now, what's happened? Has somebody been at your books?"

"No." She took a long breath and exhaled. "I'd rather be talking to both of you since you're both in this business."

"Business? What have we been doing, robbing the till?"

It was a joke but she leaped on it. "Just the opposite, Mr Denis. There's not a shortage. There's too much."

She rustled through the book, took out one after the other of numerous bank receipts. Some of them were made out in favor of Larry Hoaglund for his sizable expenses. Their dates stopped several months after the opening of the French Café.

"Salaries are in another book," she explained, bringing up a more modern-looking ledger from under the horde of paper in an unlocked steel box.

It seemed a confusing mess, chiefly because he didn't know what she was driving at.

"I do wish we had Miss Marina here. She'd know all about it, since the payments come out of an an account in her name. They're all made out to Mr Hoaglund. It must be that he borrowed the money from her."

"You must be mistaken. That doesn't make sense."

"Now, wait a minute. I've got it now," Rosa said animatedly. "It must be because after Miss Marina loaned Mr Hoaglund the money to put into the French Café, she carried on financing it. That would explain all this—" Rosa blushed, realizing that the cat had been let out of the bag.

Denis gasped, outraged. "You are out of your mind – are you trying to say Marina's lied to me all these months? Almost two years. She knows what a lie like that would—" He broke off, seeing Rosa's expression. "You aren't lying. It is true, isn't it? . . . I don't believe it. I can't take this."

"Please, Mr Mallory, please don't get upset . . . she did it for you. She certainly didn't want to hurt you. And you've done wonders with the Café."

"My God!" he said, more to himself than to her. "How could she do this thing, knowing how I felt?"

She ventured, "It wasn't so bad, really. Miss Marina was just being generous. She's always been like that. She wanted you to have a nice position. You know. Important and successful. I can understand that."

He had a deep passion against unearned gifts. Often unwanted, they always entailed a favor in return. He thought that Rosa might understand. He cleared his throat. "My father was an unhappy failure. Eventually, he took to drink, spending what little we had. Afterward, he always came home with a little gift for my mother. She got so she hated them. Once he stole something off a counter to give her. But there was always a catch. She was expected to forgive him."

"I think I understand," she said quietly.

He ignored this. "I got so I hated favors. There was always a catch."

"I'm so sorry. I'd rather be shot than hurt you or Miss Marina. She's been so good to me. Can't you" – she put one hand out, pleading – "Can't you see your way to forgiving her?"

"The doubt will always be there. *What does she want of me in return?*" he asked hoarsely. "Next time she lies to me, the question will come up. And the next."

"No, no. You don't understand at all. She's not like that. Mr Denis, where are you going?"

He shrugged. "To find out from Marina, naturally."

"Please, Mr Denis, she meant it only – Mr Denis?"

But he was already walking out on to the gravel. He probably wasn't aware that she had spoken to him.

Twenty-Four

M iss Ethelind Skinner, Marina's high school math teacher, was pleased to be recognized but, as always, there was a careful reserve about her. "Well, Marina, your mathematics must be somewhat improved since you were in my class. You are surely making a profit."

Marina sat down in the empty chair at her table. "Not me. Mr Hoaglund. Do you like the Café, Miss Skinner?"

"Within reason. It's very like an ice cream parlor. How you've encouraged them to come way out here is an interesting question. I must say, it's unlike those heavily cushioned banquettes down town. These are better for the posture, actually."

"Yes, ma'am. That's why we put them in," she lied. "As for mathematics, I leave that to our friend Rosa Santini. She's a whizz at it. Wants to know where every penny goes."

"Good girl. Italian, of course. They always were good at money, clear back to the medieval and Roman days." Her lightly wrinkled face softened in a way that Marina had seldom seen. Though Ethelind Skinner's entire life had been forced into a mathematics groove, where she had been needed when she was starting out, her real love was history.

"Tell me, girl, I've read about you in the columns. Are you really as happily married as they say?"

Marina's hands clasped instinctively. "Oh, I am. I mean, we are. And our little girl. You'll be seeing our Greg in one of your classes some day. I suspect she will be better than I was."

Miss Skinner chuckled drily. "She could hardly be worse. But you'd better hurry. I'm to be retired in less than two years."

"Oh, no! I don't see how they can get along without you. Maybe, if we're doing well after we get the upper restaurant in – it'll be very elegant, you know, really super – we could hire you as Greg's tutor. With math and history and things like that."

"Ah!" Miss Skinner's grey eyes took on new life. "That would be something to look forward to. Not that it's likely, but one never knows."

"Speak of the devil – I mean, speak of angels and you hear the beating of their wings. My husband is coming down the stairs now. Isn't he handsome?"

Miss Skinner looked behind her and up the staircase. "Very well set up. Irish, probably?"

"I don't know. He had some English ancestors long ago. He's awfully nice. He looks a little stern now, but that's his business look. You musn't mind it."

"Not at all. I like it," Miss Skinner said. "It gives a man character."

Marina rose from her chair and half stood up, waving to Denis. "Over here, darling. I want you to meet someone."

He usually brightened up for her sake, if for no other reason, when she introduced him to a friend of hers, but things must have gone wrong in the Café kitchen today because he carried on looking steely as he approached them.

She was momentarily relieved when he met the elderly school teacher and acknowledged the introduction with a handshake. Then he said with icy politeness, "Marina has quite a few friends, but not many in the teaching profession. I must congratulate her."

Marina felt the sting in that and knew Miss Skinner had noticed it. He had never behaved to her like this before, either alone or with friends. What on earth was the matter?

Miss Skinner, a little red-faced, touched Marina on the hand, inclined her head coolly to Denis, and directed her goodbye to Marina. "Perhaps we will meet again and have more time. I've left my payment in the saucer with the bill."

She left them standing there as she walked out between the balcony tables and around to the staircase.

Marina almost fell into her chair. "Well, I never!"

"You never what?"

She stared at him. "Darling, where did this mood come from? I hardly know you."

He looked after the teacher's slightly bulky departing figure. "You should have torn up her bill. Surely, you are making enough profit now to afford a simple lunch ticket."

She did not know what she looked like at this moment but she felt as if she had fallen into an icy pond; yet her lips were dry. She moistened them. "You mean Larry is making a profit. I know you are doing all the work, darling, and he gets the credit."

"But don't you get the cash? That's not very businesslike of you."

Her confusion was compounded by the question of how much he knew and the disaster if he knew the truth about her ownership.

Oh, God! she thought. I love him as he is, but why couldn't he have less pride and accept a gift-horse when it looks him in the mouth? Her own metaphor found her torn between hysterical laughter at the absurdity of refusing a fat profit and tears at what might very well be his real reaction.

She picked nervously at his coat sleeve. "Darling, it's only a loan. He didn't have enough to get on with it. You know how it was at first."

"You lied to me. I can't begin to count the times. Maybe you could count them. Try."

She had never seen him like this, showing very little of the depths he felt, only the cold sarcasm that must always have been hidden beneath the humor and the warm passions he usually showed her. She began to be frightened of him. Not physically. Never that. But worse. Mentally. Was he going to freeze her out of his mind, his heart, over something so trivial?

She put out one slender, pale hand, not quite touching him. "Darling, please, please don't let this come between us. I'm sorry!

I could say that six days from Sunday but it wouldn't tell you how awfully bad I feel about doing such a dumb thing. I should have told you. I know I should have."

Her voice was low, but she felt on the verge of hysteria and two young men and a woman at the next table must have heard her. They looked over and cast disapproving frowns at Denis.

He must have noticed it. Absently, he pushed Miss Skinner's chair back under the table beside him and leaned on the chair back. "I suppose the salary paid me did not come from Larry, or the money for our honeymoon."

She almost stammered in her excitement, "You earned it. Every cent. Don't you realize that? Anybody else would have paid you for it. Darling, don't you understand? You earned every cent."

"I wonder if anyone else would have been as generous. Bought husbands must come more expensive now than they used to."

"Darling . . ."

His calm was what unnerved her. He was pale and his dark eyes were like the vague depths of a deep well.

"If what you've admitted is true, and you are actually my employer, I'll give my notice to you. When I'm replaced I'll send you money each month until the debt is paid."

She tried to rise but couldn't make it. Her legs gave out and she sat down slowly, her legs shaking. "You don't mean – what about Greg? She worships you."

She saw some of the hurt in his face then. "I know you'll be fair about my seeing her. Without her I don't think I could—" He swiped a hand quickly over his mouth. She thought it trembled a moment. "At least Greg has never lied to me."

She clutched at his hand on the chair back. Her voice was broken. "Don't. Darling, don't leave me like this. We've got to talk. I've got to explain why I did it."

He removed his fingers with care, not hurting her but with a finality that was worse than being hurt. "I know why you did it. You did it because you thought I could never live up to your standards by myself. It's all been said. Don't you understand? I can't trust you to tell me the truth. Go and sell the place to Blake Cavenaugh. He can live up to your lifestyle. That's all."

She drew her cold hand back into her lap, borrowing some of the warmth that had been in her body so few minutes before. She felt her mouth manage to get the words out: "You're impossible. Nobody can reason with you now. When you change your mind and see how small this really is, I'll be waiting."

Even that didn't seem to move him. She watched as he turned and walked . . . where? She had no idea.

Denis. She whispered his name, willing him to come back, but he walked away and didn't look back.

Twenty-Five

He passed Rosa Santini as he came out on the highway, but he didn't realize she had called to him until he was past the "Jason Estates" in small letters. It was just as well that he didn't respond. He had been preoccupied with a jumble of nightmarish thoughts.

He had no place to go, nobody he wanted to talk to and, even if there'd been a friend he could turn to, nothing remained to be said. There had been times when the cool, almost indifferent friendship of men with whom he had worked at the *Evening Journal* might have served: he might have welcomed someone who knew nothing of the fallen stack of cards that had been his recent dream. In all the almost two years he had known the incomparable woman in his life, he had never seen her as that despicable thing, a serial liar.

How many dozens – no, hundreds of times she had pretended that Larry Hoaglund owned the French Café! Over and over, even catching herself revealing the truth and quickly changing it to the lie. Of course, she might lie once. And be sorry. But not over and over again. There hadn't been a day passed that she hadn't spoken of the French Café and her quarter of the Baths as if they had belonged to Larry.

After the profits began to show, she still hadn't told him the truth. Today, she had tried to deny it at first. Another lie. How easily she told them!

After considering the lies in his mind over and over he saw that either he could never trust her again, or he must destroy the prejudice of a lifetime. That, he thought, would be impossible.

188

Cars speeded by him around the cliffs toward the famed Sutro Baths, which he was surprised to see ahead of him after what must have been endless walking. He was amused to see these tin lizzies, Buicks, Chevrolets and several expensive cars making thirty-five or forty miles an hour with ease. He passed around the corner of Sutro Heights and made out another walker going downhill, a tallish fellow carrying a small load on his shoulders.

Good Lord! A child. He wondered who this excellent father might be, entertaining his son. Or daughter. And on a cloudy day. It was far from nice weather. That was genuine filial love for you, he thought with some admiration.

I wonder what Marina would say.

Absurd thought. Would he be able to forget? Could he come crawling back to say he didn't care what she had done? Of course he cared. The truth was that he had never known anyone else who was part of his life and his heart like Marina and the little girl who was part of Marina.

But he couldn't forget. Could there be another reason why she had given Larry the money? Why had this idiotic thought come into his head? He knew better. Didn't he?

Why would she ever have genuinely loved him when there were a hundred males she must have known in her life, each of them with more of whatever she could want of a man?

His brain wandered over this idiot idea, knowing it was ridiculous, but why had she given that enormous amount of money to Larry Hoaglund? He had no answer, none that came to him now. Later, surely later, he would find reasons for what she had done.

The idea began to obsess him. A good, honest reason. The most obvious answer would be that she wanted to give him a job where he would make enough money, but if it was kept secret as it had been . . .

Did anyone except Larry and Rosa know? That would be even more shameful.

His thoughts were buried deep and it took a male voice two greetings before he realized he was the object of this attention.

189

The man he had seen far ahead, strolling down toward the Great Highway with a small load on his shoulders, had stopped and was waiting for him.

Jason Kyle. Another couple of steps and Denis got a greater shock. The little bundle clinging to Jason's neck and giggling was Denis's own daughter, Greg. He hurried his steps.

"Perfectly safe," Jason told him cheerfully. "She loves a ride now and then. I have my daughter's permission. You certainly were deep in thought. Saving the union?"

Denis ignored that. He had been angered to think this eternal nuisance would be giving his daughter the attention he had never given her, but he hadn't lost all his common sense. Clearly, Greg was enjoying herself and if Denis had been too busy to give her attention, there was no reason why his beloved child should suffer.

With an effort he recovered a little politeness. "You certainly are giving her a treat."

Jason was quite civil. "Thanks, old man. I was without any earthly enterprize and, not having the incentive of working beside a beautiful bride, I took the next best thing. I tried to make my granddaughter happy." He looked back over his shoulder. Greg had stretched her small arms out to Denis.

"Papa! Papa!"

Denis couldn't help grinning and appreciated Jason's generous comment: "You can see whom she really wants, old fellow. Her daddy."

"Thanks. I'll return the compliment: if I had the sense you're showing, I would have taken her for a ride myself. Do you often walk down here? Those breakers don't look very safe to me. A lot of undertow, they say."

"Well, I'm no Olympic champion, I can tell you. Pretty cold and overcast on days like this." Jason wrinkled his patrician nose at the gloomy sky. "I wouldn't live out here. How Hoaglund can acquire lots and sell houses in this district is beyond me." He reached behind him, took Greg down and then suggested to Denis, "Shall I transfer her to your shoulders? That's where she wants to be."

Pleased and flattered, Denis agreed. "If she really wants me to carry her." He accepted the little load as Jason draped her around his neck and Denis was enormously touched when the child hugged his neck and propped her small, pointed chin on his rumpled hair.

"Yes, I'd say she really wants you," Jason assured him. He looked around at the meagre handful of people, perhaps tourists, timidly wading in the surf as it washed up on the beach. Several brave souls were picnicking against piled up sand and rocky outcrops.

"Brave souls," Jason murmured. "Your little princess likes to be walked along the wet sand out there. Did you know that?"

"No. I've been too busy, unfortunately." But Denis found Greg's devotion reassuring as she peered down beside his cheek and touched it with her lips.

Jason stopped. "I sometimes cross the highway here to Playland at the Beach. Do you ever have a taste for those peach turnovers they have when trade's good?"

Denis laughed in spite of his previous mood. "I used to love them when I was a kid. I had them once or twice. Seems to me there are a few working over there, even today."

Greg pounded her feet against her father's shoulder and urged him in her unclear English, "Do, Papa. Do."

Jason studied the highway. "Wait 'til the Ford gets by."

They strode across the highway. No one was around the Playland except on the Ferris wheel, where two young lovers were so locked in each other's arms they didn't know they were momentarily stranded on the top of the wheel. Beyond the Ferris wheel another pair, even younger, wandered around among the deserted stalls.

The man in charge of the front stall was making up apple and canned peach turnovers. He was elderly, thin, and sported a full mustache which was tobacco-stained. He wasn't too impressed by his three new customers and unenthusiastically went on frying dough, then folding it into turnovers concealing the cut peach slices. Then he shook his sugar shaker over each turnover.

With one hand Denis was getting out a silver dollar, which was still the standard coinage in the city. Before he could order, Jason said, "Give us two and cut one of them in halves."

Denis watched Jason take up the two halves of the turnover, which dripped the pleasant odor of fried sugar and juice. Obviously, Jason knew Greg should not have much of the sweet, half-cooked dough. That impressed Denis, though he said nothing.

Greg ate the small piece of the turnover she had been given and licked her fingers. Then she leaned away from Denis's shoulder and touched her grandfather's jaw with her moist lips and kicked at Denis in her excitement. "Goody!"

"I think she likes it," Jason murmured to Denis. "She's had the apple but never the peach. Tell me, Mallory, do you often walk down this way? I've never seen Marina here."

Denis put away his loose change. "I've never been at the beach since I was here with my parents about fifteen years ago."

The turnover seller paid no more attention to them but perked up a bit when another man and woman parked on his side of the highway. They looked back across the highway at the rolling tide growing stronger now, and Jason gaped at the sight. "Good Lord! He's everywhere."

At his tone Denis looked up. The woman, a pretty redhead with her hair catching the wind loosely, was unknown to him – but there was no mistaking Blake Cavenaugh, swinging a cane and looking jaunty.

Denis grimaced. "What the devil is he doing here at the beach? I can't see that fellow enjoying wandering around those wild breakers in this weather. He's no explorer."

Jason pulled a strand of Greg's bronze hair, the little that had been produced so far to Marina's persistent worry, and Greg frowned. Then she giggled and wadded her small fist up, pretending to punch him. He gave her his forefinger to play with but his mind was on something else as he remarked quietly, "Probably hopes you will persuade my daughter to sell the French Café to him."

It was said so easily, almost indifferently, that for a minute Denis didn't get all of its significance. He pulled himself together mentally and asked without inflection, "Then you know who owns the French Café?"

With just a shade of surprise Jason said, "I couldn't help knowing. Good old Blake told me."

Worse and worse. Of all people, Denis felt that the worst person to know the truth would be Cavenaugh. Naturally, he would assume that Denis had stolen Marina from him because of her money; and first off, he had talked Marina into setting him up in business.

Why had she done such a thing and seen to it that Cavenaugh knew it? Surely, she knew Cavenaugh was his most persistent enemy? One could hardly blame the man for thinking Denis loved Marina for what she could do for him. Why had she told him? There could be a dozen, a hundred reasons, but Cavenaugh was sure to have a conniving use for the knowledge.

Jason looked at Denis strangely. "I get the feeling you really didn't know Blake knew about it." As Denis said nothing, Jason went on. "Probably some female in the bank tattled. Or Hoaglund himself might have told him. Anyway, Blake wanted me to put my oar in, persuade Marina to sell to him."

Denis smiled. He was puzzled. Jason seemed to be on his side. It was surprising. Jason had never liked him, but since he and Marina had lived in Jason's house, he had noticed a gradual change in the man.

"Well, I'm tired of playing the sucker. At first, Blake persuaded me that you were in this for my girl's inheritance. Now . . ." He shrugged.

"Would it be any use to tell you, Marina and I may be splitting up over her money? I figured I had made a going proposition of the Café. It seems I haven't. I was simply paid a big salary because my wife held the purse strings."

Jason's eyebrows went up. He chucked Greg under the chin. "Don't get excited, sweetheart," he told her and she went back to licking the fingers of her left hand. To Denis he said, "Blake is coming. Don't bring up the subject. He knows too much about my family anyway . . . Hello there, Blake."

Cavenaugh pushed the redhead forward. She pouted but then, getting a good look at Jason, moistened her lips and gave him a big smile, holding out one hand daintily. "Do introduce me to this – these gentlemen, Blake. My! San Francisco scenery has improved lately."

Cavenaugh said roughly, "Run along, Chili. Wait for me in the car."

"Well!" She glanced over at Denis, then back at Jason, who, though older, seemed to exude financial security. "Better luck next time, mister . . ."

Denis watched his father-in-law turn her off. He figured he himself was not the friendliest guy in the world but Jason Kyle could out-freeze anyone. His eyelids came half over his pale eyes like window blinds. His smile, if you could call it that, flicked on and off. He nodded but did not address her. She took the hint and backed away, eventually going over to the turnover man and ordering a turnover. For payment, she indicated the three men with her head.

"Sorry about that," Cavenaugh told the men, chiefly addressing Denis. "Couldn't get rid of her. She was with me when I saw you two in the distance. Could it be that you were talking about Hoaglund's café? I hear it's doing very well. It's classy enough to make a handy addition to my – sorry, Jason – our estates. An added incentive, actually."

Cavenaugh glanced at Denis, saw that he wasn't going to take the nibble, and reached over to tickle Greg under the chin. The child reacted with what Denis considered very good taste, shrinking from his touch, but he went on in his friendly way. "Well, well. We only need Marina to have the whole family here. How is my ex-fiancée? Working hard, I daresay."

"She will soon be a match for you, Blake," Jason put in, with what Denis thought was light sarcasm, but a glance at Jason revealed be might well mean it.

Cavenaugh was enthusiastic. "Good girl! Maybe she will be

coming in as a partner in the estates, eh, Jason? You'll have to be putting up a little more collateral to beat that daughter of yours."

The son of a bitch, Denis thought, seeing Jason's faint wince at what sounded very like a threat to his present partner. Make that *junior* partner. It was startling, but there appeared to be a definite split coming between Marina's father and his erstwhile buddy.

Denis was being prodded by Greg's feet. Obviously, the child had no more use for Cavenaugh than Denis did. Or even than Jason Kyle, now that Denis saw the sharp edges in their relationship. Unless Marina's father played a deeper game than Denis had guessed, Cavenaugh wasn't getting anywhere with Jason. He wasn't surprised when Cavenaugh grumbled, "What the devil is that girl doing at the turnover stand? Does it take all day to eat one turnover? Chili, make it snappy, will you, sweetie?"

Chili the redhead sauntered over to Blake and hooked an arm in his. "Come on, sweetie. No more business for now."

Making the best of his failure to get a reaction on his hint to buy the Café, Cavenaugh took his girlfriend's arm and, wishing the other two men a good morning, strolled out toward the highway with her.

"There goes my next payment on the estates," Jason said and pretended to pinch his granddaughter's elbow. "Shall we give them a few minutes before making our way back to the café?"

"You go," Denis told him. "I'll take Greg home. See you later. I don't know just when."

Jason hesitated. "You aren't . . . ? Difficulties at home aren't too bad, I hope."

"Don't worry about it, and don't worry about Greg. I'll see that she gets home safe."

Jason moved away reluctantly. "This damned weather! Makes everything so gloomy. Well, see you later."

Greg struggled a little on her father's shoulder. "Gamfer! Gamfer!"

"See you at home, sweetheart." Jason looked over at Denis. "Better go and find a new money-bags, I reckon. I don't think my partnership with Blake is going to see many more good days."

With his daughter's arms fastened around his neck, Denis watched Jason walk away. Strange, he thought . . . a rich fellow like Kyle can have as much trouble finding a job as I'm going to have.

Twenty-Six

J ason Kyle hadn't noticed a sound in the house, and there was no sign of Denis's Ford in the garage all night, which explained his daughter's ghastly pallor and big eyes at breakfast the next day. She looked up from the breakfast table so quickly when Jason came in that he felt a little hurt, because obviously he wasn't the person she had hoped to see, but out of either cowardice or delicacy he didn't mention the fact that his son-in-law was missing from the house.

He played the painful scene as easily as possible, bringing up an entirely different subject when he kissed her forehead and sat down in his accustomed place across the table from her. "Good morning, my dear. Did you work late? I didn't hear you come in . . . Morning, Raymond . . . Yes, the usual for me – mushroom omelet, tomato juice and some of those little pastries you do so well."

Raymond nodded but made no attempt to wish him a good morning. His reserve was greater than Jason's and his personal opinion was that no member of the nouveau riche Kyle family was in his class, as a gentleman or a cook. But he liked the money and was fond of Marina, so he never dreamed of quitting.

As soon as he left the room, Marina smiled at her father. It was a dreadful, watery smile and made Jason most uncomfortable.

"What good taste you show, Father! You don't mention our missing member."

He poured his coffee, looked to see if she needed a refill and tried to be matter-of-fact. "I'll certainly admit your Denis works a twenty-four-hour shift. I don't know how he does it. I never did, even when I was his age."

She looked at him but didn't pursue that particular matter of today's lateness. "He wants to prove something. On his own. He's been working far too hard so that the big, new restaurant upstairs can be built."

"My dear girl—" He accepted his omelet and the pastries, drank his tomato juice, and said over the rim of his glass, "I'm convinced he never knew it was your mother's money that is making everyone's fortune. Blake told me long ago."

"Oh, God! I should never have kept it a secret." She buried her face in her hands, saying in a muffled voice, "It was stupid. Stupid!"

"Yes, it was." He took up his fork and ate for a moment before he added, punctuating his words in the air, "A lie is only good if it can be kept secret. You are not a very good liar, my dear."

She nodded.

He watched her. "You've learned your lesson. But you've got to convince him, and I'm afraid that will be more difficult than keeping the lie. I met him yesterday. He looked rather like you look this morning. Now, don't, for heaven's sakes, begin to cry."

She sniffed, wiped her eyes with the napkin and asked him, "Did he seem terribly angry?"

"Worse. He seemed as if he had been kicked in the belly. I felt sorry for the poor sap. Damned if I didn't. He was quite reasonable when he saw me with the little princess. You know. He didn't act jealous, just a decent fellow. I could almost like him."

"I should never have played that trick on him. I might have known he'd find out. But I wanted that to be just a little later, when he'd enjoyed the taste of success. Father, he's so perfect."

"Well, I wouldn't say that. When your mother and I quarrelled, we – at least, she had it out openly, in our early years. Those were wonderful times. She threw a teapot at me once. Then it was all over. These silent fellows with complicated pasts are always difficult. He is too proud. And he expects perfection. Impossible.''

She had never known about those early years of her father's marriage. But it was no use to tell him that Denis and his complexes were what she loved about him. She changed the subject. "He did come home. I was still at the Café. He left Greg with Miss Calley and was gone about ten minutes later, she said. I haven't seen him since.''

"My advice, my dear, is to keep on being your usual charming self, and hope it rubs off on him." He did look as if he doubted his own advice but didn't say it aloud.

She gave a huge sigh and in return for his support, she asked, "How are you getting along with Blake? Has he made you any more payments? How many estates has he sold?''

His eyes looked toward the ceiling chandelier as if he might find solace there.

She asked, "Is he still cheating you? Good heavens, Father!''

"Well, he keeps digging up investments I put in for on margin. Investments that all went bust. That means I lose the entire price.''

She was moderately sorry but he could see that her own troubles took precedence. "You aren't buying anything else his companies control, are you?''

He finished his omelet and poured himself some more coffee. "No, I've learned my lesson." He studied his coffee cup as if the answer might be there. "From here on in, I'm only interested in sure things. The bank may have something I can trust. Nothing to do with Blake's gang, but I've got to get hold of some money to swing it.''

"Father, I wish I . . . But you know where I've put most of the money Mother left me. Maybe next year.''

He nodded. "I was afraid of that. However, it serves me right. I've no one but myself to blame.''

She thought he looked disappointed and she felt guilty, but it was too late to do anything about it now. All the same, she felt like a dog to refuse him. And he was being so damned nice about

199

it. She gave a huge sigh and was about to pursue the matter when a phone rang somewhere in the house, making Marina jump. Even Jason looked around tensely.

Seconds later Raymond stuck his head around the kitchen door. "For Miss Marina. The Santini person."

Marina cried, "Oh, my God!" and started out on a run.

Jason called, "Easy does it, dear. Take a breath first."

Marina made an angry gesture, brushing away his words, and vanished into the hall. She hesitated before going next door to the big, formal dining room, and then rushed to her father's study which was more private.

"Yes, Rosa. It's me."

"If you missed Mr Denis last night, he spent the night here in our little room where people wait when there's a crowd. He slept on one of the couches. And he wasn't alone."

"Not alone? What do you mean?"

Rosa chuckled. "Nick is helping to clean up when we close. And last night, he brought back that accordionist to sleep as he'd had a quarrel with his daughter."

"Never mind that. What is his mood?"

"The accordionist?"

"No, damn it! My husband."

"Very calm. A little embarrassed, I think."

"Maybe – oh, please God! Maybe he's getting over it."

Rosa hesitated. "Well, I gave him a tongue-lashing about money. I told him I'd said fibs to my darling husband about money. I can't recall when, but what the devil! He smiled just a little. He's eating breakfast now."

"Thanks, Rosa. You've made up for yesterday. I'll hurry."

"I sure hope I've made up a little. I know you were mad at me. Nobody had a better right."

"Thanks, honey. Got to go." She hung up and hurried into the breakfast room.

"Your breakfast is getting cold," Jason pointed out.

"Never mind. I'm afraid I'll have to go. I want to get out to the Café with Greg. I thought if anyone could soften Denis, she could. Poor little mite. She asked me why Papa didn't come to say 'good-night' to her last night."

"Good luck, my dear."

But he didn't act as if he was at all sure either one of them would have much luck today.

Marina was several hours too early for the opening of the French Café but Rosa Santini had never lost a customer yet. She was dishing out tiny pastries fresh-made at dawn by a bakery near her apartment, and coffee which young Nick Santini was pouring for a half-dozen customers who had come by in hopes of finding breakfast early. They were four well-dressed, ageless women in pleated taffeta gowns, with fur pieces hanging from their stout necks. They were accompanied by two elderly men and all were seated at two tiny tables by the stream, which someone, perhaps Denis, had turned on.

"Rosa, you were a born moneymaker," Marina said, though this morning's pre-breakfast was on the house. It was good business, as no one knew better than Rosa.

Rosa shook her head while greeting Greg warmly with her outstretched hands. "I owe you. I was so dumb. Anyway, according to these ladies, they are going to be steady customers when we open earlier. It was Denis's idea, you know."

"Is he here now?"

"Well, he is and he isn't. He's perched on a ladder trying to nail up decorations for Halloween. Over on the side of the building. The south side where it's curtained off."

Anxiously, Marina looked over at that area of the building.

"I hope he isn't taking chances."

Rosa scoffed, "He's not that far gone."

Marina flushed a little. "I realize our quarrel is no monumental affair. Kind of silly, actually."

"Tell him that." Then Rosa cut her reply short. " 'Scuse me. I'm summoned." One of the women, feeding up free while they waited for the Café to open, called to Rosa who hurried over to oblige her.

Marina took the wide-eyed and fascinated Greg around the balcony toward where Denis was working on rolls of crêpe paper. She called to him, "Hi, darling. Greg insisted on seeing you . . . Wave to Papa, sweetheart. That's it."

With his legs wound around the ladder's rungs Denis peered a long way down between the rungs, where Greg was waving her hands, especially her fingers, and calling, "Papa, Papa."

He called back, "Hello, princess. How do you like the colors? Orange and black. Like witches."

Greg cried back, enthralled.

Marina said, "Hush, sweetheart. Papa is busy. He'll come home when he's through."

"Pretty soon, princess." But he addressed this purely to his daughter. "We're going to have witches, goblins and pretty little lights – but not near the crêpe paper."

Marina laughed.

"Yes. No more risks, especially with Blake Cavenaugh hanging around," he continued. Denis looked down at her between the rungs of the ladder. He didn't look quite like her Denis, more the pleasant co-worker. "I have my suspicious about his part in that fire," he added.

"Good God!" She hadn't once thought of that. But it had caused Cavenaugh to get what he wanted, most of the Kyle bathhouse. "Is it possible?"

"Possible. But it can't be proved."

"How horrible! Damn him! Not that it wasn't for the best in the long run."

He didn't reply to that but she wondered if it was an opening to a peace treaty between Marina and Denis. Unfortunately, he gave no sure indication of it.

She didn't have the courage to ask him if he would remain at the French Café, or, indeed, in San Francisco. She had no reason to believe he would stay at the Golden Gateway, even if he was working now. Still, though very small, it was a good sign.

She called up to him, "The sun is out. I might drive Greg down to Ocean Beach if the air is warm. Will you need me for the lunch or afternoon crowd?"

He was back at work hammering nails and twisted crêpe paper. He answered without looking at her. "Not until tonight. We've got reservations for two parties and several tables already, with more to come. You'll be needed then."

You will be needed.

Not by me, apparently.

She said brightly, "OK. Shall I tell Yee to plan for you tonight before you go to work?"

"Tell him not to bother. I'll get a bite at the Café before the evening crowd."

She said, "Sure," and as she started back around the balcony she added, "Greg says goodbye."

But he didn't hear her. He had started to pound again.

She had her pride, too. She hoisted Greg and went on up the stairs to the highway.

Twenty-Seven

O ver the next few weeks, in spite of himself, Denis hated
being away from "home" – Jason Kyle's home, that was –
at night. He was genuinely astonished not to enjoy sleeping
alone, as he had done so all his life. Even when his mother and
father couldn't afford two bedrooms in their various rooming
houses, Denis had always slept comfortably enough in a kitchen
on a army-surplus cot that could be folded up and put away in
the daytime. At one place he had been put in the bathroom in the
empty tub and made it reasonably comfortable with a blanket,
sheet and pillow. When he was out on his own, he had slept
alone, except for a few hours here and there with an occasional
girlfriend. Now, it was different. Marina had made it so.

Jason himself suggested more than once that he come back,
and he wanted to return! But he couldn't ever trust her again, he
told himself.

When he wasn't thinking of Marina he wondered about little
Greg every hour of the day. What was she doing now? Had she
gotten over her awful croup? Why had she sneezed that evening
as Nick Santini was watching over her while Marina "glad-
handed" the guests at the French Café? Greg needed watching at
all times. She was wildly curious, a born explorer, and no one
worried about her interest in the holes and corners of the Golden
Gateway more than he did. The building was not new, and some
of it was still shut off, unused until work was finished on the
fancy restaurant off the upper balcony.

But all work had stopped when Denis found out about
Marina's ownership. Larry Hoaglund had explained to him that

Marina now refused to give any orders about the half-built property.

Larry arrived at the French Café one morning to try and settle the matter but got nowhere.

"Denis, old buddy," he began for perhaps the hundredth time, "there was nothing more to it than to put your wife's money to work for both of you. Now, it's all the way you wanted it."

"My wife is rich again?" Denis asked ironically.

"She always was, buddy. A man's wife's property is also his. That's law. No changing it now."

Denis took a breath. He was really bored with explaining. "No one ever understood. I didn't want to marry her until I could work for a salary. From you. The idea was that after a while we might be able to buy you out."

Larry lost his temper, not for the first time. "Damn it! I don't want all the responsibilities of a café. Worse: two cafés. I want nothing to do with cafés except good food and a place to pour my libations. For me, the God-damned thing is a white elephant. I couldn't wait to unload it. Marina paid me off yesterday for my share and, as far as I'm concerned, that's the end of it."

Denis looked at him, puzzled. "I get satisfaction every time we have a good night. We have problems, sure. Right now, I'm trying to wean my father-in-law's chef away, paying Jason for the right, of course – and Marina, for the loss of her pet chef. If I offer him enough, it will be a first-class operation. You think rows of houses out in foggy Richmond are better than the French Café?"

Larry laughed. "I prefer houses. They don't complain about the food or not getting waited on, or a bad night's business."

Denis made a gesture, dismissing the conversation. Larry started to leave but looked over his shoulder. "Buddy, are you still ready to kick my hide?" Not getting an answer, he admitted in farewell, "Anyway, I like you in spite of your idiotic pride. You're one honest man. Always have been."

Denis smiled, shook his head, and went back to work exchanging Thanksgiving turkeys and pilgrims for Halloween goblins. Obviously, Larry didn't understand. But Denis didn't care for him as he cared for Marina, who had been his whole life, then left him wondering if anyone in the world could be trusted. He had never considered Larry the soul of honesty anyway.

Denis thought very little about Nick Santini during these long weeks of what he would look back on as quiet misery of his own making. But one morning as Denis was making a breakfast of coffee and raisin-bread toast, furnished by Rosa's baker friend, Nick Santini appeared in the Café kitchen.

He reminded Denis that he would be in to clean up the café kitchen as soon as he got in from school.

It occurred to Denis that the boy was getting very little out of life, thanks to his schooling and especially the work at the French Café before school and in the evenings. He mentioned it lightly, hoping Nick wouldn't be too proud and take offense.

He was jarred when the boy said casually, "Well, Mr Denis, I reckon you do what you have to and I do what I want to."

Denis chuckled. "You want to work all those hours? When do you do your homework? In fact, when do you sleep?"

Nick pulled the sleeves of his rain-slicker down over his thin wrists. "I get it all in. I'm going to be famous, and that takes a plan."

"A plan."

"I'm still after that camera I told you about."

"Yes, I remember. You haven't got it yet?"

The boy was quite matter-of-fact: "Ma had a little operation."

"What? Good God! Why didn't you tell me so?"

Nick drew back, affronted. "I got my feelings. You'd think I was Salvation Army. I ain't. I mean, I'm not that stuff. Ma would strap me good. We got it done and she's going to be good as new. Only, I got set back a little."

"Does your aunt know about this?"

Nick looked around into the dark corners. "Gosh, no! She better not. She and Ma don't hit it off too well. They used to argue all the time. Now, they're just – you know, polite. Ma's awful proud."

Denis lost a taste for his raisin-bread toast. He set it down and forgot it. "Look here, boy. Marina and I are your friends. So is Mr Kyle. You should have come to us. What kind of operation was it?"

Nick shrugged. "It's all paid for. Don't mean nothing."

Denis went on quickly, "How can I help you without your mother getting huffy?" Pride! Was it worth all the suffering?

"I've got a raise coming in May, sir."

"So they tell me."

Come to think of it, he could give the boy the raise earlier than May without using Marina's money. It would take less than fifty dollars off his own salary to buy the camera.

"Keep your fingers crossed."

"Yes, sir. Please don't give it a thought. We're mighty well fixed. Long as Ma don't think it's charity."

"I know how it is, Nick. I had a mother just like yours."

Nick gave him a singularly attractive grin that made his freckles light up. "Kind of a trial sometimes, ain't they, sir?"

"Sure are. But you wouldn't have anybody in their place, now, would you?"

"Gosh, no!" He went tramping up the stairs and called back to Denis, "You need me to go on watching the little princess now and then, mister, after I get off school?"

"Sure thing, if you can make it. It's good for a little extra."

"Can do. Wow! I'm late for math class."

I could stand to have two kids if they were like that one and our own Greg, Denis thought. For a little while he was almost happy. But there was no point in enjoying his good spirits by himself. He would be glad to employ Nick whenever he could. He had come to trust the boy more than any other employee, except Rosa, whom he'd now forgiven for accidentally telling him about Marina's lies.

Early in the afternoon his father-in-law came in, proudly showing off his granddaughter's ability to walk.

"Well – toddle," Denis corrected him, but was amused all the same at the older man's claim.

Jason Kyle let Greg give a ginger kiss to her father, who was covered with cobwebs and dust. Both men laughed when the child was set down on the floor of the balcony and demonstrated her walking ability. She hugged Denis's trouserlegs and then wrinkled her nose.

"Dirty, Papa."

"Dirty is the word," Jason agreed. "I hope you take a bath before you go sauntering though the café this afternoon."

Denis promised to do so and after tweaking Greg's small nose, he went over to wash up in the lounge restroom. There was one of the new showers in a cubicle beyond and he began to unbutton his shirt on the way, after calling to Jason, "Keep Greg away from that boarded up area over the rocks on the Golden Gate side."

"My dear boy, I wasn't born yesterday," Jason reminded him.

Denis went into the shower and Jason spoke to an early customer who remembered the Kyle bathhouse and wanted to know what had happened to the other half of the Baths.

Having finished scrubbing, Denis dried and then dressed in a reasonably smart suit. He had to admit the result was not quite what he would have liked. The suit was all right but during the past weeks, running now into long months, he looked older. No question about it: his private feelings were beginning to show. He wondered if there wasn't something in Rosa Santini's most recent advice to "forgive and forget". He himself was hardly a perfect specimen. Why should he expect it of the one person he had loved best in his narrow world?

He hadn't been gone very long, less than half an hour, but Jason and the admirer of the Kyle Baths as well as little Greg were gone now and Denis went over to the kitchen, passing the accordionist who was fussing with his instrument. The young chef, humming "The Sheikh of Araby", began to sharpen his knives, looking regal if not bloodthirsty, while his assistant, an excellent young sous-chef, peeled potatoes and broken eggs and handled any other chores.

Rosa Santini came down the stairs at the same time, signalling to Denis. "Shall we?"

"Sure thing. Look like a good day?"

She nodded. "Swell. It's raining and church is over. It's Sunday and there's nothing else to do, so they're heading our way."

She went back upstairs and Denis watched the chain go down. The first of what seemed to be a reasonably good crowd of men and women, though few teenagers as yet, started down the stairs, chattering away. The sight always gave Denis a pleasant little thrill, the only successful thing he had ever been part of. He reminded himself that it was not he who was the success but his wife. Without her money, there would have been nothing.

He crossed to the busy semicircle of the balcony and introduced himself, shaking hands with anyone who held out a hand. From the moment he first did this, they flocked to shake his hand, which both surprised and pleased Denis. As usual, the women were elegantly dressed, all with hats on, many of which had plumes – the way the hats were worn a couple of years before in New York and the stylish spas. The men were dressed a little more sportily. That was the San Francisco way.

Trailing along, looking a bit out of place and self-conscious, were several boys and girls, the girls heavily bundled but opening their coats so their winter finery could be seen.

The Gateway had started out as an informal gathering place, but it seemed to Denis that they were now nearly all dressing up a little. He liked it. Marina must like it.

He banished that idea for the moment.

Since Marina wasn't coming on duty until evening, Denis escorted them, two by two, then four here and there. He found small, individual tables for each of the two elderly ladies and they appreciated his smile as well as his recommendations from the small but carefully chosen menu.

Though it was generally considered common, several ordered the hamburgers, called "minced steak" during and since the war. It was a choice sirloin or fillet, and was the most popular dish in the house. Denis wished it was always excellent, but that depended on the chef's level of sobriety.

When Jason came by a short time later he seemed to be crushed by disappointment.

"What the devil is wrong?" Denis asked, genuinely concerned. "You look terrible."

Jason was grim. "I've got reason, believe me. I've just been told, nice as you please, that Blake is going to hold up the rest of his building for a year as the estates haven't been selling fast enough."

Denis considered the matter. He had wondered why the building of the estates was going so slowly. Jason probably hadn't received more than the first down payment on the properties. People were complaining about the climate out here – the fog and the wind.

"My God! I've been counting on my next share of the profits." Jason sank slowly into one of the little balcony chairs.

Denis lowered his voice. "Marina can probably help you. The Café is doing well. I've seen the figures."

"Not enough," Jason muttered, leaning on one hand and sheltering his eyes as if he couldn't bear to face the truth.

"It can't be as bad as that." Denis added, "Is Marina at home? Tell her about it when you take Greg back to her . . . Greg, honey, you're going home to Mama." He turned around. "Greg?"

His voice had raised and Jason looked up. "She's here on the balcony. Little princess, we're going home to Mother." He got up, looked around, and then squinted up at the skylight as if, by some miracle, the high ceiling, where only the rain falling on the skylight was visible, would illuminate the figure of the little girl. "Princess?" And then, with just an edge of anger, "Greg! Don't play games. Where are you?"

Denis kept calm for the moment. "Where did you actually last notice her?"

"She was following me and that friend of Blake's who told me the bad news. After we'd talked—"

"Never mind." Denis was striding along the balcony. "Greg, it's Papa. Where are you hiding?"

He looked into the lounge and the rest rooms, then glanced around the area where construction had stopped. He looked behind the huge, billowing velvet curtains hiding part of the building works. There were a hundred places where she might be hiding. Or lost.

He looked around, calling again. He said finally, "Think, man! When was the very last second that you consciously saw her?"

Jason was looking pale and unnerved, partly over his own problems, but they were now superceded by the question of what had happened to his granddaughter.

Denis said, "Find the night man. He's on duty now. Tell him to get on the search with us. And Nick. Yes, Nick might know. He's due in any time."

He was rattling around all of the dark recesses that worried him, though common sense told him that they would find Greg in some pleasant spot not too far from where she had left Jason.

"And get someone on the job near the Café in case any of the food or the good smells bring her back."

It began to seem like five or six hours since Jason had lost Greg. It was less than an hour. But no one had seen or heard her. Even the patrons were getting into the act. Several of them asked if they could do anything.

The women, especially, were concerned, thinking of their own children. Jason had gotten breathless running up and down the stairs calling Greg, and Denis noticed that his hands were now trembling – Denis understood his feelings perfectly. Jason wouldn't give up, though. He insisted it was he who must find the little princess.

One by one, the searchers and their well-meaning assistants returned empty-handed.

Nick Santini showed up at three forty and heard the story in bits and pieces. He tossed his books into a corner, tore off his jersey, then stopped and said to Denis, "It's likely a place she's wanted to go but never could. Look, Mr Denis. Let's think of all the places she wanted to go and we took her for a walk around the Golden Gateway instead. What's the one she wanted to see most?" He and Denis both thought of it together.

"The sealed-up place over the rocks."

Denis added, "Hell, there's no way of getting out there. But I'm going to try it." He started around the balcony toward a small staircase leading upward into the boarded-off area.

Nick ran after him while the others were trying to puzzle it out before following. "Look, Mr Denis, you can't get through there to the outside, but I can."

To the outside terrified Denis. He began angrily, "I'm getting out there if I have to worm my way through on my belly."

"Yes, sir," Nick agreed, giving up the fight until they got there but he knew that Denis was much too tall, his shoulders too broad to make it.

Beneath a series of crossed boards that had been bolted in place there was one hole, scarcely larger than a badger's tunnel. Denis listened for a few seconds. "I think I hear her. Poor lamb. She's crying. Poor baby!" He groped at the boards.

"She can't get back," Nick said. Instead of tearing away the boards, he crawled along, saw an opening after he had gone a few feet, and wriggled on while Denis was still tearing away the boards.

Denis saw that Nick had gotten out on the ledge. He wanted to push on and seize his child, but common sense once more came to his aid. He remained where he was as Nick held one hand out. Denis could hear Greg's tearful voice. "Nickie!" she cried.

"Give me your hand. No! Give it to me. That's it. Good girl."

Denis couldn't hear them for an instant but then the childish voice, laughing through her tears of fright, said, "My hand."

There was a scream which followed that nearly tore Denis's heart out, but Nick's calm young voice reassured him. "See? You're all right now. Hold tight . . . Mr Denis, tear away some more boards. That's it – I'm coming back. Here's Greg."

Denis carefully drew her back through the hole. "That's my brave girl."

"Papa . . . Papa." Her arms were around his neck. She was freezing cold, but he managed to bundle her into his jacket.

Nobody paid much attention to Nick, who got back to safety much ruffled by the wind and rain, but he was grinning.

Within a minute or two they were surrounded by at least half of the rescuers, led by Jason Kyle, looking grey-white and sick. Greg grinned mischievously with tears of joy still chasing each other down her cheeks.

"Gamfer, I was bad."

"You were bad indeed," her father told her.

Then, knowing how deeply Jason felt, Denis said, "Yes, and here is grandpapa. And all these nice people who want to thank Nick for his brave work." He beckoned to Nick with one hand.

Nick reached out, winced and put out the other hand. "Sure thing, princess. Safe and sound. It was cold out there, wasn't it? Mr Jason, she called for you several times out there, sir."

It was probably Jason's proudest moment. There were tears in his usually cold eyes. He held out his arms and Denis gave Greg to him, seeing that her grandfather's shaking hands were controlled and he could handle her.

Of one accord the group applauded and Denis felt that Jason had needed that boost to his ego and his pride.

Twenty-Eight

T rying to be businesslike about the whole thing, Denis found
his hands shaking a little and, though not usually a religious man, he heard himself thanking God in a way he hadn't
remembered since babyhood.

The Café was returning to normal, and Denis got hold of
himself while he was trying to be calm over the wall-phone to
Marina. "We had a little problem with the baby, but it's all right
now, dear."

"What's all right, darling? What happened? Denis, tell me
straight out. Was she hurt? Or you?"

"No, no. She just wandered off. Poor lamb. Jason has her now
and I'll drive them home right away. Matter of fact, both of them
are fine. I'll explain this evening. Don't cry, dear. Please. Everything is all right."

"Oh, Denis!" She sounded a little hysterical. "I know it's
worse than you said. Never mind. Just come home with Father
and the baby. You say Greg is all right?"

He played it down. Jason was only human. He wouldn't need
any hint of his mistake.

"Jason is nervous but he's going to be fine. He and Greg are
happy waiting for me in the car now, and we're bound for
home."

"Thank God! Can I expect you home for sure?"

He didn't go into details and he didn't mention apologies on
either side. That would come later. He had realized there was
more to be grateful for than just a life of pride.

"I'll be there in minutes, darling."

"I'm 'darling' again, thank God! But do, please, be here. I love you."

How long ago those days of separation had seemed! Now, they had caught up with him and almost caught up with the child he and Marina loved as dearly as they loved each other. It was, after all, because he had quarrelled with Marina that the building work had been left dangerously half finished.

Jason Kyle's estate loomed up around a corner of the cliff and Denis's Ford slid on to the parking area in front of the garage. Denis hadn't realized just how excited he was until he saw Marina running toward the car, hatless, coatless, and her lovely flaxen hair streaming out of its pins around her head.

"Darling, you're home! Really home!" she was yelling against the sunny afternoon breeze. She reached up, received the sleepy Greg from her father and still managed to kiss Denis.

There was a tangle for a minute but it was all straightened out as they went up the cement steps, with Marina talking all the time and Mr Yee making way for them.

In the late afternoon light Marina saw her father's face and cried, "Father, you look terrible, but I do love you. Greg, baby, you've been a bad little girl but we all forgive you. And Denis, my darling!"

Denis leaned over Greg's head with her feathery hair flying, and kissed Marina's cold but inviting cheek. He tried to look into her eyes but things were a little hectic as they all piled into the living room. Straightaway, Mr Yee – who was unimpressed by Prohibition – came in and asked them what cocktails they favored.

Marina was so glad to have her entire family – Greg, Jason *and* Denis – around her that she basked in warmth and happiness. Denis perched on Marina's big overstuffed chair near the fireplace, which burned low, and Jason, looking tired and worn out, sat in the rocking chair making faces at Greg across the room.

When Rosa Santini came by with Nick shortly after to see how they were the evening was complete.

It was Greg who broached the photography idea.

"Nickie, click-click!"

Immediately everyone thought this was a great notion. Nick got out his little box camera and was working with it when Jason suddenly got up, with his chair still rocking. He was almost his urbane self.

"Excuse me, ladies. Gentlemen. I've an idea," and he went off into his study, somewhat to everyone's surprise.

Minutes later, he returned with the magnificent camera Marina had brought back to him from her honeymoon with Denis. He held it up.

"This work of art needs a professional to operate it. I'm sure my daughter wouldn't mind if I gave it to today's rescuer with the thousand thanks of the entire Kyle-Mallory family."

He handed it to Nick, who was so astonished and embarrassed he wouldn't touch it for a moment. Then he looked over at Denis. "Sir, is it all right?"

"It certainly should be. Don't you think so, darling?"

Marina said enthusiastically, "Wish I'd thought of it myself. But you bet! It's perfect."

She hugged Greg, who was interested but not impressed by this activity that made everyone so happy.

Rosa said briskly, "That ought to keep you out of mischief, Nick."

Nick was stunned. He accepted the camera from Jason's hands and examined it fearfully, turning it over gently, touching it as if it were made of precious metal.

"I–I can't thank you, sir. I just can't. I'll keep it" – he looked around, all his freckles seeming to shine – "forever."

Everyone felt as if, in some way, he or she had contributed to this happy moment but only Denis, and perhaps Rosa, knew what it meant to Nick.

Denis was deeply touched by the gesture, but somewhat

troubled too. He wondered why Jason had made this perfect gesture, which was so untypically generous.

It was a happy evening with much planning of how the new restaurant would run when it was ready, but, as Denis himself pointed out, "We can't overlook the French Café. That's done wonders. No one expected it to be such a success."

"I did. It was the management, or I should say – the manager," Marina pointed out proudly.

"The management with the owner," Denis gave in. "I've decided the present owner is the best one we'll ever find."

Throughout this conversation Jason said nothing. He sat thoughtfully studying his fingernails and occasionally glancing at Nick, who was ecstatic over his new camera, and a softer expression replaced the urbane sophistication that was typical of Jason Kyle. The guests both left early, Rosa, who had work to do, and Nick, who was still in a daze, though quite willing to go back to work at this hour.

As they were leaving, Nick stopped by Jason and in a low voice said, "It's not just thank you, sir. Nothing so great ever happened to me before." He wanted to say more but couldn't put it into words and had to get into Rosa's car with head hanging and the camera hugged to his thin young chest.

Jason was very much his old self, but Denis felt that there was more to his attitude than appeared on the surface. He waved good-night to the boy, said he understood, and turned away.

Denis and Marina went to bed that night in an almost euphoric mood. Jason came upstairs later and, for some reason, shook hands with Denis. Then he kissed Marina and, last of all, his granddaughter.

Sometimes after dawn the body of an elderly male was found where it had been washed up on the shore. Three boys came running to report it, more excited than shocked. The police easily identified it as Jason Kyle.

"Funny thing," one of the officers said on reporting. "There was this little package with a turnover in his pocket. Good as new. A note says it's for the little princess – somebody sure loved kids. Maybe he didn't have any of his own."